THE CRIMES OF GWENDOLYN GORMLY

(WELSH VILLAGE MURDER MYSTERIES)

K T MILL

dark neon

ISBN: 978-1-913132-19-4
Published by: **dark neon**

http://www.darkneon.com/

The Welsh Village Murder Mysteries

The Crimes Of Gwendolyn Gormly is the third book in the series of Welsh Village Murder Mysteries.

Also available…

Welsh Requiem
Who Killed Inspector Stoat?

K T Mill was born in a South Wales valley and now lives close to a seaside village which bears some resemblance to the village described in this book (but which, fortunately, does not suffer from a great many peculiar crimes and murders).

TABLE OF CONTENTS

1. Snow In The Air

There was snow in the air. Occasional soft flakes pattered against the big picture-window overlooking the terrace of Gwendolyn's Wine Bar.

"Don't worry," said Maggie Pountice, "it won't stick."

Ruby was not so sure. It was a long way to her cottage at the top of Fern Hill. The night was dark, the road was rough and potholed. It was a difficult walk at the best of times. If the snow settled, the road would become treacherous. "I think," she said, "I'd better be going. Just in case."

"Going where?" There was no mistaking the harsh, accusatory voice of Gwendolyn Gormly, the owner of the wine bar. "You've only just ordered this bottle of wine and you'll have to pay for it whether you drink it or not."

Gwendolyn placed a large wine glass on the table directly in front of Ruby and proceeded to fill it, almost to the brim, from a bottle of New Zealand sauvignon blanc which she was holding in her well-manicured right hand. Her well-manicured left hand was holding a smouldering cigarette which, according to the signs liberally dotted around on the walls, she was legally forbidden to smoke. Being a staunch upholder of the law, Gwendolyn obeyed the signs to the letter: the cigarette smouldered but she never once put it to her lips.

A blast of cold air brought in a flurry of snowflakes as the door to the terrace was opened and quickly closed again. "You've got the wine in, I see. Oh, Gwendolyn, my love, I wonder if you'd be good enough to bring another glass?"

It was Ruby's friend, Muriel Greenalge. As Muriel took off her snow-flecked overcoat and hung it on a nearby coat stand, Gwendolyn Gormly strode away from the table, her stiletto heels clacking noisily over the imitation marble flooring: "There's wine glasses on the bar," she shouted. "Get one yourself."

"This place has really gone downhill," Muriel grumbled after she had returned from the bar, holding a wine glass in her hand. "It was so nice here when Gino was running it. Oh, sorry, Ruby, I didn't mean to…"

Ruby had developed a close friendship with the wine bar's previous owner, Gino Ricci. When Gino had suddenly left in mysterious circumstances, rumours started going around that he had deserted Ruby for another woman.

"I've told you before," said Ruby, "there was nothing between me and Gino. Nothing sexual…"

Maggie Pountice rumbled her disapproval. In her opinion, there were some things that should not be talked about in public and sex was top of that list.

Ruby decided to rephrase what she had been about to say. "There was nothing *romantic* between us is what I mean. We got on well together, I wouldn't deny that, but…"

Muriel slapped down the latest copy of the local newspaper, The Clogwyn Clarion, upon the table, cutting off Ruby mid-sentence. "Have you seen this?" She flipped through the pages and found the advertising section towards the back. "The mystery of Coot Hall's new owners thickens. There. Take a look!"

Ruby pulled the newspaper towards her. A boxed display advertisement dominated page 27. It was headlined in bold text: "**The Retreat. Clogwyn Bach's Luxury Spa. Staff Wanted!**"

"Spa?" said Maggie Pountice. "That's where you go to take the waters, isn't it? We haven't got no waters worth the taking of round here."

"It's not that sort of spa," Muriel explained. "Look, this is what the advert says: 'Opening this spring, The Retreat will be a unique resort where guests will be able to refresh the body and revive the spirit in an idyllic spot where the magic of nature combines with luxurious surroundings and world-class fine dining.'"

"Coot Hall's not what I'd call no idyllic spot," rumbled Maggie. "It's a big, ugly, cold, horrible old building. Luxurious surroundings, be buggered!"

"The grounds are pleasant enough," Ruby said. She had become familiar with Coot Hall after visiting it on several occasions following the untimely death of its previous owner, Sir Clifford Coot. "It's just the house itself that leaves something to be desired."

The tapping of stilettoes announced the return of Gwendolyn Gormly. "Having a good time, ladies, I see. Now that there's the three of you, you'll be wanting another bottle of wine, I expect."

"I'm not drinking that filth!" Maggie Pountice snapped with distaste. She had a tankard of Guinness in her hand. She did not approve of any drink that was served in anything less than a pint glass. Mild ale was her preferred tipple, though she was also partial to a good bitter. Neither mild nor bitter was served in the wine bar so she had settled for a Guinness.

"Oh, Gwendolyn," said Muriel, "I wonder if you would get me a dish of olives?"

Gwendolyn glared at Muriel with a stony expression. It was an expression which suggested that there were some tasks of so demeaning a nature that Gwendolyn would not even consider lowering herself to perform them; fetching a dish of olives for Muriel Greenalge was one of those tasks. The clattering of stilettoes was all that broke the frosty silence.

When Gwendolyn had disappeared into the nether regions of the wine bar, Muriel whispered, "I only hope she falls off those high heels and breaks her bloody neck."

Ruby and Maggie stared at Muriel. As a rule, Muriel was polite to the point of obsequiousness. Ruby could not remember ever hearing her say an unkind thing about anyone. Gwendolyn Gormly did, however, tend to bring out the worst in people. Even so, there was a tone of bitterness in Muriel's voice which suggested that she had some particular reason for disliking Gwendolyn.

Muriel noticed the surprise on Ruby's face. "Well," she said, "the thing is, Gwendolyn and I have had our little disagreements."

"Who hasn't?" muttered Maggie Pountice. "Gwendolyn's man mad, that's her trouble. She went after my late, dear husband like a thing possessed. No man's safe when she's around."

"Hmm." Muriel paused to think about that. "She's never gone after my Emrys."

Maggie raised a cynical eyebrow. "As far as *you* know," she rumbled.

"What she *has* done, though, is she's tried to ruin our business."

Muriel and Emrys Greenalge ran the local newsagent and grocery store, "Food'n'News". As there was no supermarket in Clogwyn Bach, this was a vital source of essential supplies in the village. "Food'n'News" sold everything from tea-bags to chocolate digestive biscuits. Ruby had discovered that if she gave Muriel prior notice she was even able to obtain rare and strange exotics seldom seen in that remote part of west Wales, ranging from black peppercorns to jars of lime pickle.

"How did Gwendolyn try to ruin your business?" Ruby asked. "She's not planning to open her own grocery shop, is she?"

"She claimed she found rat droppings in our liquorice allsorts!" Muriel hissed through clenched teeth. "Reported us to the Food Standards Agency, she did."

"No!" Maggie Pountice gulped down the rest of her Guinness, wiped the foam from her lips and said, "I've bought your liquorice allsorts many a time. If it goes to court, you can call me as a character witness."

"Oh, it won't go to court. The inspector called round a couple of days ago. Said he'd never seen a shop as spick and span as ours. Rat droppings indeed! Why would Gwendolyn say such a thing?"

"Because she's an evil bitch, that's why," said Maggie. "She closed my little shop down, didn't she. For years I was running Maggie's Mystic Emporium on the High Street and then I was late with my rent a couple of times due to circumstances beyond my control and she went and booted me out and opened her own shop."

"Gwendolyn's Grotto," Muriel said. "A lot of tourist tat is what she sells, if you want my opinion."

"She gets cheap Chinese tarot decks," Maggie muttered darkly, "and charges French prices for them!"

"And now this wine bar is going the same way," Ruby added. "I mean, it was so nice and friendly when Gino was running it…"

Muriel nodded. "The wine was better too. The stuff Gwendolyn serves is half way to being vinegar. I reckon she buys bottles of cheap plonk and sticks expensive labels on them…"

"Is everything to your satisfaction, ladies?" They had been so engrossed in conversation that they had not seen or heard Gwendolyn clicking her way across the room towards them.

A dispassionate observer might have concluded that the three faces that turned to grimace at Gwendolyn Gormly gave the distinct impression that everything was not to their satisfaction. Maggie Pountice smiled and said, "If everything isn't just perfect, Gwendolyn my love, I just don't know what isn't."

Gwendolyn was speechless for a second which, by her standards of speechlessness, was a very long time indeed. For a fleeting moment she wondered whether she had just been paid a compliment. Then she remembered it was Maggie who had spoken and dismissed the idea as absurd.

"Finish up your wine, ladies, and I'll get you another bottle," Gwendolyn said. "After all, I'm not running a charity here, you know."

"The most charitable thing she could do is get out of Clogwyn Bach for good and all," Maggie said when Gwendolyn was out of earshot. "Preferably in a hearse."

"There's many around here who wouldn't spill a tear if Gwendolyn met a sticky end," Muriel added. "She's a nasty piece of work. One day her crimes will catch up with her, you mark my words."

Little did Muriel know how prophetic her words would be!

2. HELL HATH NO FURY...

"She was after Coot Hall, you know," Muriel said.

Ruby, who had been staring through the plate glass window of the wine bar, increasing worried by the relentlessness of the falling snow, snapped out of her reverie at the mention of Coot Hall. "What? You mean that Gwendolyn wanted to buy the place?"

"You remember she was flirting with Arthur Smiddle, the estate agent, a few months back? And then, she fell out with him. Called him all kinds of names I wouldn't even want to repeat. It turns out she'd made an offer on the Hall but the seller turned her down. Gwendolyn blamed Arthur Smiddle."

"Where would Gwendolyn get enough money to buy Coot Hall?" Maggie asked. "It must be worth millions."

"Where does Gwendolyn get money to buy whatever she takes a fancy to? Like this wine bar, for instance?"

"She has gentlemen friends," Maggie said ominously.

"I'm surprised Coot Hall is considered to be such a desirable property," Ruby said. "The grounds are nice, I suppose. But the Hall itself. Well, it's so big and rambling and..."

"Ugly?" Muriel suggested.

"Well, yes. It is. Exceedingly ugly."

"I wonder who bought the Hall in the end?" said Muriel. "Nobody seems to know, do they?"

Ruby opened her mouth to say something, thought better of it, and closed her mouth again.

"I heard it was a rich American," Maggie said. "The rumour is that he's had dungeons installed. There'll be swingers' parties there."

"What's a swingers' party?" Muriel asked.

By way of answer, Maggie lowered her eyebrows and made a low, disapproving, grumbling noise like a bulldog with dyspepsia.

"Look," said Muriel, turning her attention back to the newspaper advertisement, "it says here they are looking for a 'sous-chef', plus a groundsman and a holistic masseur."

"A masseur!" As far as Maggie was concerned, that confirmed her darkest fears. "No good can come of that, believe you me."

"I had a massage once," Muriel objected. "It did wonders for my sciatica."

"There's massages and there's massages," Maggie said cryptically. "Massages is just the tip of the iceberg. Mark my words, before you know what's happening they'll be having Black Masses. And nudity!"

"That's not what I heard," Muriel said. "I heard the Hall was going to be used to home lamas."

"Llamas?" said Ruby. "The things with long necks that spit at you?"

"Tibetan monks," Muriel said. "The ones that meditate and blow trumpets."

"I only hope you're right," said Maggie. "Good in a fight, your Tibetan monks. Kung Fu. They all have the Kung Fu, you see."

"I thought that was Shaolin Monks," Ruby said.

"Same sort of thing." Maggie gave the impression of being an authority on monastic martial arts. "What I'm saying is, you don't want to get into a fight with a monk."

There was a long pause. The three women sat staring at the steamed up window beyond which the snow continued to fall in the blustery darkness over the unseen bay.

Finally Muriel said, "I knew a Benedictine monk once."

"Dirty fighters, the Benedictines," Maggie said. "Did you know it was the Benedictines that invented the Grobbit hold?"

That remark brought an effective end to the conversation. Neither Ruby nor Muriel knew much about Benedictine monks. Their knowledge of the Grobbit hold was even sketchier.

"Anyway, getting back to your love life, Ruby," Muriel said. "I suppose Gino's just an old flame now that you and Nye are…"

"Oh, really!" Ruby gave a devil-may-care laugh that sounded a good deal less devil-may-care than she had intended. "To listen to you two talk, you'd think I have a string of lovers! There's nothing of that sort between me and Nye. For your information, I like Nye Clump, we share some interests, but that's as far as it goes."

Maggie chuckled. "You got to admit though, he's a tasty little number, Nye is."

Ruby had met Aneurin Clump (known to his friends as 'Nye') at the Clogwyn Bach Summer Fayre the previous July. He was charming, intelligent and good-looking. Ruby had liked him from the outset. He sometimes visited the wine bar in the evening. That Ruby also had taken to visiting the wine bar in preference to the Cat and Ferret pub, which had formerly been her favoured night-spot, may not (some people said) have been entirely coincidental.

Just then another cold gust of air swept into the wine bar as the outer door was briefly opened and shut again. The three women turned to see who had entered. It was a slim, middle-aged, middle-height man with neat, fair hair and vivid blue eyes. He was wearing a long, dark overcoat which was liberally sprinkled with snowflakes. "Am I glad to be in the warmth at last!"

"Aye, aye," said Maggie under her breath. "Casanova's arrived then." And she winked broadly at Ruby.

"Nye!" said Ruby. "I didn't think you'd bother coming in this weather."

"We kept a seat for you," said Muriel.

Nye Clump took off his overcoat, dusted the snow from it and hung it on the coat stand. "The snow's getting quite heavy now," he said.

"Don't worry," said Maggie, "it won't stick."

*

They had nearly finished their third bottle of wine and Ruby was feeling in a flushed good mood. Nye, on the other hand, was taciturn. He was swirling the wine around in his glass and staring at it as though trying to figure out the solution to some complicated problem.

"Nothing wrong, is there?" Ruby asked.

Nye looked up as though he had only just noticed Ruby's presence. "Oh," he said at last, "I was just thinking about Gwendolyn."

"Gwendolyn?" Ruby said the name in much the same tone that Muriel had said "rat droppings" in their earlier conversation.

"Yes. She worries me."

"She worries us all," Maggie said. "What's she done to you, then?"

"Oh, nothing. Not yet, anyway. Though there's still time. It's just this thing Ruby and I are going to tomorrow."

"What thing is that?" Muriel asked.

Ruby avoided Muriel's gaze. It was a topic that she had hoped Nye would have had sufficient diplomacy not to mention. Nye's diplomatic skills clearly fell short of Ruby's expectations.

"Oh, you know," Nye said, in a tone that suggested it was a trivial matter of no conceivable consequence. "The Retreat."

"You're going to The Retreat?" said Muriel.

"The *two* of you?" said Maggie.

"You dark horse!" Muriel nudged Ruby with an elbow, almost causing her to spill her wine. "You didn't say a word about that to us."

"It's really nothing," Ruby blustered. "I mean, it'll probably amount to nothing. Nye has some connection. With, you know…"

"Nathaniel Snibb," Nye said.

"Who?" said Muriel and Maggie in unison.

"The man who bought Coot Hall. I happened to bump into him. Somewhere. He thought there might be some work for me. I mentioned Ruby. The fact that she's an actress..."

"*Was* an actress," Ruby said.

"…and, well, he thought there might be a job for her too. At The Hall, I mean."

"What kind of a job?" Muriel asked, eager for all the latest gossip to pass on to customers in her shop.

"Not a masseuse, I hope!" grunted Maggie, suspiciously.

"Voice training," Nye said. "Public speaking. All that kind of thing. They'll be doing workshops, you see, for their clientele. Public speaking goes down very well among that sort of person, apparently."

"But what's that got to do with Gwendolyn?" Muriel interrupted.

"What?"

"You said you were worried about Gwendolyn."

"Ah yes. Well, you see, Nathaniel Snibb has appointed a man called Lennie – or 'Guru Lennie' as he likes to be called – as, well, sort of the figurehead. It will be Guru Lennie who will be running The Retreat on a day-to-day basis. It will be Lennie's photograph in the brochure, Lennie who welcomes the guests, Lennie who does all the press interviews and whatnot."

"But what has that got to do with Gwendolyn Gormly?" Muriel persisted.

"The job was supposed to have been Gwendolyn's. Nathaniel Snibb promised her the job, do you see. And then suddenly he changed his mind."

"Oh dear," said Muriel.

"Hell hath no fury like Gwendolyn scorned," added Maggie.

"Quite," said Nye. "I have an awful presentiment that this won't end well."

3. The Talk Of The Village

It was still snowing the next morning when Ruby called around to Bessie, her next door neighbour, for a cup of tea and a slice of *teisen lap* fruit cake on the pretext of asking Bessie's advice on the best outfit to wear on her visit to Coot Hall that evening. In fact she was much more interested in finding out what Bessie had to say about Gwendolyn Gormly.

In the ten months or so since Ruby had moved to Clogwyn Bach she had discovered that barely anyone had a good word to say about Gwendolyn. On the one hand, Ruby could understand Gwendolyn's unpopularity: she was aggressive, argumentative and had a vicious streak that ran through her like the words through a stick of Porthcawl rock. On the other hand, Ruby had known plenty of aggressive, argumentative and vicious people in her life but none of those had been as universally loathed as Gwendolyn.

"Gwendolyn has always felt short-changed by life, I think," Bessie said. "When she was a teenager she wanted to be…" Bessie paused. She looked out of the kitchen window. "There's weather for you!" she said irrelevantly. "One thing I can't abide is snow. Still, it won't stick. Not here. It never does."

"Bessie," Ruby said, "what did Gwendolyn want to be that was so bad that you can't even bear to say it? Come on, I'm a woman of the world. It doesn't matter to me whether she wanted to be an exotic dancer in the Moulin Rouge or a streetwalker in the Cardiff docks."

"She wanted to be an actress," Bessie blurted out.

"Ah," Ruby nibbled at a slice of *teisen lap* and took a long slurp of tea from her mug. "Yes, that *is* bad."

"She used to be full of big ideas about acting in films. She saw herself as a femme fatale, a blonde bombshell, I think. Like Marilyn

Monroe. Or Diana Dors. She had the looks in those days. And the figure."

"So what was holding her back?"

"She couldn't act."

"I see. Yes, that can be a disadvantage. But in the acting profession the lack of acting ability is not an insurmountable barrier." Ruby smiled. "I mean, look at me!"

"Oh, but you can act!" Bessie said with fervour. "You have the talent."

Ruby raised a sceptical eyebrow. "Go on, then, name something you've seen me in!"

"Well, there was…"

"And if you mention the dancing kitten, I swear to God I'll throttle you."

To Ruby's lasting shame, the one performance of hers that everyone remembered was as a dancing kitten in a television commercial for cat food.

"Mrs Carter-Ricketts," Bessie said.

"Who?"

"You remember. Midsomer Murders. You were the nosy neighbour who'd seen what the vicar was up to in the marrow beds."

"Oh, yes!" Ruby was pleased that Bessie had remembered that. It had been quite a small part but Ruby felt that she had played it sympathetically. "Yes, I was quite good in that, I suppose. But anyway, getting back to Gwendolyn. The fact that she did not succeed in her desired career hardly explains why everyone dislikes her so much."

"It made her bitter and twisted," said Bessie.

"That's as may be. But even so…"

"She accused Muriel Greenalge of having rat droppings in her liquorice allsorts!"

"So I've been told. And she also forced Maggie Pountice to shut down her shop due to late payment of her rent. I can understand how that might breed resentment. But those are hardly crimes against humanity are they? I mean, it's not as though Gwendolyn has murdered someone."

Bessie furrowed her brow and lowered her voice. "Don't be so sure."

"What?"

"You haven't heard the rumours, then?"

"No. I mean, I don't know. What rumours are you talking about?"

"Ken Collop."

"Who?"

"Gwendolyn's live-in lover. It was Ken, not Gwendolyn, who owned Maggie Pountice's shop. When he died, Gwendolyn inherited the shop. And quite a lot more besides. That's why she's so well off. Died very suddenly and very unexpectedly did Ken Collop. A heart attack was the official reason."

"But you don't believe that?"

Bessie was looking unusually grim. "Nobody in Clogwyn Bach believes that."

Ruby was unable to get any more information from Bessie on the supposed scandal surrounding the death of Ken Collop. There was always a great deal of salacious gossip and innumerable unfounded rumours swirling around in Clogwyn Bach. Ruby supposed that this was just another one of them. The local people did not care for Gwendolyn's brashness so they fabricated stories to defame her.

Ruby finished her tea and was about to go home when she remembered that her ostensible reason for calling on Bessie had been to get her advice on which outfit to wear that evening.

"Either a long, black evening gown with high heels or a pair of slacks with comfortable shoes," was Bessie's advice.

"But I haven't got a long, black evening gown with high heels," Ruby said.

"Problem solved," said Bessie.

"I'll call round at seven, then, shall I?"

Since Ruby did not drive and Bessie did, she had wangled a lift from Bessie. Nye Clump had assured her that Bessie would be very welcome to attend the little get-together at The Retreat. "Who knows," he had said, "there might even be a job for her?"

Knowing her as well as she did, Ruby was quite certain that Bessie would not accept a job even if she were offered one. Having spent her life as a teacher, Bessie had not the slightest interest in interrupting her comfortable retirement with anything so inconvenient as a job. But Ruby also knew that Bessie was dead keen to get a first-hand look at the developments at Coot Hall. The goings-on at The Retreat were the talk of the village. Once she had actually visited the place and met its new owner, Bessie would have the "inside story" which, when she related it to her friends, would make her an overnight celebrity.

"When are we supposed to arrive there?" Bessie asked.

"Half-past seven."

"Then we'll leave here at twenty-past. That should get us there ten minutes late. It's always bad form to arrive on time."

4. A Late Arrival

That evening, Bessie's little yellow Mini Minor scrunched to a halt on the gravel driveway at the front of Coot Hall. The turreted hideousness of the building was thankfully obscured by the darkness, for the sky was thick with clouds and no moon was visible.

"We probably shouldn't stay too long," Ruby said, looking at the big flakes of snow that were already beginning to settle on the car's windscreen, "just in case we get snowed in."

Bessie laughed. "You needn't worry about that. This snow won't settle. It never does around here. It's a very mild location due to being so close to the sea, you see."

Mild or not, once she stepped outside the car, Ruby pulled her coat closer around her and stuck her ungloved hands deeper into her pockets. "I hope you are right," she said. She could not help but notice the plumes of vapour her breath made in the air.

There were electric lanterns fixed on the walls at either side of the monumental portico which, with its triangular pediment supported by four mighty columns, gave the impression that it had been designed by an architect of limited abilities who had recently taken a holiday in Athens. The portico loomed over a pair of huge oak doors each of which was furnished with a weighty brass knob and a brass lion's head from the teeth of which depended a thick brass ring that served the function of a doorknocker.

"Which knocker do you think I should knock?" asked Ruby. "The one on the left or the one on the right?"

But before a decision could be made, one of the huge doors creaked open and there, standing in the gap thus formed, backlit by lights from inside the house, crouched a small, skinny figure whose stooping form positively oozed hostility. "Yes?" it snapped.

"Is Mr Snibb at home?" Ruby enquired.

"What's it to you?" snapped back the stooping form.

"We are expected," said Ruby.

"Not by me, you're not."

"By Nathaniel Snibb," Bessie interposed. "I am Bessie Morgan. My friend is Ruby Lake." The crouching figure made no reply, so Bessie added, "The actress."

The figure turned around and stumped back into the house. Assuming that this meant that they had been granted entry, Ruby and Bessie followed in his wake. The man, they now saw, was dressed in a long, black tailcoat, his greasy hair hung limply over his collar and the bottoms of his trousers were frayed. Whether he were a slovenly servant, an eccentric millionaire or an undertaker who had fallen on hard times it was impossible to say. What was certain, however, was that he was a man of few words and those of a mostly disagreeable nature.

"In there!" he snapped, pointing a grubby finger towards a room on the right of the huge, echoing hallway, and, without once turning around, he continued to shuffle off into the shadowy nether regions of the house.

The room to which the disagreeable little man had pointed was behind a big oak door which, at that moment, was firmly closed. Ruby tapped hesitantly upon it. Her tapping was greeted by silence. She then proceeded to thump upon the door with rather more vigour. A thin, warbling noise proceeded from the room beyond. With a little imagination, the warbling might be construed to be a human voice. What that voice might have been warbling was anyone's guess but Ruby decided to interpret it as words approximating to "Come in." She pushed open the door and entered the room.

It was a room which she had entered once before when the previous owner of Coot Hall, Lady Patricia Coot, had been in residence. On that occasion, the room had been decorated with predominantly floral motifs that extended from the curtains and the carpets to the covers of the settee. The new owner obviously preferred more sombre furnishings. The predominating theme was crimson velvet. Crimson velvet curtains had been drawn over the windows, the carpet was, if not velvet, at least some sort of deep, plush material of a crimson hue, and the huge armchairs and chaise-longue were upholstered in the sort of decadent, dark crimson velvet which one expects only to see in theatrical productions of Victorian melodramas and in the more traditional type of bordello.

Perched, sparrow-like, on the edge of the chaise-longue was a tiny, fragile-looking, elderly woman wearing a long, black satin dress, a beige cardigan and an expression of enthusiastic bewilderment. "Oh good!" she warbled, "have you brought me some tea?"

Ruby was at a loss for words. Bessie was not. "I'm afraid, madam," she said, "you may have mistaken us for the domestic staff. We have no tea."

The little woman looked crestfallen but in the very next second she had cheered up again, "Are you gypsy fortune tellers?"

"Alas," said Bessie, "that is an accomplishment to which we cannot lay claim. We are merely guests of Nathaniel Snibb."

"Oh, Natty!" chirruped the woman. "He's a scream, isn't he! I'm Mrs Lowri Williams-Jenkins but you may call me…"

"Lowri?" suggested, Ruby, extending a hand.

"…Mrs Williams-Jenkins." She glanced at Ruby's extended hand for a few moments as though trying to think what to do with it. Having thought and come up with a blank, she smiled at Ruby and said, "And you are?"

Ruby withdrew her hand. "Ruby Lake. But you may call me Ruby."

"And I am Bessie," Bessie added simply.

"How lovely to meet you," cooed Mrs Williams-Jenkins. "I say! You haven't seen anyone with some tea, have you? I was promised a fairy cake, you know."

"And here it is!" boomed a voice from the doorway. A tall man with a flaring mass of whiskers entered carrying a tray bearing a teapot, a cup and saucer and a plate upon which sat two dainty fairy cakes. He placed the tray upon a low table near to where Mrs Williams-Jenkins was perching. As he poured the tea, he glanced at Bessie and Ruby and said, "Is there anything I can get for you ladies?"

"Well, a cup of…" began Bessie. But Ruby interrupted her sharply. She knew that once Bessie started drinking tea, a few minutes could rapidly become a few hours and it was Ruby's intention to make this visit as short, snappy and business-like as she possibly could. "I'm afraid we really haven't got much time," she said. "Would you be Nathaniel Snibb, by any chance."

The bearded man gave a volcanic laugh of such volume that, for a moment, Ruby feared for the safety of the chandeliers. "No! Not me! Ebenezer Estyn Evans is who I am. The chef of this establishment. I don't normally serve tea, of course, but the place is a bit short-staffed just at the moment."

Ruby and Bessie introduced themselves. Ebenezer Evans asked them what they were doing in the Sitting Room when everyone else was gathered in the Vermilion Saloon. Ruby explained that they had been directed to the room by the man who had answered the door.

Ebenezer Evans let rip with another earth-trembling guffaw. "You don't want to pay any attention to old" (Ruby did not quite catch the next word but it sounded to her like "Crickspittle"). Then, lowering his voice to Level 5 on the Richter Scale, which was his closest approximation to a whisper, Ebenezer added, "He's a bit soft in the head, if you know what I mean."

"Did he call the man Crickspittle?" Ruby whispered to Bessie once Ebenezer had turned to leave.

"I think he said Craigysbytol. It's a Welsh name."

Ruby raised a sceptical eyebrow. "Crickspittle suits him better."

Leaving Mrs Williams-Jenkins to her tea and fairy cakes, Ruby and Bessie followed Ebenezer Evans out of the Sitting Room, across the echoing hallway and into an even larger room, sumptuously decorated in shades of red with gold trimmings, in which several people were standing around, drinking cocktails. Ebenezer strode straight up to a slim, balding man wearing old-fashioned round spectacles and a well-tailored dark suit. A woman of middling years and imposing aspect was standing next to him.

"I found two of your guests wandering around the place, lost," Ebenezer boomed. "Ruby Lake and Bessie Morgan." Then, turning to Ruby and Bessie, Ebenezer added, "I don't know if you've already met but just in case you haven't, this is your host, Nathaniel Snibb."

Nathaniel beamed at them through his old-fashioned spectacles. "Oh, Ruby!" he exclaimed. "And Bessie! I am so glad you could make it. And this is Clarissa Winthrop, my, er... a friend of mine."

The woman standing next to him smiled lazily. "Charmed," she said, with supreme indifference.

"Oh, but, my dears, you haven't got a drink." Nathaniel gave the impression that the absence of a drink was an insupportable prodigy in nature. He snapped his fingers at a woman wearing a black dress and a white apron, just like a maid in a French farce. She tottered over carrying a selection of drinks on a silver tray. "What will you have?" said Nathaniel to Ruby and Bessie. "We have champagne, malt whisky, brandy…"

"Bronwen!" Ruby exclaimed. To her surprise, the young woman doing the French maid impression was Bronwen Price, a local girl who came once a week to clean Ruby's cottage. "What are you doing here?"

"Oh, hello, Ruby. Well, I used to work here when Sir Clifford and Lady Coot had the Hall, you see."

"Bronwen knows the place much better than I do," Nathaniel said. "She helps out here from time to time. I had no idea you knew one another. Such a small world, what?"

"Everyone knows everyone else around her," Bessie said, taking two glasses of champagne from Bronwen's tray, one of which she handed to Ruby. Bronwen had already walked off towards a small, plump man wearing a brilliantly embroidered kaftan who gave the impression of being in urgent need of alcohol.

"Ruby," a man's voice said. "You're late. I thought you might have changed your mind."

Looking somewhat flustered, Ruby turned to face the man speaking to her. "Nye! I didn't notice you standing there!"

"I could take that as an insult." Nye gave her one of his most charming smiles.

"Hello, Miss Morgan," Nye added.

"Nye and I know one another from way back," Bessie explained. "He was a disruptive influence. He stuck chewing gum in the girls' hair."

"You'll be pleased to know that *that* is something I very rarely do these days, Miss Morgan." For Ruby's benefit, Nye added, "Miss Morgan was the strictest teacher in our school. And also the prettiest."

Now Bessie was looking flustered. "That was a very long time ago," she mumbled. "And you can call me Bessie. You are not in detention now!"

"Have you met the Guru yet?" Nye asked, glancing across at the plump man in the multi-coloured kaftan. "He's quite a character."

Ruby shook her head. "So that's the famous Guru Lennie, is it? I thought he'd be taller somehow."

"Mystical ability is not dependent on height, it would seem. Come on, I'll introduce you."

Pushing past a small gaggle of people standing around, drinking and gossiping, Nye led Ruby and Bessie towards the improbable guru. With a round face and slightly bulging cheeks, Guru Lennie looked like an overgrown hamster. Nye made the introductions and Guru Lennie's broad smile gave the impression that nothing in the world could, at that moment, have given him greater pleasure than meeting Ruby and Bessie.

"My darling petal!" he chirruped, clasping Ruby's slim fingers in his pudgy hands. "I've been so looking forward to meeting you." He released Ruby's hands and swooped upon Bessie's, "And you, my dear, you are seeking, I presume?"

Bessie withdrew her hands from his marshmallow-like clasp. "I am seeking a comfortable chair. If that counts."

For a brief moment, Ruby worried that Guru Lennie might be offended by Bessie's abrupt manner. Her worries were dispelled when the guru made a strange snorting sound in his nostrils which gradually grew into a full-throated laugh. "I'm just the same," he said, merrily. "A good sit-down is the best tonic. Well, make yourself at home, my petal. The soft furnishings are yours to command."

"But first," interrupted Nye, "let me introduce you to the assembled throng. You've met Nathaniel. Had you met him before?"

"Not at all," said Ruby. "Bessie and I don't move in such exalted circles."

"It's Nathaniel who bought this hideous building," said Nye in a low voice. "He's got plenty of money to spare thanks to his pickles."

"Pickles?" said Bessie. "Did you say pickles?"

"I did. You are not familiar with Snibb's Scrumptious Pickles, then?"

Bessie looked blank.

"Crunchy on the outside, squidgy in the middle."

"I have no idea what you are talking about, Aneurin Clump."

"You see," Nye was smiling at Ruby, "Miss Morgan – I mean Bessie – still treats me like a snotty-nosed kid. That's just the way she used to talk to me when she was my teacher.

"Nathaniel Snibb," Nye went on, "is a pickle magnate. He rose from poverty to wealth through the wholesale manufacturing and marketing of jars of onions in vinegar. You may not be aware of the fact that the Great British public cannot get its fill of pickled onions. Early in his life, Nathaniel noticed this insatiable craving and resolved to do everything in his power to satisfy it. As a result, he is now rolling in so much spare cash that he barely notices the few million it takes to buy and furnish a mouldering heap like Coot Hall."

"But why on earth would he want it in the first place?" asked Ruby.

"He has found spirituality. His lifetime's devotion to the pickled onion may have brought him wealth but it has not fulfilled the cravings of his soul. Then he met Guru Lennie. They were on a television chat show together, I believe. They hit it off at once due to a shared enthusiasm for pickled gherkins. No doubt at some stage their conversation turned from gherkins to mysticism, possibly under the influence of alcohol, which is another passion shared by the two men. Guru Lennie told Nathaniel of his lifelong ambition to set up a spiritual regeneration centre. Nathaniel got out his chequebook. And this," Nye waved a hand to indicate both the room in which they were standing and also everything that lay beyond it, "is the result."

"And how, if I may enquire," Bessie asked, "did *you* get involved in all this?"

"Guru Lennie was looking for local talent. He found me. And Ruby, of course."

"I haven't decided yet," Ruby interjected, "as to whether or not I am interested in being found. Maybe by the end of the evening…?"

"And what talent, precisely, have you to offer, Aneurin Clump?" Bessie asked.

"The Celtic Twilight," Nye replied. "I take it you have not read my book, 'Arthurian Legends – From Brittany To Beddgelert'?"

"Strangely, I've missed out on that one," said Bessie.

"It was Number twelve in Amazon's list of bestselling Anthropological Folklore books for a while!"

"*Arglwydd mawr*! People actually buy books on Anthropological Folklore?"

"Indeed they do. And if you are interested in the Celtic roots of the Arthurian legends, I'm the chap to come to."

"But I thought you were a French teacher!"

"I was for a while. But my heart wasn't in it. Have you any idea how ruinous to the soul it is to hear bored teenagers chanting '*Je suis, tu es, il est, elle est…*' day after day, month after month, year after year? My real interest lay in the legends of our land. So I chucked in my job and started writing books, teaching courses, going on cruises…"

"Cruises?"

"As a lecturer. You get a nice room, decent pay, adequate food and a lot of bored adults chanting 'Arthur, son of Uther Pendragon, Merlin his wizard, Guinevere his wife, Excalibur his sword'. Beats teaching French any day. But let me not bore you with all that. You should be mingling. Let's see, who shall we mingle with? I don't suppose you know the two people over there, do you?" Nye indicated a short, pale, ethereal-looking, dark-haired woman wearing a lacy white dress and a man with a military bearing and equally military moustache; they were standing over by the mantelpiece.

Ruby and Bessie agreed that neither the man nor the woman were familiar to them so Nye led the way and made the introductions. The man was Sergeant-Major Selwyn 'Stonker' Stippleton, who was to be the physical training instructor at The Retreat ("The body is the temple of the spirit!" he explained with a leer), and the woman was 'Madame' Evadne Miskyn, a self-proclaimed "celebrity astrologer" and mystic, who was to be The Retreat's "spiritual consultant".

Ruby, Bessie, Nye, Sergeant-Major Stippleton and Madame Evadne Miskyn were busy making desultory small talk when the doors to the room were opened and in slithered the servile Crickspittle, beetle-like in his obsequiousness. Everyone turned to look at him. "There's a late arrival," he said.

Striding into the room from behind the cringing Crickspittle came the statuesque form of none other than Gwendolyn Gormly.

5. An Experiment Is Planned

"I have heard, Miss Gormly," said Mrs Williams-Jenkins, "a great deal about you…" She tapped the side of her nose significantly before adding: "I'm sure you understand what I mean…"

At Guru Lennie's behest, the assembled throng had begun to migrate from the Vermilion Saloon into the Sitting Room. Mrs Williams-Jenkins, who had now finished her tea and fairy cakes, was sitting in the middle of the chaise-longue with Ruby to her left and Gwendolyn Gormly to her right. Bessie sat in an overstuffed armchair next to Ruby.

Gwendolyn furrowed her brow and set her jaw. "I don't know what you've heard about me, sunshine," she said, "and I don't really care. Fact of the matter is that people around here talk too much. Meddling in other people's business." She aimed a gimlet glare in Ruby's direction. "Whatever you've heard about me is just the filthy imaginings of narrow-minded people."

"Oh!" Mrs Williams-Jenkins took a small frilly handkerchief from a pocket of her cardigan and dabbed at the corners of her mouth as though to remove some annoying drops of grease, "I think, my dear, I may have expressed myself poorly. What I meant to say was that it has been intimated to me that you possess what we used to call the 'second sight'."

Gwendolyn paused a moment to think about that. Having thought, she smiled. Having smiled, she said, "Well, it's not something I talk about much but I do hear voices."

"Oh!" Mrs Williams-Jenkins dabbed at her lips again. "And what do the voices tell you?"

"All kinds of things! Good fortune that is to be. Bad fortune that is to follow. Births, marriages, deaths, divorces…"

"Don't suppose they tell you who'll win the three-thirty at Goodwood, will they?" a gruff voice interjected.

"Oh, Sergeant-Major Stippleton!" Mrs Williams-Jenkins coquettishly wielded her frilly handkerchief like a fan in front of her face, "You startled us!"

Sergeant-Major Selwyn 'Stonker' Stippleton leaned over the two women and beamed a terrifying smile from beneath his bristling moustache. "Did I hears you aright, ladies? Was it the mysteries of the spirit world you was talking of? Only, see, I has had numerous experiences of that malarkey myself, so I has. Out in India it was. They has what they call fakirs who is able to commune with the spirits of them what has passed beyond the veil. Well, one fakir I met, in a little mud-hutted village west of Agra it was, he tells me that one day I will live in a great hall in the far, far west. And here I am. In a great big hall in west Wales."

Gwendolyn yawned.

There was a tinkling laugh as Madame Evadne walked into the room. "Don't believe a word that he says. Darling Stonker suffers from an excess of imagination."

Ignoring the Sergeant-Major's incoherent denial, Madame Evadne continued, "However, I believe I heard you dear ladies discussing the mysteries of the afterlife. This is the greatest of all mysteries, is it not?"

Ruby could not help smirking. Madame Evadne reminded her of a seaside fortune teller whose booth she had once visited and who had spouted a preposterous lot of twaddle about parting the veil and making contact with the dear departed. Ruby thought her smirk had been small enough to go unnoticed. She was wrong.

"I notice you smirking," Madame Evadne said bluntly.

Ruby affected a look of sombre seriousness. But too late. Once a smirk has been spotted it is not easily forgotten.

"No need to apologise," Madame Evadne added (Ruby had not even considered the possibility of apologising but in the interests of decorum, she said nothing). "A doubting mind is a good mind. I think we should conduct a little experiment, don't you? The souls of the departed are with us at all times, hidden by a mere shimmering chiffon that separates their dimension from ours."

Ruby struggled a losing battle against the smirk which was, in spite of all her efforts, creeping back onto her face.

"But we can make contact. Oh, yes, we can! All we need is the sincere desire to communicate with the departed. And a planchette."

"What did she say?" asked Mrs Williams-Jenkins. "A blanket?"

"A planchette," Madame Evadne enunciated with exaggerated clarity.

Gwendolyn Gormly aimed a look of derision at Madame Evadne. "She means a Ouija Board," Gwendolyn explained. "We have some very nice ones for sale in my emporium. Perhaps you know it? Gwendolyn's Grotto in Clogwyn Bach. None of your rubbish. Proper wooden boards, not the cheap cardboard variety."

Madame Evadne let loose with one of her tinkling laughs again. "Oh, we don't need a Ouija Board. They are but toys for the simple-minded."

Gwendolyn glowered and was about to say something withering but, catching sight of Nathaniel Snibb, who was ogling Gwendolyn with spaniel-like eyes, she thought better of it and contented herself with a silent sneer.

From the corner of her eye, Ruby thought she saw Nathaniel Snibb winking in Gwendolyn's direction but when she turned to look at the pickled onion magnate, he was ostentatiously rubbing his eyelid as though the wink had been caused by a speck of dust.

Ruby leaned closer towards Bessie. In a whisper, she said, "Did you see that?"

Bessie nodded grimly. "He winked at her."

"Dust?" whispered Ruby.

"Lust, more like it," Bessie replied.

"You should all concentrate on your hara," Madame Evadne commanded. "For those of you who are not familiar with the hara, it is the centre of your spiritual energies and is located, well…" She fluttered her fingers in front of her stomach, seeming vague on her hara's precise location.

Ruby had no intention of concentrating on her hara. She was not at all enthusiastic about the spiritualistic experiment which Madame Evadne was in the process of organising. It had been Ruby's intention to come to Coot Hall, meet its owner, discuss the possibilities of undertaking some freelance work for him (since Ruby's finances were in a state which was far from healthy) and then depart with the greatest of speed. She might have been prepared for a small glass of dry sherry somewhere along the way but she felt that communicating with the spirits of the dead was taking it a bit far.

"I'm afraid," she said aloud, to no one in particular, "that I shan't have time to participate in this, er, experiment."

"Oh, but my dear!" cried Mrs Williams-Jenkins, "you simply must! There may be someone here even as we speak who wishes to make contact with you."

As a rule, Ruby went to great lengths to avoid living people making contact with her and she was damned if she was going to let herself be at the beck and call of dead people.

Finding herself close to Nathaniel Snibb, she smiled at him and said, "I believe there was something you wanted to talk to me about."

"You came recommended," Nathaniel said. Ruby assumed her recommendation had come from Nye Clump. "But as for the final arrangements, that's all up to Guru Lennie. I may own Coot Hall but I entrust its running completely to the Guru."

"Did I hear my name mentioned?" The plump kaftan-wearing hamster of a man waddled up, smiling broadly between a pair of enormous, rosy cheeks.

Ruby briefly explained that she was in a bit of a hurry and all she really wanted to know was what sort of job was on offer and what kind of remuneration was being suggested. She would then go home, consider the offer and let Guru Lennie know her decision in a few days.

Guru Lennie chuckled. "Oh, you make it sound so formal and dull, my petal. I promise you, if you take a job at The Retreat it'll be more like fun than work. Let me show you around."

"What?" Ruby had been to Coot Hall before. She did not, she said, need to be shown around. But Guru Lennie would not take No for an answer. "There's been a lot of changes since you were here last, my rosebud. You'll be amazed. Won't she, Natty?"

"Beg pardon?" Nathaniel Snibb said. "Oh, changes, yes, there have been a few changes. Facilities. Décor. Soft furnishings. That sort of thing."

"Feng Shui," added Guru Lennie. "To harmonize everything at a spiritual level."

"I really must be getting back home," said Ruby, looking ostentatiously at her wristwatch.

But the guru had already taken Ruby's arm in a surprisingly firm grasp and was leading her out of the Sitting Room. Ruby glanced in desperation at Bessie, hoping for a last minute rescue, but Bessie was deep in conversation with Sergeant-Major Stippleton and she did not notice Ruby's predicament.

"It's a fabulous building, isn't it!" gushed Guru Lennie, his chirruping voice echoing around the walls of the huge central hallway. "I expect you've noticed a few alterations already."

Ruby glanced at the walls. "There used to be a great many pictures of gloomy Victorian gentlemen with whiskers." The walls were now decorated with a mixture of batik-printed silk drapes and occasional watercolours of naked nymphs and satyrs dancing by moonlight.

"You knew the previous owner, Sir Clifford Coot?" Guru Lennie asked.

"Not to speak to," said Ruby. "The first time I met him was when he was already dead."

"Passed on," said Guru Lennie. "The 'd' word is not one I care to use. Then what, if I may be so bold, is your precise connection with Sir Clifford Coot?"

"I found his body and then I found his murderer."

"Really!" the guru's eyes grew wide. "How exciting! Perhaps we shall be able to contact Sir Clifford's spirit later on?"

"Sadly," said Ruby, who felt there was nothing sad about it, "I shan't be able to stay for the, er, séance."

"Experiment," Guru Lennie said. "We prefer to call it an experiment."

"Yes, quite. Anyway. If you could just give me the details of the sort of work you had envisaged. I mean, which I might be able to do. At The Retreat, I mean…"

Guru Lennie waved his hand to dismiss the idea. "Plenty of time to talk business, my dear. The Retreat won't be opening until the spring anyway. We are still recruiting, you know…"

By now they had moved across the hallway and entered another room. "This is the Lounge," the guru said. As in the Sitting Room and the Vermilion Saloon, the predominant colour scheme was crimson with gold trimmings. The furniture was fussily old-fashioned, elaborately carved legs and overstuffed velvet upholstery being much in evidence.

"Did you design this?" Ruby enquired.

"I chose the fabrics."

"Very tasteful."

Having had a quick gawk at the Vermilion Saloon, they strode across the great hallway again towards the room adjoining the Sitting Room.

"I know this room of old," Ruby said, "It was Sir Clifford's study."

"We prefer to call it the Drawing Room."

It looked, to Ruby's untutored eye, like an elaborately decorated smoking room in an old-fashioned gentlemen's club.

"There used to be a huge mahogany desk just there." Ruby pointed towards the centre of the room. "Oh, and over there, by the window, there was a grand piano."

Guru Lennie gasped. "How fabulous! Perhaps we should have a piano here too. In case we have any guests who fancy a quick tinkle on the ivories."

"Nye Clump plays the piano, I believe." Ruby had said it without thinking. She had not wanted to give the impression that there was anything between her and Nye. Rumours were already circulating freely in the village. If she was not careful, stories about her and Nye sharing romantic evenings in dimly-lit piano bars would soon be doing the rounds.

"I know Nye very slightly," Ruby added. "Hardly at all, in fact."

Guru Lennie winked at her. "Your secret's safe with me, petal."

"No!" said Ruby. "Honestly! We've met a few times. In public places. That's all."

"Nye Clump certainly has many talents."

"Yes indeed!" said Ruby.

Guru Lennie gave her a suspicious look.

The time had come, Ruby decided, to put the big question: "Why is Gwendolyn Gormly here?"

Guru Lennie looked confused. "I thought you knew Gwendolyn."

"I do."

"Then isn't it obvious why she's here?"

"She's not blackmailing you, is she?"

Guru Lennie tittered, uncertain whether or not Ruby had been making a joke. "Auras," he said.

"Auras?"

"She reads them."

"Gwendolyn?"

"And chakras."

"She reads those too?"

"Aligns them, my pet, she aligns them."

"Really? I had no idea."

"She has a poster in the window of her shop. Gwendolyn's Grotto. She is qualified in reiki, iridology, primal therapy and Glorphangler's technique."

"What's Glorphangler's technique?"

The guru shrugged. "She's very secretive on that subject. It's one of the forgotten secrets of the ancients."

"But she runs a wine bar. How did she discover one of the forgotten secrets of the ancients?"

"To tell you the truth, I wondered that too. I suppose it may have been revealed to her. That's often the way with forgotten secrets."

"And what are Mrs Williams-Jenkins's special talents?"

"She hasn't got any as far as I know. Why do you ask?"

"Well, won't she be working here?"

"Oh, I certainly hope not! No, she's a sweet old trout but I don't think I'd want her in charge of our paying guests."

"Then why…?"

"Why's she here tonight? She's a benefactor, you might say."

"She has more money than sense, you mean?"

"I wouldn't have phrased it that way. Let's just say that she is making a small contribution."

"But I thought Nathaniel Snibb was rolling in money. Thanks to his pickled onion fortune. Surely, any contribution she might be able to make would be petty cash as far as he's concerned."

Guru Lennie ruminated upon that before answering. "Lowri – Mrs Williams-Jenkins, that is – she has contacts. With other…"

"Seekers?"

"Exactly."

"And you are hoping she will be able to put in a good word for you? Drum up some business, as it were?"

"Word of mouth is the best publicity, so they say. Though when The Retreat opens we shall, of course, be inviting the press."

"You've been talking to Tegwyn, then?"

"Who?"

"Tegwyn Pritchard, chief reporter with The Clogwyn Clarion."

"We were thinking more along the lines of the Sunday Times, Vogue, GQ."

Guru Lennie led Ruby back out into the main hall and towards a door at the rear end, just beyond the Sitting Room. Once through the door, he flipped on a light switch. This caused a low-slung electric candelabra to illuminate the room which, unlike all the others in the house, was devoid of furniture other than bean-bags and scatter-cushions which formed soft mounds upon the sumptuous woollen carpet.

"The Meditation Room," Guru Lennie announced. "It's not finished yet, of course. We shall have speakers hidden in the walls so that meditators may listen to the sounds of nature – waterfalls, bumble bees, gentle rain pattering on dandelion leaves, all that sort of thing – while communing with the Infinite."

The guru aimed a cherubic smile in Ruby's direction. Apparently he was expecting a few words of unbridled enthusiasm.

"Nice," Ruby said, hesitantly.

The guru's smile faltered.

"Then, through that door," (he pointed to a door at the far end of the Meditation Room) "is the gym." Guru Lennie seemed unenthusiastic about the notion of hard physical exercise and had no more to say on the subject of the gym. He led the way back into the main hall, switching off the electric candelabra as he did so. "Now, here, across the hallway we have the yoga studio…"

But before he could take Ruby to inspect that, a booming voice called out from the open door of the Sitting Room. "What d'you think you are doing, you two?" It was Sergeant-Major Stippleton, stomach-in, shoulders-back, standing to attention, red faced, moustache bristling, teeth-clenched. He called to them like a foghorn trying vainly to attract a negligent ship's attention to the iceberg looming at it through the mist. "On the double! Quick-march! By the left! One-two-one-two-one-two…"

As though by a Pavlovian reflex, Ruby and Guru Lennie found themselves striding towards the summoning voice, arms swinging in the manner of soldiers on a ceremonial parade.

"What does he want us for?" Ruby whispered out of the corner of her mouth.

"Oh, the experiment, my petal," said Guru Lennie.

"You mean the séance?"

The guru smiled indulgently. "Whatever you wish to call it, we mustn't be late for it."

"Oh well," thought Ruby, "since there's no way to get out of it, I may as well enjoy it."

6. Wandering Spirits

"There are a few items that we need," said Madame Evadne. "First, we must have a crystal wine glass. We will also need some pieces of paper with the letters of the alphabet written upon them. Oh, and two more pieces of paper with the words 'Yes' and 'No'. Then we must have a large, well-polished table – such as the one conveniently placed in the middle of this very room."

Mrs Williams-Jenkins could barely contain her enthusiasm. She was positively beaming and tapping her fingertips together as though clapping soundlessly. "Oh, just wait until I tell Winifred. That's my dear friend, you know. Miss Winifred Hicks. Of the Derbyshire Hickses. She will be so annoyed to have missed this. A séance. A veritable séance. How enormously exciting!"

When Madame Evadne had first suggested making an attempt at communicating with the spiritual world, it had sounded as though she had only that moment thought of the idea. However, Ruby suspected that her so-called 'experiment' might not have been quite as spontaneous as Madame Evadne would have them believe. Within seconds of asking for a crystal wine glass, one had been placed at the centre of the great oak table. Meanwhile, Guru Lennie was arranging, around the glass, a circle of small white squares of cardboard bearing the letters 'A' to 'Z' and the words 'Yes' and 'No'. The cards had all been prepared in advance, that was quite obvious.

"Ladies and gentlemen, ladies and gentlemen, may I have your attention, please!" Guru Lennie was clapping his pudgy hands together, causing his gaudy kaftan to flutter like the wings of an overweight bird of paradise. "Madame Evadne Miskyn has kindly consented to guide us in an experiment to make contact with the world beyond the world."

"What did he say?" piped up Mrs Williams-Jenkins. "World beyond the world? What does that mean? Mars?"

Guru Lennie's face creased into a dimpled smile. "The world, I should say, that is ever present but rarely seen. The world that is beyond time and which shall never die."

"I have no idea what the fellow's talking about," Mrs Williams-Jenkins complained.

"The spirit world, madam. I am referring to the world beyond the veil of our apprehension."

"Ah!" said Mrs Williams-Jenkins. "Ghosts! Why didn't you say so? What good's a séance without ghosts, hey? A few trumpets and some ectoplasm would be nice. But I'd be prepared to settle for a couple of wailing banshees."

"If I might prevail upon you all," continued Guru Lennie, "to seat yourselves around this table, I shall then ask our medium," (here he wafted a hand in the direction of Madame Evadne) "to explain the protocols of the experiment."

"I'm having nothing to do with it!" Bessie told Ruby. "There are some things you shouldn't meddle with."

"Oh, come on!" Ruby replied. "It's only a bit of harmless fun."

"Let's see how harmless you think it is when Lucifer arrives hot and steaming from the Pit!" And, to Ruby's incomprehension, Bessie started speaking in Welsh: "Gwr neu wraig a fo ganddynt ysbryd…"

Ruby interrupted her. "You know very well that I don't understand a word of what you are saying."

"A man," said Bessie, "or woman," and she lowered her brows meaningfully towards Madame Evadne, "that hath a familiar spirit, shall surely be put to death. Leviticus Chapter 20, verse 27."

In spite of the fact that Bessie had long ago given up any claims to the Methodist faith in which she had been raised, she continued to have a deep-rooted fear of the God in whom she claimed not to believe. She also had a frighteningly compendious knowledge of the sterner Biblical warnings and curses in both Welsh and English.

"I take it, then, that you will be sitting out of this?" said Ruby.

Bessie gave Ruby a severe look by way of answer.

"And so shall I!" exclaimed Ebenezer Evans in the sepulchral tones of an old-time evangelist. "If you want my opinion, the dead should be left in peace. What self-respecting spirit would come down from Heaven at the behest of some meddling fools pushing a wine glass around on a table? And if the spirits thus summoned be not from Heaven, then whence come they?"

Ebenezer Evans had a carrying voice; his words carried the full length of the room. Madame Evadne, who, at that moment, was making some finely-tuned adjustments to the layout of the cards around the wine glass, affected not to have heard him. Guru Lennie, however, reacted with his usual cheerful ebullience: "The spirit world is beyond our comprehension. Sometimes spirits wander the earth for untold years, often unaware that they have even passed from the land of the living. I'm quite sure that any spirits who may visit us tonight will come with good will. Yes, yes, I'm quite, quite sure of that."

"Well, I'm not!" rumbled Ebenezer Evans. "So if nobody objects, I think this good lady," here he looked at Bessie, "and I will go and indulge in more uplifting activities – to wit, a cup of tea and a slice of seed cake in the kitchen."

Being wholly agreeable to that suggestion, Bessie walked arm in arm from the room in the company of Ebenezer Evans. When they had left, several silver candle-holders were placed upon the table and the candles they held were then lit. Next, the electric room lights were extinguished. Madame Evadne asked everyone who remained in the room to take a seat at the table. The shadows cast by the light of the candles, and also by the flames of the fire that burned in the open grate, flickered over their faces dramatically.

"Very well," said Madame Evadne, "the time is ripe. We must begin."

7. The Séance

"I should like you all to place one finger, very lightly, upon the base of the glass," said Madame Evadne.

At the centre of the table the crystal wine glass had been inverted so that its rim rested upon the highly-polished table top. In clockwise order around the edge of the table sat Madame Evadne, Nathaniel Snibb, Clarissa Winthrop, Guru Lennie, Nye Clump, Sergeant-Major Selwyn 'Stonker' Stippleton, Gwendolyn Gormly, Ruby and Mrs Lowri Williams-Jenkins.

Clarissa Winthrop was the first to respond to Madame Evadne's injunction. Reaching out a bony hand, she carefully placed a well-manicured finger upon the base of the glass. "Maybe we'll summon one of my old lovers," she chuckled. "Preferably a rich one who'll tell me where the loot is hidden."

Mrs Williams-Jenkins muttered "How common!" under her breath. Ruby, who was sitting next to Mrs Williams-Jenkins, heard the remark quite clearly and smiled at her to express her agreement. Fortunately, Clarissa Winthrop did not hear the remark. Had she done so, Ruby suspected, she would have wasted no time in telling Mrs Williams-Jenkins what she thought of her in words of one syllable. There was about Clarissa an air of barely-suppressed aggression which, although disguised beneath a thin veneer of 'good breeding', reminded Ruby of Gwendolyn Gormly.

Gwendolyn was the next to put her finger upon the inverted glass. "How many rich old lovers have you had, anyway?" she said, smiling at Clarissa. "And what did they die of? Exhaustion?"

Clarissa returned Gwendolyn's smile. Ruby tried to think where she had seen a smile like that before. Suddenly it came to her – it was the sort of smile which the actor Christopher Lee would give when playing Count Dracula, just before sinking his teeth into a particularly succulent neck.

Ruby got the feeling that this might not be the first occasion on which Clarissa Winthrop had crossed the path of Gwendolyn Gormly. The two women kept eyeing one another with barely suppressed malevolence.

"Now, come along, everyone, don't be shy," Guru Lennie said enthusiastically. "The spirits can only communicate once we provide them with our combined life forces."

One by one, each person reached across the table-top to rest a finger delicately upon the upturned wine glass. By the time Ruby reached across, there was barely any room left for her fingertip. The base of the glass was completely obscured by fingers. Finger upon finger upon finger now formed a criss-crossed stack rising several inches above the glass itself. Ruby's finger rested upon Mrs Williams-Jenkins's finger. The final finger, placed upon Ruby's, belonged to Sergeant-Major Selwyn 'Stonker' Stippleton.

"Now, please, relax," intoned Madame Evadne, "and let the spirits guide the planchette. Is there anybody there?"

"Stupid question," whispered Mrs Williams-Jenkins. "There's nine of us here. Are we all supposed to answer?"

Madame Evadne rephrased the question: "Is there anyone from the spirit world who would like to communicate with us?"

The wine glass trembled.

"You're pushing!" Gwendolyn accused Clarissa.

"Not me! It was you. I felt your finger twitch."

"Ladies, ladies," said Guru Lennie, placatingly, "we need to be silent or the spirits may not answer."

The wine glass trembled again.

"I ask once more," said Madame Evadne, "is there anyone on the spirit plane who would like to speak to us?"

Slowly, haltingly, the glass began to slide around the table. First it made for the card bearing the letter 'K', then it slithered towards the letter 'Z', then, after a few more hesitant movements around the shiny surface of the table, it suddenly zoomed with speed and conviction to the card on which was written the word 'Yes'.

Mrs Williams-Jenkins gasped. "Oh! How exciting!"

"Who is there?" droned Madame Evadne.

The glass quivered. It slid across the table top towards the 'X' but changed its mind before arriving there. Then it suddenly made a bee-line for the 'E' and, in quick succession, the 'M' and the 'I'.

"Is it Emily?" Madame Evadne asked.

"Yes," the planchette answered.

"Emily was a street urchin, a flower-seller, in Victorian times," Madame Evadne explained. "She often pays us a visit. Where did you live, Emily?"

The planchette began to spell out a name: 'W', 'H', 'I'…

"Whitstable!" Sergeant-Major Stonker Stippleton said.

"Whitechapel," Madame Evadne corrected. "Emily lived in a squalid attic room in Whitechapel."

"Well, if you knew that," protested Clarissa, "why did you go through that whole rigmarole of making her spell it out?"

Madame Evadne raised her eyebrows in plain astonishment. "But if I'd just told you that's where she lived you might not have believed me."

Ruby opened her mouth to say something, thought better of it and closed her mouth again.

"And have you a message for someone, Emily?" asked Madame Evadne.

"Yes," said the planchette.

"Tell us, Emily, for whom is your message?"

The glass trembled, then it moved in a small circle, then in wider and wider circles. It seemed to be hunting for the right card. It slid past the 'A', then the 'B', the 'C', 'D', 'E', 'F', 'G' and 'H'. It paused by the 'I' a moment then had a change of mind and slid back the way it had come, eventually touching its rim to the 'G'.

"Is this a message for Guru Lennie?" Madame Evadne asked.

The glass sped across to the 'No'. Then it went back to the 'G', then the 'W', the 'E' and the 'N'.

"It's for me!" Gwendolyn exclaimed.

"What is your name, my dear?" Madame Evadne enquired.

"Gwendolyn!" Gwendolyn replied, irritably. "Everybody knows who I am. Gwendolyn Gormly."

"Is your message for Gwendolyn Gormly?" Madame Evadne asked into thin air.

"Yes" came the planchette's response.

Gwendolyn laughed. "I don't know who's pushing the glass but whoever it is, you can stop having your bit of fun now."

Guru Lennie looked shocked. "Oh, I'm quite sure nobody was pushing it, my dear. We are but the servants of the spirits, our hands are the tools through which they speak."

"Pull the other one," said Gwendolyn. "I know how this Ouija stuff works. I'll bet it was Clarissa, trying to play a joke on me."

"I wouldn't sink so low," said Clarissa.

"That's not what I've heard," riposted Gwendolyn. "In fact, certain members of the Hell Fire Club have seen you sink a good deal lower. So I've been told."

"The *what* Club?" asked Mrs Williams-Jenkins.

Ruby had heard of the Hell Fire Club. It was a members' only establishment in the nearby village of Clogwyn Mawr. She did not know exactly what went on within its walls but she did not think it was poetry reading.

"Ladies, ladies, please…" chirruped Guru Lennie. "We must have silence if Emily is to continue with her message. Please, Madame Evadne, continue."

A tremble ran through Madame Evadne's entire body. "Emily is crying," she said. "Is something troubling you, Emily?"

The glass did not move.

"Emily, darling, you know you are among friends. Please continue with your message. What do you wish to tell us?"

The glass trembled hesitantly. Then it began to slide jerkily over the polished table top, never moving far and never moving quickly.

"Emily seems nervous," Madame Evadne explained. "Give her a moment. I'm sure that, once she's calmed herself, she will vouchsafe her message."

And sure enough, a few seconds later, the glass started moving faster and faster, spinning around in circles at the centre of the table before finally darting out to touch card after card in quick succession: 'G', 'W', 'E', 'N', 'D', 'O', 'L', 'Y', 'N'. "Gwendolyn," said Madame Evadne for the benefit of anyone who may not have been paying attention. The glass continued: 'G', 'O', 'R', 'M', 'L', 'Y'. "Gormly," said Madame Evadne. The glass went on: 'I', 'S'.

Gwendolyn laughed. "Oh, this is going to be good. I can see where this is going. What will little Emily say about me, I wonder?

Not 'Gwendolyn Gormly is going meet a tall, dark stranger' or 'Gwendolyn Gormly is going to win the Lottery', I don't suppose. OK, whoever's pushing the damn' glass, carry on having your fun. It's all water off a duck's back as far as I'm concerned."

Guru Lennie was sitting tight-lipped, his usual jovial demeanour no longer in evidence. Ruby got the impression that Gwendolyn's interruptions were testing the limits of the Guru's endurance. "Please continue," he said to Madame Evadne.

"Emily, my darling," said the medium. "Can you complete your message, my sweet? You told us that 'Gwendolyn Gormly is' but you didn't tell us *what* she is. Please, Emily, finish your message."

The glass did not hesitate this time. It zoomed across the table, picking letter after letter in rapid succession: 'G', 'U', 'I', 'L', 'T', 'Y'.

Suddenly there was a sharp movement and a harsh cracking sound. The crystal wine glass shattered beneath the stack of fingers resting upon it and lay in fragments upon the oak table.

Mrs Williams-Jenkins gave a cry of astonishment. Sergeant-Major Stippleton let forth with a plain-spoken imprecation which would have been unexceptional in the barrack room but was not entirely polite in genteel society. Clarissa accused Gwendolyn of deliberately smashing the wine glass and Gwendolyn accused Clarissa of pushing it around the table in order to spell out the accusatory message.

"This is all a nasty trick!" Gwendolyn spat out the words like bullets from a gun. "'Gwendolyn Gormly is Guilty'. What the bloody hell is that supposed to mean? Guilty of what?" She looked around the table from person to person, fixing each with a penetrating glare. Madame Evadne Miskyn the medium was smiling beatifically as though still entranced by her spirit flower-girl's message and not at all bothered that it pointed the finger of guilt at Gwendolyn. Nathaniel Snibb looked vaguely embarrassed but whether his embarrassment was due to the unpleasant message, Gwendolyn's angry response or simply the whole silly business of pushing a wine glass around on a table it was impossible to tell. Clarissa was smirking. Nye Clump was staring through narrowed eyes at Gwendolyn. Guru Lennie was shaking his head and tutting. Sergeant-Major Selwyn 'Stonker' Stippleton was holding Gwendolyn's hand (something which, in the heat of the moment, Gwendolyn had not noticed) while muttering "Now, now, Gwendolyn, my love, a stiff drink is what you need." Ruby was looking blank, as she so often did in times of high drama. And Mrs Lowri Williams-Jenkins was patting her hands together like a trained seal and wittering away about how jolly exciting this all was.

"You!" Gwendolyn suddenly snapped. She was pointing at Madame Evadne, whose beatific smile withered in an instant. "I warned Lennie about you."

"*Me?*" wailed Madame Evadne.

"Oh, now, just a moment, ladies," burbled Guru Lennie, "this really is not the time or the place for…"

"Evadne Miskin, you are a fraud!" continued Gwendolyn.

"*Me-ee?*" Madame Evadne managed to draw the word out into two syllables.

"You were nothing but a seaside fortune teller. There was that little scam you were running, wasn't there. With an assistant. Get the punters to write their questions on a piece of paper and hand them to your assistant. The paper was supposedly burnt in a candle flame but in reality it was snuck into a secret compartment under your table. There was a hole in the table and a crystal ball on top of the hole. You gazed into the crystal ball, read the question and came out with the answer. Fraud is what that is. Nothing but fraud!"

"Well, really!" wailed Madame Evadne. "I've never been so insulted."

"Don't worry, love, I've got plenty more insults where that one came from and you deserve them all."

"Now, now, really, I'm sure there's been some mistake," Nathaniel Snibb said. "We all need to have a nice drink and calm down."

Ruby was left wondering why Gwendolyn had taken such an active dislike to Madame Evadne. But no more was said on the matter that night.

8. Snowbound

Ruby, Bessie and Mrs Williams-Jenkins were sitting in armchairs close to the log fire in the Sitting Room. The others had dispersed themselves through the labyrinthine structure of the house. Ruby had been given to understand that the permanent staff such as Guru Lennie, Ebenezer Evans, Sergeant-Major Stippleton and Madame Evadne, had their own rooms. The owner, Nathaniel Snibb and his lady friend, Clarissa Winthrop, although not resident at the Hall, were staying the night. Goodness knows where Nye Clump had got to. And as for Gwendolyn Gormly, Ruby neither knew nor cared where she was.

Bronwen was pouring coffee from a silver pot into three dainty little cups. "I'll get some more logs for the fire," she said, as she put the pot down upon a highly ornamental table mat. "Oh, and I'll bring you some biscuits to have with your coffee."

Ruby put up a negating hand. "We can't stop. It's very thoughtful of you, Bron, but it's already later than I was planning to stay. As soon as we finish our coffee, Bessie and I will be off."

"So shall I," said Mrs Williams-Jenkins. "Wilkins, my chauffeur, will fetch me in the Bentley. I told him to be here at nine o'clock sharp. What time is it now?"

Bessie looked at her wristwatch, "Almost twenty to ten."

"How odd!" Mrs Williams-Jenkins sipped her coffee meditatively. "Wilkins is normally so punctual. I shall have stern words with him."

"How far away do you live?" Bessie asked. "If it's not too far, I'll be happy to give you a lift."

"I'm not sure you'll be able to," Bronwen said.

"What do you mean?"

"Open the curtains."

"The curtains?" said Ruby.

"Open the curtains and you'll see exactly what I mean."

Ruby went over to the huge velvet curtains hanging from rings on a long wooden curtain rail and she pulled them back with a flourish. In the darkness beyond the window, illuminated by the pale light seeping from the Sitting Room, huge flakes of snow could be seen falling in profusion. Snow was mounded up on the windowsill. The garden was deeply covered in snow. Snow, in short, was everywhere in evidence.

"Oh!" said Ruby.

"Myn uffern i!" said Bessie, who only cursed in Welsh when she was upset. "The snow's settling."

"I thought," said Ruby, "you said the snow never settles here."

"It doesn't! Well, only once every few years, anyway."

"But we have to get back home," Ruby protested.

"There's no chance of that," Bronwen said. "Not until the snowploughs get out. And I don't think they'll be here until tomorrow at the earliest."

"We can't stay here all night," said Ruby.

"Why not? There's plenty of space. Have you any idea how big Coot Hall is? There are lots of bedrooms."

"They won't have been aired," Bessie said. "We can't stay in damp bedrooms. We'll catch our death."

"Wilkins will be here soon," Mrs Williams-Jenkins insisted. "Nothing short of the Four Horsemen of the Apocalypse would prevent Wilkins from getting through."

The door to the Sitting Room creaked open and in waddled Guru Lennie. "We've just had a phone call," he said. "For Mrs Williams-Jenkins. Your chauffeur sends his regrets but he can't get the Bentley started and the driveway of your house is two feet deep in snow."

"Blast the fellow!" said Mrs Williams-Jenkins. "Then I suppose I shall have to stay overnight after all. I shall require two eiderdowns – *not* duvets – and lots of soap and talcum powder."

"I think that may be arranged, Madame. Now then, ladies…" Guru Lennie turned to Ruby and Bessie, "please feel free to make yourselves at home. You are the first guests to stay at The Retreat and I want to make sure your stay is a memorable one."

9. The First Crime

Ruby lay on her bed staring at the vermilion birds and golden flowers embroidered on the sagging canopy. She had never slept in a four-poster bed before and she feared that she might find the experience claustrophobic. Not that she planned to retire for the night just yet. Nathaniel Snibb had invited everyone down to the Drawing Room for what he called a "small nightcap". Ruby felt that, after the excitement with the planchette and the frustration of being snowed in, a few relaxing glasses of something pleasantly alcoholic would go down a treat.

Mr Crickspittle, whom Guru Lennie described as his "butler", had shown Ruby and Bessie to their rooms on the first floor with all the grace of a spider leading a fly towards its web. There was something about that man that made Ruby's skin crawl. He seemed to seethe with contempt and hatred for everyone and everything but he reserved a particularly high level of seething for Ruby.

Ruby's room was dank with an incongruously high ceiling. Its walls were covered with an old-fashioned green-and-red-striped wallpaper disfigured by numerous irregular brown blotches of dampness. Upon the floor was a frayed and worn woollen mat of an elaborate oriental pattern which must once have been attractive but now would be likely to attract only the most disreputable of moths that had fallen on hard times. And dominating the bedroom was the four-poster bed, its four carved pseudo-Doric columns supporting the dusty canopy at which Ruby was currently staring.

She looked at her watch. It was almost ten o'clock. Nathaniel had suggested meeting for drinks at quarter past ten, which gave Ruby just enough time to get a quick bath and freshen herself up. She wished she had brought a change of clothing. But, of course, she had not had any intention of staying; so slipping into a long black evening dress was not an option (even if she had owned a long black evening dress, which she did not). She heaved herself off the soft feather-mattress and took a look in the long mirror attached to a door of the wardrobe.

Her beige chinos were not the most elegant attire for a cocktail party in a country house but they would have to do. Towels and toiletries had been set out for her but since her room did not have *en suite* facilities she would be obliged to use the bathroom at the end of the corridor. Mr Crickspittle had tersely informed her that the bathroom was shared with some of the other guests "so it's no good complaining if there's no hot water."

She picked up the big pink bath towel draped over the back of a chair next to a small dressing table and set off towards the bathroom. Her room was in the west wing of the house. Bessie's bedroom was directly to the left of Ruby's. Mrs Williams-Jenkins's room was facing Ruby's, on the other side of the corridor. Adjoining Mrs Williams-Jenkins's room was Guru Lennie's room, directly across the passageway from Bessie.

A staircase at the north-eastern end of the corridor led upwards to the second floor where both Bronwen and Sergeant-Major 'Stonker' Stippleton had their rooms. Nathaniel, Clarissa, Madame Evadne, Nye Clump and Gwendolyn Gormly had rooms in the east wing so (Ruby supposed) they would not be sharing the west wing's bathroom. Ruby only hoped that nobody had got to the bathroom before her. She longed for a good, relaxing soak in the huge Victorian cast-iron bath which she had seen when she had gone to wash her hands earlier. It would be just too disappointing if someone had already commandeered the bathroom for their own bathing pleasure.

Still, she thought, if the worst came to the worst, she would just wait until whoever was taking a bath had finished. The 10:15 deadline for drinks in the Drawing Room would surely not be rigorously enforced. If she happened to wander down at half past ten, that would hardly be a crime, would it!

The door to the bathroom was, in common with all the other doors in Coot Hall, made of solid oak. It was, therefore, not possible to see if there was a light on inside the room. However, the danger of entering while somebody was already within had been thoughtfully avoided by the simple expedient of fitting a small labelled dial just above the brass handle of the door. The dial was connected to a locking mechanism on the inner side of the door. When the door was locked, the dial said "Engaged". When it was unlocked, the dial said "Vacant". Ruby's luck was in. The dial said "Vacant". She glanced along the corridor to make sure that nobody else was approaching with the intention of using the bathroom and, having ascertained that the coast was clear, she rapidly turned the door knob, slipped quickly into the bathroom and banged the door shut behind her.

She was astonished to find that, in spite of the "Vacant" sign on the door, the bathroom was already occupied. In fact, there were two people there. One of them was Sergeant-Major Selwyn 'Stonker' Stippleton. The other was Gwendolyn Gormly. Sergeant-Major Stippleton was lying, unmoving, on the floor with his eyes staring wildly and a ghastly pallor clouding his face. He was making a horrible rattling noise in his throat which, Ruby thought, sounded like the sort of noise a person might make when being strangled with a pair of tights – which, by a curious coincidence, is precisely what was happening to him at that very moment. The legs of a pair of Nylon tights had been wrapped around Sergeant-Major Selwyn 'Stonker' Stippleton's neck, forming a sort of tourniquet or garrotte which could be tightened by pulling on the two leg-ends of the tights – which was exactly what Gwendolyn Gormly was doing.

"Oh my God!" cried Ruby. "You've killed him!"

10. Guilty Or Innocent?

"Of course I wasn't strangling him!" Gwendolyn Gormly was standing by the big, open log fire in the Drawing Room. Looking magnificent in a tight, leopard-spotted silk blouse, black miniskirt and six-inch stilettoes, she was holding a large glass of malt whisky in one hand and a pungent cigarette fitted into a long, black cigarette-holder in the other hand. "I don't know how any idiot could think I was strangling him. He's got muscles on his muscles. He'd overpower me in seconds."

Clarissa Winthrop, who was standing on the other side of the fireplace looking slightly less magnificent than Gwendolyn in a crimson silk blouse, tight white midi-skirt and four-inch stilettoes, sniggered lasciviously.

"Besides which," Gwendolyn paused to give Clarissa a condescending glance from beneath her mascara-heavy lashes, "why would I even want to strangle the man? I barely know him. Like I said, you'd have to be an idiot to think I was strangling him."

Gwendolyn shifted her condescending glance from Clarissa to Ruby.

"But I saw you!" Ruby protested. "Sergeant-Major Stippleton was lying on the floor of the bathroom with a pair of tights wrapped around his neck and you were pulling the ends!"

Gwendolyn rolled her eyes and made a tutting sound. "Any fool could see that I was trying to resuscitate him."

"Well, it didn't look like you were."

"I don't care what it looked like. That's what I was doing. The tights were tied around his neck and I was trying to undo the knot."

"Why were you even in that bathroom?" Madame Evadne asked. "Your room is in the east wing. As is mine. We have our own bathroom."

"That one was already taken," Gwendolyn said. "I could hear sounds of splashing and singing coming from inside. I happened to bump into Clarissa in the corridor and she told me there was another bathroom in the west wing. So I went to that one."

Clarissa chuckled and Gwendolyn looked daggers at her.

From the chaise-longue came a sound like a Saint-Bernard dog clearing its throat. This curious noise was being produced by the recumbent form of Sergeant-Major Selwyn 'Stonker' Stippleton who, at that moment, was in the process of recovering painfully from his recent near-death experience.

"He's looking a little better now, I fancy," opined Nathaniel Snibb.

"He's very pale though," added Guru Lennie.

"His aura is glowing more brightly," Madame Evadne observed, optimistically.

"I wouldn't say so," hissed Gwendolyn, who did not much care for amateurs trying to read auras.

"Smelling salts are what the poor man needs," said Mrs Williams-Jenkins.

"I have some aspirins in my travelling bag," Nye Clump said. "Perhaps, in the absence of smelling salts, they might do?"

"Peace and quiet would do him a lot better than having all of us crowding around making a fuss," Bessie said pragmatically.

Just then the door to the Drawing Room opened and in walked Bronwen. "I've phoned Doctor Davies," she said.

"How long before he'll be here?" Nathaniel Snibb asked.

"He only lives down in the village," said Bessie. "He'll be here in ten minutes, I should think."

"I'm afraid not," said Bronwen. "He won't be coming. Not tonight, anyway."

"What do you mean, he won't be coming?" Nathaniel Snibb said. "You did explain the urgency, I trust."

"The roads are completely impassable," Bronwen said. "If it goes on like this, it could be days before he'll be able get here."

"Then what are we to do?" asked Nathaniel.

"Doctor Davies suggested giving the patient a stiff brandy and hoping for the best."

"That can't be proper medical procedure, surely," protested Nathaniel. "Are you sure the man is a real doctor?"

Mrs Williams-Jenkins piped up in answer to that. "Oh yes. He's a marvellous doctor. I had a terrible pustule, you know, in a most painful location. He gave me some cream that cured it almost overnight."

This observation caused a temporary pause in conversation. Nobody was inclined to ask for further details but nor were they completely sure that Mrs Williams-Jenkins's resounding endorsement of Doctor Davies's medical competence when confronted by painful pustules was entirely relevant to the present circumstances.

It was Nathenial Snibb who eventually broke the silence. "I'll get the brandy."

"It doesn't make any sense," Nye Clump said. "You say that you went to the bathroom, Gwendolyn, and there you found Sergeant-Major Stippleton unconscious on the floor with a pair of women's tights wrapped around his neck. If we are to believe your story…"

Gwendolyn's eyes blazed. "You can believe whatever you like for all I care, sweetheart! It's the bloody truth!"

"Yes, well, what I mean is, that means that someone else must have tried to strangle him. Someone in this house."

"It could have been an intruder, I suppose?" suggested Guru Lennie.

"In this snow?" said Bronwen. "I can't see how anyone would have managed to get here, let alone to break in."

"So where was everyone at the time it happened?" asked Nye.

"I was with Natty," Clarissa Winthrop said.

Nathaniel Snibb coughed.

"With Nathaniel Snibb, I mean," Clarissa corrected.

"We were discussing business," Nathaniel added, "related to the opening of The Retreat."

"And everyone else?" Nye asked.

"I was in my room," said Mrs Williams-Jenkins.

"Me too," said Evadne. "In *my* room, I mean."

"We were all in our rooms," said Bessie.

"Except for me, of course," said Ruby. "I was on my way to the bathroom. As you all know."

"I was in the kitchen with Ebenezer," Bronwen said, "getting the sandwiches and canapés ready."

"Can-a-*what?*" said Clarissa Winthrop.

"Canapés, my dear," sneered Gwendolyn Gormly. "It's French for 'nibbly bits'. They are served in all the best places." She paused to take a good swig of her whisky, "Which may explain why you've never heard of them."

It was at that moment that Ebenezer Evans entered the room bearing a large tray of plates heaped with little triangular sandwiches, savoury snacks, roasted nuts, olives and cheeses. "Voilà!" he said with the panache of a magician unexpectedly producing a mongoose from a top-hat, "Please help yourselves, ladies and gentlemen."

Sergeant-Major Stippleton pulled himself into a sitting position against the back-rest of the chaise-longue and said, "If you've got any cheese-and-pickle sandwiches, I'll try to force a few down."

Ebenezer Evans, who was well aware of the Sergeant-Major's culinary preferences, had been sure to prepare a fine selection of cheese-and-pickle sandwiches and soon, after eating a few of them, washed down with a generous measure of Nathaniel Snibb's Rémy Martin, the colour began to come back into the invalid's cheeks.

11. Tights Of Death

"I'll tell you everything I remember." Sergeant-Major Stippleton was on his second glass of Rémy Martin and, while he had not yet returned to his habitual appearance of rosy good health, he was nevertheless managing to stride about the room with a glitter in his eye and a boom in his voice. "I'd gone into the bathroom to have a…"

Nathaniel Snibb gave him a warning glance. "We don't need the details, Sergeant-Major. There are ladies present."

"…to have a wash-and-brush-up, I was about to say."

"Ah."

"I entered the bathroom with the intention of combing my hair, brushing my eyebrows and moistening the ends of my moustache when suddenly the room goes spinning around me, everything goes black, stars twinkle across my vision, fireworks explode somewhere in the back of my skull and I wakes up with a rotten headache and a feeling like my throat has been wrapped in the coils of a boa constrictor."

"That would have been the tights," Clarissa Winthrop said, spitefully. "The ones Gwendolyn was strangling you with."

"You keep your filthy mouth shut!" Gwendolyn warned, "or I'll come and shut it for you!"

"Ladies, ladies, please!" Guru Lennie said. "Nobody is accusing anyone of anything."

"She's accusing me!" Gwendolyn protested.

"Please continue, Sergeant-Major," said Nathaniel Snibb. "Are we to take it that you did not see your assailant?"

"If I'd 'a seen him…"

"Or 'her'," Clarissa interjected.

"…he'd have ended up in a much worse shape than what I am now, I can tell you that. These hands," (here he held up his hands for the appreciation of the assembled throng) "is weapons of mass destruction. Trained to kill, these hands is. I dares not leave them out of my sight for fear of what they could do. But sneaking up on a man while he's grooming his moustache. That's not Queensbury Rules, is it? That's not the actions of a gentleman, that isn't!"

"You certainly received a hefty wallop on the cranium, that's for sure," Nathaniel said. An earlier examination of the Sergeant-Major while he lain recumbent on the chaise-longue had revealed the presence of a painful swelling on the upper-back part of his head. It appeared that he had received a blow from a blunt instrument and it was that which had rendered him unconscious.

"The first thing I remembers seeing was this lady here." Sergeant-Major Stippleton glanced towards Gwendolyn Gormly who was sitting in a large leather armchair with her legs nonchalantly crossed, drinking a glass of malt whisky. "I opens my eyes and there she is, bestraddling me, as you might say, with her hands tugging at the two legs of a pair of tights, the gusset of which, if you'll forgive the expression, was choking the very life out of me."

"Very fancy tights they were too," said Clarissa Winthrop. "I recognised the label." The tights, having been removed from the Sergeant-Major's neck, were now draped across the back of an upright chair. "'Nuits de Montmartre'. Quite an exclusive brand. Expensive. Not the sort of tights you'd expect women around here to be wearing. I suppose it's worth finding out if anyone here has that brand of tights."

Madame Evadne shook her head. Ruby pointed out that she had no need of tights as she was wearing chinos and, in any case, she had never heard of the 'Nuits de Montmartre' brand. Clarissa Winthrop expressed the opinion that the tights in question were vulgar and she would not touch them with a barge pole. Neither Bronwen nor Bessie were in the habit of wearing tights. Mrs Williams-Jenkins said "Tights?" as though the concept was unfamiliar to her, and all of the men denied any knowledge of the garment in question. Which just left Gwendolyn.

"Yes, they are my tights. I never denied it, did I? I had a spare pair in my overnight bag. Someone must have crept into my room when I wasn't there and filched them."

"Who'd do such a thing?" Madame Evadne asked.

"Any one of you might have!"

Guru Lennie looked horrified. "Really, I find it hard to believe that any of the people here in this room would stoop so low as to steal a pair of tights."

"Nuts!"

"I beg your pardon?"

"You heard me." Gwendolyn Gormly put down her drink, pushed herself out of her chair and made a stately progression (or, at any rate, as stately a progression as is possible on six inch stiletto heels) towards Guru Lennie. "Now, I don't know whose idea this was, but when I find out I won't be in a pleasant frame of mind."

Gwendolyn turned to Sergeant-Major Stippleton and gave him a look that could curdle milk. "Look, chum," – Gwendolyn prodded him in the chest with a daggerlike fingernail – "I don't know what your game is but you know as well as I do that someone clobbered you on the head and throttled you with them tights. Then I arrived in the bathroom thinking to run myself a nice, relaxing bath, and what do I find? *You*, is what I find! Flat out on the floor, looking more dead than alive. If it hadn't been for my quick thinking, dead is what you'd have been by now. I got down on my hands and knees to loosen them tights, as well you know. When Ruby strolled in, that's what I was doing."

"Well," conceded the Sergeant-Major, "that is possible, I suppose."

"Possible! I'm telling you, that's what happened."

"Such a shame that you can't prove it!" said Madame Evadne.

"Oh, I can prove it all right! The Sergeant-Major here has proved it already. And Ruby can back him up."

"Me?" Ruby said. She had already made it clear that she had seen Gwendolyn in what looked like a very guilty position, apparently strangling Sergeant-Major Stippleton.

"Yes," said Gwendolyn, "you. Was he," (here she prodded the Sergeant-Major with her fingernail once again) "making any sound when you found us?"

Ruby thought a moment. "Well, yes, he was. He was gurgling."

"And yet he claims that he was out for the count, having been knocked over the bonce and garrotted. Now if it'd been me who'd knocked him out and strangled him, and if, having been knocked out and strangled, he'd gone unconscious, how come he was up to gurgling when you, Ruby Lake, found us?"

"I… I suppose he must have recovered a bit."

"And d'you think an unconscious, strangled person would recover if someone was strangling him even more, like you reckon I was? 'Course he damn' well wouldn't. He recovered because I'd managed to loosen the tights, thus allowing him to suck in enough air to do all the gurgling you heard. Stands to bloody reason, I'd have thought!"

"She has a point," Mrs Williams-Jenkins said. "Given the evidence, I should say that you have all done this lady a grave injustice by accusing her of strangling Sergeant-Major Stippleton when it would seem that, on the contrary, she is responsible for saving his life."

"Well," said Guru Lennie, "I can see how that might be a possibility."

"For God's sake, never mind all the blather," hissed Gwendolyn, as she picked up her empty glass and handed it to the guru. "Just fill that up with whisky, can't you."

"I wonder," said Mrs Williams-Jenkins, "if I might have a quiet word with you, Miss Gormly?"

Gwendolyn took the whisky glass which Guru Lennie had just that moment topped up and, when the guru stood there smiling at her, she said, "Hop it!"

Guru Lennie flushed red and mumbled "Well! Really!" but he took Gwendolyn's advice anyway and hopped it.

Gwendolyn sat on the settee next to Mrs Williams-Jenkins and they began talking together in hushed tones. Ruby pretended to pay them no attention, giving the impression that she was listening to Bessie who was nattering away about something or other; but Ruby was, in fact, watching Gwendolyn like a hawk. Due to the hubbub of talk throughout the room, Ruby was unable to catch precisely what was being said but she heard occasional snatches of conversation. From this she gathered that Mrs Williams-Jenkins had been altogether unimpressed by the spiritual shenanigans of Madame Evadne and, moreover, she had formed a clear impression that Guru Lennie was "a charlatan of the worst sort". However, of Gwendolyn she had formed a far more favourable impression.

"You have the true second sight, I believe?"

Ruby could not hear Gwendolyn's reply but from the broad smile which illuminated Mrs Williams-Jenkins's face, she assumed that it had been in the affirmative.

"Do you do private consultations, by any chance?"

Again, Ruby could not hear Gwendolyn's answer, but she assumed it involved a discussion of remuneration. Money, it seemed, was no object as far as Mrs Williams-Jenkins was concerned.

"My dear Miss Gormly, I should very much like to introduce you to my good friend, Miss Winifred Hicks. She should have been here tonight you know, but for her infirmity. Her legs, you see. She has terrible trouble with…"

But that was all that Ruby was able to hear of the conversation for in the next moment, Bessie was tapping her on the shoulder. "Mr Snibb," she said. Ruby glanced around and saw that Nathaniel Snibb was standing there, "was asking if you'd like to have a nightcap?"

Ruby could not have cared less about a nightcap but she made polite conversation and thanked Mr Snibb for his kind offer. "Plenty of drinks in the cabinet," he was saying. "Please feel free to help yourself."

When Ruby glanced towards Mrs Williams-Jenkins, Gwendolyn was nowhere to be seen.

12. The Guilt of Gwendolyn Gormly

"What do you make of that, then?" Sitting in a big leather armchair, Nye Clump swirled the whisky around in his glass and hunched forward towards the heat of the open log fire.

"On the face of it," said Ruby, "it would seem that everything points to Gwendolyn Gormly's guilt."

"She's always been a nasty piece of work," Bessie said. "I remember when she was a little girl, she poured treacle down Tegwyn Pritchard's trousers. Someone capable of that is capable of anything."

The three of them had the Drawing Room to themselves now. It was half-past twelve and everyone else had retired to their rooms.

"There is just one thing that mitigates against her guilt," Ruby said. "Well, two things, actually. First, how would she have done it? And secondly, why."

"Well, we know how she did it," said Nye. "She bopped him over the head with a jar of bath salts."

Once Sergeant-Major Stippleton had recovered sufficiently to be capable of refilling his own glass with Cognac, Nathaniel Snibb, Guru Lennie and all the others had gone upstairs to take a look at the scene of the crime. On the bathroom floor they found a large glass jar partially filled with pink crystals. The jar had not been noticed initially since it had rolled under the huge cast-iron bath on its four ball-in-claw legs. A quantity of the crystals had spilled from the jar. The jar itself was cracked, no doubt due to the force with which it had been brought down upon the victim's skull.

"We know how *somebody* did it," Ruby corrected. "We don't know if that person was Gwendolyn. But even assuming that she had managed to knock the poor man unconscious with the jar of bath salts, the question then arises: why would she strangle him with a pair of her tights?"

"To make sure he never regained consciousness, I suppose," said Bessie.

"Yes, but why with her tights? Her own tights. Tights that are of such an uncommon brand that they can immediately be identified as Gwendolyn's?"

"Baffling," Nye said. "Tights, I mean! Not an obvious murder weapon, I shouldn't have thought. Not that I am an expert on these things."

The three of them stared blankly into the fire. The flames licked and crackled over the logs. Ruby sipped at the vintage port in her hand. Nye savoured his whisky. Bessie was drinking a mug of hot cocoa which Ebenezer Evans had made for her just before he went to bed.

"I don't suppose," Bessie said, "that she ever intended anyone to find the tights. If Ruby hadn't happened to pop into the bathroom, Gwendolyn would have been able to strangle him and scarper without anyone being the wiser."

Ruby sipped her port and stared into the fire again, as though looking there for inspiration. In a far corner of the room an old grandfather clock tick-tocked gloomily.

Suddenly inspiration struck. "But that doesn't make any sense," said Ruby. "Gwendolyn doesn't leave things to chance. We know that already. She's ruthless. She managed to get Maggie's shop off her by devious means. She snapped up the wine bar so fast the ink wasn't even dry on the estate agent's contract. She plans. She connives. She plots things out and she doesn't leave anything to chance."

"So?" said Bessie.

"So, she wouldn't strangle someone with a pair of her own tights in an unlocked bathroom. She'd at least have locked the door. More probably she'd have chosen somewhere more off the beaten track."

"And she wouldn't have used her own tights!" said Nye. "By golly, I think you are on to something, Ruby."

"Then again," Bessie sipped her hot cocoa, "maybe she didn't have the chance to plan it all out in advance. Maybe she was in a rush. Maybe she saw the opportunity and had to make the most of it. The Sergeant-Major was in the bathroom. Gwendolyn happened to be holding a pair of tights. She noticed the jar of bath salts. And, well, she acted on an impulse."

"So, let me get this right." Nye stood up with his back to the fire, cradling his whisky in the palms of his hands, "You both think that Gwendolyn is quite capable of killing someone. But you, Ruby, believe that the manner in which it was attempted is out of character?"

Ruby shrugged. She did not like Gwendolyn. She had never liked Gwendolyn. But she did not have absolute proof that Gwendolyn was a killer, or a would-be killer. True, the evidence was all against her. But the evidence was, as they say in TV courtroom dramas, "circumstantial". Gwendolyn was innocent until proven guilty.

"Then there's my second objection," Ruby reminded him. "Why would she want to kill Sergeant-Major Stippleton? They had never met one another before tonight."

"As far as we know," said Nye.

"Well, as far as I can remember, neither of them paid much attention to one another earlier in the evening. If Gwendolyn was planning to do him in, all I can say is she was playing it pretty cool."

"So was the Sergeant-Major," Bessie added. "If he knew her, I mean, and if there was some sort of bad blood between them."

"And yet," said Nye, "there she was, garrotting a man with a pair of her tights."

The grandfather clock ticked. The fire spat and crackled. Ruby sipped at her port. "I think she was set up."

Bessie nearly choked on her cocoa. "Set up!" She took out a handkerchief from a pocket and wiped some cocoa-spatter from her chin. "For God's sake, Ruby, you caught her red-handed. On her knees. In the bathroom. Throttling Sergeant-Major Stippleton!"

"Yes. So it seemed at the time," Ruby conceded. "But I've been thinking about that. And I have to admit that Gwendolyn's version of events cannot be completely dismissed. I mean, it certainly looked as though she was pulling the tights tighter. But I don't know for sure that that's what she really was doing. She said she was trying to untie them. Maybe she was. I mean, I only saw her at it for a moment and in the next moment I was on my knees too. Trying to untie the damn' tights. Maybe if someone had seen *me* at that moment they'd have thought that *I* was strangling him? And maybe I made that mistake when I saw Gwendolyn."

"If you believe that," said Bessie, "you've lost your marbles."

"Ruby is right, however," Nye said, sternly. "It is a principle of British law that a person remains innocent until proven guilty."

"Call the police is what we should do," said Bessie. "Let them sort it out."

"Not much point in that," said Ruby. "Doctor Davies couldn't get here and nor would the police be able to. The snow's several feet deep out there and it's still falling heavily. Nobody will be able to get up here until the roads have been cleared. Or until it thaws. And who knows when that will be? It could be days."

"Well, whatever British law may say," said Bessie, "it's perfectly obvious that Gwendolyn Gormly is guilty."

"Oh, is it?" – Bessie froze when she heard the voice behind her. While the three of them had been talking around the fire, Gwendolyn Gormly had crept into the room, the usual give-away clatter of her stilettoes muffled by the deep, shag-pile carpet. "Well, Bessie Morgan," Gwendolyn said, "when it comes to the crunch you certainly discover who your real friends are, don't you."

Bessie turned to face here. "I didn't mean that you did... what you appeared to have done..." she blustered. "What I meant was..."

Gwendolyn smirked broadly. Her blonde beehive hairdo quivered slightly as she shook her head. "No, no, Bessie, my love. You meant it all right. I know what you all say behind my back. Ruby thinks I'm as guilty as sin, don't you? You'd all be happy if I was sent away and put behind bars." She took a swig of whisky from the crystal tumbler she was holding. Then she took a leisurely puff on her cigarette and blew out a long, contemptuous stream of smoke.

"I've changed my mind," said Ruby. "I was too hasty to rush to judgement. I've thought about it since and I am now quite certain that you are innocent."

Gwendolyn stared at her as though unable to believe that Ruby was being serious. Then she said, with much less swagger than was typical of her, "Of course I'm innocent."

"I think so too," Nye added.

Gwendolyn looked at Bessie. After a few moments, Bessie said, "Judge not lest ye be judged."

A look of sudden anger flashed into Gwendolyn's eyes. "And what is that supposed to mean?"

"It means," said Ruby, "that Bessie thinks you're innocent too."

Gwendolyn took another swig of whisky. There was a tremble in her voice when she spoke. "Everyone else thinks I did it. Do you have any idea how it feels to be stuck in a house with people who think you are a killer? No, of course you don't. Well, I can tell you, it's starting to drive me nuts. The sooner I get out of this hell-hole the better."

"Not much chance of that in this weather," said Ruby.

"We'll just have to make the best of it, I suppose," said Nye. "Until either the snow melts or they finally get the snow-ploughs out. Look on the bright side, though. I mean, it could be worse. At least we are in a pleasant situation. Amongst good company."

"Good company?" said Ruby. "I'm not so sure about that. Somebody in this house tried to kill Sergeant-Major Stippleton. What's to say they won't try again?"

"No good worrying about that," said Bessie, philosophically. "All we can do now is go to bed and get a good night's sleep."

But a good night's sleep was not to be theirs. Because at half-past three in the morning, they were awakened by a scream.

13. The Second Crime

Ruby had not slept at all which explains why she was the first on the scene. Following the attempt on Sergeant-Major Stippleton's life, Ruby's mind had been so active that she had eventually given up any attempt at sleeping and so she had come downstairs to the Drawing Room.

The room was warmer than her bedroom thanks to the fire which was still smouldering in the grate. By the light of a small lamp set upon a table at her elbow, Ruby was alternately reading a novel and glancing through the window at the continually falling snow. Even though the novel was by Ed McBain, an author who was usually guaranteed to grip her interest, she could not concentrate. She kept wondering if Gwendolyn could really be as innocent as she claimed; and, if so, who then was the guilty party?

Ruby had opened the curtains in order to be able to watch the snow. On the one hand, the gently falling flakes were strangely relaxing. On the other hand, she rather hoped they might stop falling soon so that the snow-ploughs would be able to get out and start clearing the roads. While Coot Hall was not a disagreeable place in which to be isolated, she far preferred the familiar comfort of her own small cottage and she fervently hoped that her isolation would not be prolonged much longer.

By chance she had happened to be looking out through the window at precisely the moment when a body fell past it. Her first reaction was to blink her eyes. Her view through the window was illuminated by exterior lights set upon ornamental lampposts which lined the track leading from the road to the front door of Coot Hall. Since the lights were behind the falling body, Ruby saw it only in silhouette. So it was quite possible that what had appeared to be a human body had been something much more innocent – snow falling from the roof, perhaps? It was equally possible that her eyes, tired from reading and unable to see clearly into the darkness beyond the window, had conjured up an imaginary shape that, for some inexplicable reason, happened to look rather like a falling body.

It took but a moment to dismiss these conjectures since neither a mass of falling snow nor an optical illusion was capable of emitting a penetrating scream. And a penetrating scream was precisely the noise that had been emitted by the falling shape just before it made a great 'thump' upon striking the ground.

Ruby put down her book, leapt from her chair, ran from the Drawing Room, flicked on the lights in the great, echoing hallway and, after throwing back the bolts, pulled the front door open and… stopped. She was wearing bedroom slippers. Slippers and dressing gowns had been provided for all the guests. But the snow beyond the door was more than two feet deep. It would be practically impossible for her to go outside and investigate further.

She needed to summon help. She looked around for some way of rousing the household with the greatest of speed. She did not have to look far. To the left of the great staircase which ascended from the centre of the hallway stood a dinner gong – a circular, slightly convex brass disc suspended by two wires fixed to a wooden frame. Attached to the right-hand side of the frame was a small hook. Suspended from the hook was a big wooden stick, like a drumstick with a padded end. Ruby picked up the stick and began to strike the gong with all her might. It made a much greater racket than she had been expecting. In fact, by the time, Nathaniel Snibb arrived at the top of the staircase, Ruby's ears were ringing and she felt slightly dizzy from the exertion.

"What on earth is the matter?" Nathaniel cried, tiptoeing briskly down the staircase into the hallway. "Is the house on fire?"

Other people were arriving by now: Nye, Clarissa, Guru Lennie, Sergeant-Major Stippleton. Bessie was there too, frowning with concern.

"I saw someone," Ruby yelled. "Didn't any of you hear anything?"

"We heard the bloody gong." That was Gwendolyn. She was standing at the top of the staircase wearing a Japanese silk dressing gown lavishly embroidered with dragons. Her beehive hairdo was immaculate. Remarkably immaculate, Ruby thought, for someone who had just rushed from bed having been woken by a dinner gong at half-past three in the morning.

"I heard something," said Mrs Williams-Jenkins, who was wearing an altogether more practical tartan woollen dressing gown and had her hair in curlers. "I thought it was an owl. Owls scream quite loudly, you know."

Ebenezer Evans, Bronwen and even the slithering Crickspittle had arrived by now. Ruby looked at them all. One person was missing. "It's the medium!" she cried. "Someone's killed Madame Evadne!"

Guru Lennie screamed. He looked as though he was going to faint but Nye caught him by the shoulders and kept him standing upright until he had recovered somewhat.

"Whatever is the matter with you?" Nathaniel Snibb asked, casting a disapproving eye at Guru Lennie. "Evadne is no doubt fast asleep in her room. I fail to see what is so remarkable about that."

"It's almost as though the guru knows something we don't," Clarissa said. "Or would like us to think he does."

"What did you see, Ruby?" Bronwen asked. From previous experience, she knew that where Ruby went, strange events, sometimes involving mysterious deaths, were quite likely to follow.

"I was sitting in the Drawing Room," she said, "reading an Ed McBain book…"

"Good choice!" said Mrs Williams-Jenkins, approvingly.

"…when suddenly someone fell past the window."

"Some *one* or some *thing*?" asked Ebenezer Evans. He stroked his bristling beard and flashed his eyes for dramatic effect.

"Some*one*," Ruby said with what she hoped sounded like a degree of confidence, "dropped like a stone from whatever lies above the Drawing Room window to whatever lies below it."

"The terrace lies below it," Nathaniel Snibb said. "And above it is one of the guest bedrooms. Let me see, now, which one would that be? Do you know, Bronwen?"

"It's the Brecon Room, sir." All the bedrooms in Coot Hall had been given names of picturesque Welsh locations. Guru Lennie had picked the names for their supposed connections with the spirituality of the Celtic Twilight.

"Was that Madame Evadne's bedroom?" Ruby asked. "Maybe she fell from the balcony."

"No," Bronwen said. "Evadne was in the Splott Room directly opposite the Brecon Room."

"Who was in the Brecon Room, then?"

"Oh yes, very clever. I see what you've done," Gwendolyn Gormly pushed her way to the front of the gathering, her silk, dragon-embroidered dressing gown caressing her voluptuous curves in a manner that was attracting a certain amount of attention from the men there, particularly from Nathaniel Snibb whose eyes were practically popping out of their sockets; only Guru Lennie seemed to be indifferent to Gwendolyn's notorious charms.

"I don't know which one of you it is," Gwendolyn said. "Maybe it's all of you? Plotting against me. Yes, I wouldn't put it past you. But it's not going to work. I can tell you that now!"

"What's she talking about?" piped up Mrs Williams-Jenkins.

"I'll tell you what I'm talking about, my love. What I'm talking about is: someone here is trying to frame me for murder."

Guru Lennie gasped. "Murder! Surely not!"

Gwendolyn gave the guru one of her most withering stares. "Don't come over all innocent with me, sunshine. You knew right away that she fell from my bedroom because it was you who arranged for me to have that room, wasn't it? So when Madame bleedin' Evadne plummets to her no doubt grisly death from my bedroom window, who gets the blame, 'ey? Gwendolyn Gormly, that's who."

"Death!" said Nathaniel Snibb. "Nobody has died, surely."

"That's why I made all that racket," Ruby said. "Because, well, something terrible may have happened. Someone should go outside and, well, see if anyone is there."

Everyone was staring blankly at Ruby, so she added, "I would have gone myself but I'm wearing slippers. You'd need a good pair of Wellington boots to go out in that snow."

"There's some Wellies downstairs," said Ebenzer. "We keep them on a rack outside the kitchen."

But the Wellington boots were not needed that night for in the next moment the front doors creaked open, pushed from the outside. Standing there, almost knee-deep in snow, was the frail, dishevelled, cold and wet form of Madame Evadne Miskyn.

Nye Clump was the first to run to her aid. He held one of her hands in his, then put his other arm around her shoulder and helped her stagger into the hallway. Crickspittle slithered across the marble floor towards the doors, shutting and bolting them with an air of moral superiority as though he disapproved of a cold, wet, dripping spiritual medium being let into the house at all.

There was by now a hubbub of chatter as people gathered around Madame Evadne. Through the hubbub, Ruby was able to make out occasional words and phrases – "Poor woman", "What happened?", "Could have been killed", "Lucky escape", "Fell from a bedroom window, did she?", "Or was she pushed…?"

Bessie, who was by far the most practical person there and could always be relied upon to take control in an emergency, quietly and efficiently began to organise everybody. She told Bronwen to go and build up the fire in the Drawing Room. She told Guru Lennie to go and fetch brandy. She told Crickspittle to go and get some towels to help to dry Madame Evadne and some blankets to put around her; and when Crickspittle whinged that it was not his place to take orders from just anyone, Bessie informed him that she was not "just anyone" and if he did not get those towels and blankets pretty damn' quickly, he would regret it very much indeed – and, to Ruby's astonishment, the odd little man took Bessie at her word and went for the blankets and towels without so much as a grumble.

Once settled in a comfortable armchair next to the roaring fire (it was roaring thanks to several large logs which had been added by Bronwen), Bessie asked Madame Evadne what had happened. The others, who were all standing around, watched in silence (apart from Mrs Williams-Jenkins who could not resist exclaiming, "Oh, what fun! Two attempted murders in one night!")

In brief, Madame Evadne said that she had gone to Gwendolyn's room, had been pushed out of the window and would have fallen to her certain death on the cobbled terrace below had not her fall been cushioned by a deep drift of snow.

"How extraordinary!" Nathaniel Snibb commented. "Do you know who pushed you?"

"Oh, I know all right," Madame Evadne hissed. "Evil spirits are abroad in this house. I felt them last night. Emily, my spirit guide, warned me. But I didn't listen." With that, she upturned her brandy glass and downed its contents in a single gulp.

Gwendolyn stepped forward. "Give me that, love. I'll get you a refill."

Madame Evadne recoiled as though Gwendolyn had struck her with a cattle prod. "Avaunt!" she cried. "Satan is in you. I knew as soon as I set eyes on you. You are evil. Evil!"

Gwendolyn shrugged. "I've been called worse. Do you want more brandy or not?"

Guru Lennie had silently padded up behind Gwendolyn and had put one pudgy hand on her elbow. "Best to leave her," he whispered. "You seem to be upsetting her."

Gwendolyn pulled the guru's hand away with the distaste she might have expressed for a slug that had set its sights on her lettuce patch. "Get your hands off me," she warned. "If you're suggesting that it was me who pushed this woman out of a window, you know what you can do with your suggestion. You can shove it where the sun don't shine."

Into the awkward silence came Crickspittle's sibilant voice. "It was from *your* window," (he pointed an accusatory finger at Gwendolyn) "that she was p… I mean, that she, er, fell."

"Well, I didn't damn' well push her!"

"How you can stand there and lie, I do not know," Madame Evadne said. "It was you. You got me to come to your room and you pushed me out of the window."

Gwendolyn sneered. "Prove it!"

"Now, now, ladies, there is no call for arguing," Ebenezer Evans rumbled.

Ebenezer's placating comment only inflamed Gwendolyn's anger all the more. "No point arguing!" she said, striding up to Ebenezer and gritting her teeth at him in what looked like a less than friendly manner. "This so-called medium just accused me of trying to kill her. It's obvious I didn't because if I had, she wouldn't be standing there now. When I decide to do something, I do it properly. Whoever pushed her out of my window was an amateur."

Here she looked around the assembled throng. "Which means it could be any one of you."

"May I ask," Ruby said and, without waiting to hear whether she may or not, she asked anyway, "why you, Madame Evadne, were in Gwendolyn's room at half-past three in the morning?"

For a moment, Madame Evadne looked flustered. She quickly regained her composure and said, "There was a draught, the shutters were banging in her room. I went to see if everything was all right."

"Gwendolyn's bedroom door was open then?"

"It may have been. I'm not sure."

"I'm afraid, "Nathaniel Snibb interjected, "that the bedrooms are not equipped with locks at present. When Coot Hall was a private residence locks were not deemed necessary. We shall have the very best security locks installed before The Retreat opens to the public, of course."

"You heard the shutters banging in Gwendolyn's room and you went to take a look?" Ruby said.

"Her room is directly across the corridor from mine. The banging was quite persistent. I knocked upon the door and when no reply was forthcoming, I turned the handle and went inside."

"Was Gwendolyn sleeping?"

"I assumed so. The curtains were drawn around the bed. A four poster bed, you know. I presumed she was a heavy sleeper. The window was wide open. So I went across to it and I…"

"Leaned out? Overbalanced perhaps?" said Ruby. "I suppose we all had quite a few drinks last night."

"I did not fall!" Madame Evadne glared at Ruby. "I've already told you. I was pushed! By Gwendolyn Gormly!"

"Oh, really!" Gwendolyn rolled her eyes. "I hope none of you are believing what this mad woman is saying! She's making it all up. Isn't that obvious?"

"Making it up!" Madame Evadne screeched. "Making it up! That's your best excuse, is it?"

"Did you see me?"

"No. It was dark. You leapt from the bed and pushed me out of the window before I had a chance to turn around."

"It wasn't me." Gwendolyn was defiant. "It wasn't me. Which means it was one of you lot. Someone standing here in this room tried to kill this silly woman. It wasn't me!"

"But surely," said Sergeant-Major Stippleton, who had by now sufficiently recovered from his brush with death to take a keen interest in the attempt on Madame Evadne's life, "if the would-be assassin had been secreted in the room, you, madam…" He aimed a wolf-like smile at Gwendolyn, "…would have noticed?"

"He's got a point," Nathaniel Snibb agreed, looking with suspicion upon Gwendolyn. "If what Evadne says is correct, by which I mean that an arctic blast was blowing in through the open window and the shutters were banging in the frosty breeze, well, even the soundest of sleepers could hardly have failed to notice. Thus, we must suppose that Miss Gormly was lying awake in her bed, cold, shivering and irritated by the banging, when some other person entered with evil intents – namely, to push Madame Evadne through the window to her icy death. Are we really to suppose that you, Miss Gormly, did not notice any of this?"

"There never was another person!" Madame Evadne screeched. "I've been telling you all along! It was her! It was her!"

"Perhaps," said Nathaniel Snibb, "if you could give us a full account of exactly what happened between your entering the room and the savage attempt upon your life, we might be able to make some deductions on the, er, true nature of the events."

"Not much to tell," said Madame Evadne. "Once I was in the room I couldn't see a thing. The room was in darkness, you see."

"You could have switched the light on," Clarissa Winthrop said.

"I didn't think of it. I mean, I would have done so only, well, I couldn't find the switch on the wall. And anyway, there was enough light coming in from the passage for me to see my way about. And besides, I didn't want to wake Gwendolyn."

"So many reasons for not switching on the light!" Clarissa said, satirically. Her smile suggested that she did not think that Madame Evadne was a credible witness.

"It wasn't the darkness I noticed, "Madame Evadne continued, "it was the cold. It was damned cold in there."

"The heating…" Guru Lennie began to apologise, "it's been a bit on the blink lately."

Madame Evadne cut him off. "It was cold because the window was open, you fool. Wide open. Snow was swirling into the room. So I went across to the window. To shut it"

"When I was a girl," Mrs Williams-Jenkins said, "we were always encouraged to keep a window open at night. So that we could have ready access to lots of good, fresh air. I never did though. I'm not awfully fond of fresh air."

"I thought," Madame Evadne ignored Mrs Williams-Jenkins's girlhood reminiscence, "that Gwendolyn might have been fool enough to have gone to the window, tottering on those high heels of hers, and had slipped and fallen. So I looked through the window just to check. And that was when I felt two hands pushing roughly on my back. I didn't have a chance. The next thing I knew, I was falling, falling, falling…"

"How awful!" Mrs Williams-Jenkins cried out, and she clapped her hands daintily together as though she was having the most tremendous fun.

The evidence was damning. It all pointed to Gwendolyn's guilt. Everyone stared at her. In the grate, a log spat out some sparks that crackled noisily in the tense silence.

"It wasn't me," said Gwendolyn.

Someone – it may have been Clarissa Winthrop – said "Hah!"

"Not only wasn't it me," Gwendolyn went on, calmly, as though relishing her spot in the limelight, "but I can *prove* it wasn't me."

"Oh, really?" said Madame Evadne. "And how would you do that?"

"I have a witness."

Each person there looked at each other person. Which one among them would be called to testify to Gwendolyn's innocence?

Gwendolyn smiled with enormous self-satisfaction. "Nye Clump," she said and she strode across to the stuffed bear against which Aneurin Clump was at that moment, leaning, or possibly trying to hide behind. "Well, speak up, man. Don't be shy. They'll be coming for me with pitchforks if you don't tell them the truth."

"Ah, yes, well," Nye shuffled away from the stuffed bear, keeping his eyes firmly cast downward, "There is, er, well, that is to say… yes, what Gwendolyn says is quite true. She can't possibly have done it, you know, because, um…"

“Oh for God’s sake!” cried Gwendolyn, “I was with Nye in his bedroom. I had been there all night!”

14. Gwendolyn Gormly, Murderer

Next morning, Bessie and Ruby were sitting at a table in the Dining Room taking breakfast. The Dining Room occupied a long, narrow area at the back of the house. Unlike the other rooms in Coot Hall, its decoration was Spartan with plain white walls and numerous large windows overlooking the Italian Garden.

In summer, the garden presented a pleasant prospect of greenery and flowers dominated by a big, low-walled lily pond in the middle of the lawn. At the centre of the lily pond was a statue of a naked man holding a large fish from whose mouth water gushed for no obvious reason. On that wintry morning, however, there were no flowers or greenery to be seen; the statue of the man and the fish were there but no water was gushing from the fish's mouth and the modesty of the naked statue was preserved by the thick covering of snow upon it.

Snow was everywhere: on the lawn, on the low walls around the pond, even covering the pond itself, the surface of which had frozen solid. Had she not previously seen the Italian Garden in more clement weather, Ruby would not have guessed that there was a pond there at all. The scene beyond the window of the Dining Room had, overnight, been transformed into a seamlessly undulating surface of pure white.

"You haven't touched your egg," Bessie commented.

"What?" Ruby glanced down and was surprised to see that, on a plate in front of her, there was an egg cup containing a boiled egg. On another plate alongside there were two pieces of toast and a pat of butter with notched edges. "Ah." She picked up a small knife and, with one swift movement, cleanly decapitated the top fifth of the egg. It was then that she noticed that there was tea in a delicate bone china cup to the right of the egg. She picked up the cup and she drank. Then she put it down again and started delving into the egg with a small silver spoon. "Delicious egg."

"One of Tom Crockley's."

Tom Crockley was a local farmer. Ruby had first met him at the village art class. They had been drawing "from life" which was the artistic jargon for drawing a nude model. Tom Crockley had been the model. The image of his voluminous naked bulk was seared into Ruby's mind.

"Tom brought his digger around first thing this morning."

"Digger?"

"A big tractor sort of thing with a scoop on the front. He cleared the snow off the drive up to the house. Should be able to get the car back on the road, I reckon. Tom says the main road's been cleared now."

"Tractor?" said Ruby who was still delving half-heartedly into the innards of her boiled egg.

"You haven't heard a word I've said, have you?"

"What? Yes. Of course I have. Tom Crockley's eggs. Crockley's farm is next to Coot Hall, isn't it? I'd forgotten."

"You," said Bessie, sternly, as she mopped up the last remnants of the substantial Welsh Breakfast which she had consumed (a Welsh Breakfast is similar to an English Breakfast but bigger: in this case, three sausages, several rashers of bacon, black pudding, baked beans, mushrooms, tomatoes, a fried egg and some fried bread), "are distracted."

"What?"

"And I know what you are distracted by. You've got the urge on you again, that's it, isn't it?"

"The urge?"

"To solve the mystery. I can tell by the glazed look in your eyes."

Ruby delved deeper into her egg with the little silver spoon but did not both eating any of it. The boiled egg was clearly not at the forefront of her mind.

"Don't you think it was all rather convenient?" she said at last.

Bessie poured out some more tea, took some toast from a silver rack and began smearing it with honey from a white ceramic pot. "Don't I think that *what* was all rather convenient?"

"Everything. Me finding Gwendolyn strangling a man with her own tights. Madame Evadne being pushed out of Gwendolyn's bedroom. What murderer would make their guilt so obvious?"

"A stupid murderer?"

"Gwendolyn may be many things. She may be nasty, vicious, foul-mouthed, scheming and greedy."

Bessie nodded in agreement.

"But the one thing she isn't is stupid."

Bessie bit deeply into her toast. Honey ran freely down her chin. "You believe Gwendolyn's story then?"

"She has a watertight alibi."

"Well, if you believe what she says…"

Gwendolyn had explained that, being unable to sleep after all the events of the previous evening, she had asked Nye Clump if she might sit and talk to him for a while. Nye invited her back to his bedroom where, according to Gwendolyn, they had spent a couple of hours drinking cocoa and playing card games.

"I don't," Ruby said, "take anything that Gwendolyn says on trust. For all I know they were having a night of illicit passion in Nye's room."

Bessie huffed disapprovingly.

"But that they were in Nye's room I have no doubt. If Nye says they were there, then they were there."

"You still trust that man? After all he's done?"

"Done? What do you mean?"

"Led you on is what I mean."

"Me? Ha! I hardly think so."

"You may put a brave face on it," Bessie said, "but everyone knows that you and Nye have been seeing one another."

"Seeing one another? Pah! I've bumped into him from time to time. In the wine bar. Or in the pub. I don't call that 'seeing one another'."

"And now here he is going off with the first cheap floozy that throws herself at him."

Ruby rolled her eyes. "You think I should be jealous? Of Gwendolyn? Ha! Besides, if Gwendolyn is to be believed…"

"I wouldn't believe Gwendolyn if she told me that water was wet and the pope's a Catholic," Bessie said.

"Now then, ladies, and how was breakfast?" Ebenezer Evans had padded into the room. He was wearing his chef's whites and had a checked tea-towel over one arm. "Oh!" His eyebrows bristled an inch or two up his forehead. "You haven't eaten your boiled egg, madam."

"What?" Ruby looked at the egg. She scooped out some of the yolk on the silver spoon, popped it into her mouth, gave a look of purest ecstasy and enthused, "I've been savouring it. It's absolutely delicious. My compliments to the… well, to you."

Ebenezer smiled broadly, his eyebrows descended to their usual locations, he leant closer to Ruby and said in a rumbling undertone – "So, have you worked out how she did it?"

"I beg your pardon?"

"I don't mean to speak out of turn but everyone knows your reputation. The murders you've solved. A local celebrity is what you are in that respect. I'm sure you must be close to working out how she managed to get away with it."

"Get away with it? Who?"

"You're teasing me, aren't you! Gwendolyn Gormly, of course. First she strangled the Sergeant-Major with a pair of tights, then she shoved Madame Evadne out of the window. We all know she's guilty. But what I can't figure out is how she did it. Mr Clump swears she was with him at the time, so she'd have had to be in two places at once to push Madame Evadne out of the window. Unless, well, you know…" Ebenezer gave a nod and a wink to Ruby.

Ruby looked baffled. "No, I don't know. Unless *what*?"

"Well, unless Nye Clump was in on it. An accomplice, as it were. Either they did it together or one of them did it and the other one provided the alibi."

"That's a disgraceful suggestion," Ruby said.

"Oh?" Ebenezer scratched his head in thought, "So you have another solution, then? No, don't tell me. Let me guess. Oh, I know. Gwendolyn probably used some device. Yes, that's it. She must have constructed a machine of some sort, a big piston maybe, that could be activated remotely, radio-controlled perhaps, so that when she pressed a button it was the piston that did the pushing out of the window."

"What are you talking about?" Ruby's jaw had dropped a good inch while Ebenezer had been speaking. "I doubt if Gwendolyn Gormly is capable of constructing anything more complicated than a bubble-bath. Let alone a radio-controlled piston. And even if she had, where is it now?"

"That's what I've been wondering," Ebenezer admitted. "No, no, you are quite right. The piston explanation has to be rejected. For the time being. Drugs, however, might be involved, don't you think? Yes, that would explain everything. Gwendolyn drugged Mr Clump, maybe she put sleeping pills in his cocoa, then she ran back to her room, pushed Madame Evadne out of the window, and then ran back again to Mr Clump's room just as he was coming out of his snooze."

"But that doesn't make any sense," said Ruby firmly. "No, really, that doesn't make any sense at all."

"Why not?" Ebenezer looked crestfallen by Ruby's dismissal of his ideas.

"Because," said Ruby, "of one very obvious fact."

"Oh? And what might that be?"

"Gwendolyn Gormly," said Ruby, "is innocent."

*

A week later, Gwendolyn Gormly was arrested on suspicion of murder. It was a particularly nasty murder – brutal and without any obvious motive. Gwendolyn Gormly had been found at the scene of the crime. The wine bottle with which the unfortunate victim had been bludgeoned to death came from Gwendolyn's Wine Bar. The evidence was overwhelming. It looked as though Gwendolyn could expect to serve the rest of her life behind bars. This time, there could be no doubting her guilt. Everybody in the village accepted that Gwendolyn Gormly was a killer.

Everybody, that is, except Ruby.

15. Innocent Until Proven Guilty

"But it's a travesty of justice!" Ruby shouted into her mobile phone. "Gwendolyn didn't do it."

She was standing in her kitchen looking out at the bleak grey landscape and watching the dripping icicles melting outside her window.

"Well, now then, Mrs Lake..." For once, Ruby did not correct him. She was too annoyed about this grotesque miscarriage of justice to be bothered about the small detail of her marital status or lack thereof. "See, I had a few words with Detective Inspector Gruttock, over in Clogwyn Mawr, and I am given to believe that they have got Miss Gormly bang to rights, as the saying is."

Ruby took the phone away from her ear. "Bang to rights," she thought. Did people say that in real life? She had once acted in an episode of a police drama on television in which a small-time criminal had uttered the immortal line, "Shove the bracelets on, Inspector. You got me bang to rights," but she was not sure that this was really an accurate representation of modern criminal parlance.

"Mrs Lake? Mrs Lake?" Tegwyn Pritchard's whining voice was squeaking from her phone in a pathetic and irritating manner. Ruby put the phone back to her ear and snapped, "For God's sake, shut up, man! Now, look, if you are expecting me to give you some juicy quotes, you are profoundly mistaken."

Ruby had had dealings with Tegwyn Pritchard, chief reporter on The Clogwyn Clarion, on previous occasions. In Ruby's opinion, he was the sort of journalist who brought the profession into disrepute. He had an annoying tendency to take quotations out of context. On one occasion, he had described Ruby as the "murder queen of the Clogwyns" which made her sound like a cut-price Lady Macbeth.

"But she was found at the scene of the crime!" Tegwyn screeched, "with a wine bottle. From her own wine bar!"

The details of the murder were already familiar to Ruby. In a small community like Clogwyn Bach news travels quickly – especially when the owner of the local wine bar is arrested on suspicion of killing someone using a wine bottle as a blunt weapon.

"That's as may be," Ruby said.

"It's true!"

"Well, even if it is, I don't know why you want to talk to me. I wasn't there. I don't even know the woman she's accused of killing. It's true that I have had some slight involvement in solving previous murders in the locality but on this occasion, I cannot be of assistance."

"Oh, no, you got the wrong end of the stick, see," said Tegwyn. "No one's expecting you to solve this murder. That's due to the fact that it's already been solved. Gwendolyn Gormly killed Miss Winifred Elizabeth Hicks, an eighty-three year old spinster, in her house, 'The Brambles', in a place called Cwmhyfryd which is up in the hills to the south-west of Clogwyn Bach. She was found at the scene by Mrs Lowri Williams-Jenkins, a seventy-eight year old widow."

"Yes, yes, all very interesting. But nothing to do with me."

"Ah, but maybe it is."

"I really don't see how it can be."

"Well, you see, I've been doing some investigating."

"Well done. I am glad to hear that investigative journalism did not die with Watergate."

"With what?" The reference was lost on Tegwyn Pritchard. His knowledge of world events extended no further than the boundaries of the two towns of Clogwyn Bach and Clogwyn Mawr.

"Never mind," said Ruby. "I'll give you twenty seconds to convince me that you have anything worth listening to. Then I'm ending this conversation. I have work to do."

"You witnessed her two previous murder attempts."

Ruby sighed. She had hoped – she had hoped with every fibre of her being – that what had happened in Coot Hall would stay in Coot Hall. Someone had been talking.

"If you are referring to the accidents…"

"Evadne Miskyn, the celebrity psychic, was pushed out of the window of Gwendolyn Gormly's bedroom."

"Pure conjecture. She might have fallen."

"Sergeant-Major Selwyn Stippleton, known as 'Stonker' to his friends, was strangled with Gwendolyn Gormly's tights."

"That is nothing but supposition and speculation. Not a shred of real evidence."

"You saw her doing it!"

"Who told you that?"

"You also saw the body of Evadne Miskyn falling from the window of Gwendolyn Gormly's bedroom."

"That's got nothing to do with anything."

"And now I discover that the woman who found Gwendolyn Gormly at the scene of her latest murder…"

"Did you say 'her latest murder'? I'm surprised at you, Mr Pritchard. Innocent until proven guilty, you know."

"…was one of the guests at Coot Hall on the night that Gwendolyn Gormly made her two previous murder attempts. Coincidence, Mrs Lake? I think not."

"Think what you like, Mr Pritchard. I have no comment to make. Goodbye."

Ruby was fuming with anger. Why did people assume that every time something dreadful happened in the district she was either already mixed up in it or that would wish to be so? But there was more to her anger than that. She was even angrier that Gwendolyn Gormly had been arrested.

According to local gossip, confirmed by Ian Tucker, the local police constable whom Ruby had phoned the moment she had heard about the arrest, Gwendolyn had indeed, been found by Mrs Lowri Williams-Jenkins at the house of a friend of hers, Miss Winifred Elizabeth Hicks. The inert body of Miss Hicks was stretched out on the floor of her kitchen. Gwendolyn Gormly was in the kitchen with blood on her hands and the murder weapon, an empty wine bottle, was resting on the floor next to the body.

It was a cut and dried case. No room for doubt. Gwendolyn had been caught red-handed, quite literally. And that was why Ruby was totally convinced that Gwendolyn was innocent.

It was all too convenient. Gwendolyn was found at the scene. If she had been the murderer, she would surely have put as much distance as possible, as rapidly as possible, between herself and the body. Mrs Williams-Jenkins had turned up at precisely the right time to find Gwendolyn there. Why had she come? Had she just happened to wander into the house at the perfect moment to find Gwendolyn standing over the corpse? And as for the bottle of wine – one which was easily identified as coming from Gwendolyn's Wine Bar… well, that strained credulity to breaking point. Of all the murder weapons she might have chosen, why would she use something that clearly identified her?

No, it was all far, far too convenient. Just as Gwendolyn's easily-identifiable tights wrapped around Sergeant-Major Stippleton's neck had been too convenient. Just as Evadne Miskyn being pushed from the window of Gwendolyn's bedroom had been too convenient.

And there was another curious feature of the murder, and also of the two unsuccessful attempts at murder which had preceded it. As far as Ruby could tell, Gwendolyn neither knew the people she was accused of attacking nor had she any particular reason to want them dead. Ruby made a decision. If the police couldn't see that Gwendolyn was innocent, Ruby would prove that she was.

16. The Quality Of Mercy

Bessie was busy baking oat biscuits in her kitchen when Ruby called around. Bessie took her baking seriously. When most people make them, oat biscuits end up being dry and tasteless. When Bessie made oat biscuits they had a zesty tang of orange and a lavish coating of dark chocolate.

"You must be mad," was the first thing Bessie said after Ruby had told her about her plan to prove Gwendolyn's innocence. The second thing she said was, "Sit yourself down at that table and I'll get the tea on."

Bessie's big, old-fashioned kitchen was filled with warmth from her Aga stove; condensation ran down the windows. When the sky is blue and the sun shines, the view from Bessie's windows is spectacular – a panorama of wooded slopes leading downward towards the broad sweep of Clogwyn Bach Bay. When, on a day like today, the sky is grey and the air is full of blustery winds and lashing sleet, the view is what an artist might term "dramatic". However, thanks to the condensation, there was at that moment no view from the windows at all.

"We have three days to prove her innocence," Ruby said.

Bessie put a mug of tea and a plate of oat biscuits in front of Ruby then she sat at the other side of the table and said, "We?"

"Well, that is…" Ruby nibbled a corner of an oat biscuit. "This is delicious, Bessie. You must let me have the recipe."

"You would only burn them," said Bessie. "Now, getting back to the subject – did you say 'we'?"

"I could conduct the investigation on my own, I suppose. But I thought… well, you were so helpful the last time."

"I was?"

"Invaluable. And what's more, I need to go to Clogwyn Mawr."

Bessie drank some tea and frowned at Ruby. "You want me to drive you there?"

Ruby did not own a car. She had, in fact, never bothered learning to drive. That was not a problem when she wanted to go down to the village to buy groceries in Muriel Greenalge's small shop, "Food'n'News", nor was it a problem if she wanted to stroll down to the pub or the wine bar in the evening. But the town of Clogwyn Mawr was a different kettle of fish. It lay on the coast ten miles to the north of Clogwyn Bach which meant it would be a twenty mile round trip. Ruby did not object to walking on a two, three or four mile hike but she knew her limits. Twenty miles was well past those limits.

Ruby had not replied to Bessie's question. She gave the impression of being so enraptured by the oat biscuit that she had not even heard it. So Bessie said, "Why?"

"Why *what*?"

"Why do you want to go to Clogwyn Mawr?"

"There's someone I need to see."

"Who?"

"You are being unusually monosyllabic today, if you don't mind my saying so."

"Who?" Bessie repeated.

Ruby mumbled something through a mouthful of oats. Bessie was not sure but it sounded like "Arthur".

"And who exactly is Arthur?"

"Arthur Gruttock. That is to say, Detective Inspector Arthur Gruttock." She took a drink of her tea. "Of the South Wales Police Force," she added just in case Bessie might not have deduced as much.

"I know who Inspector Gruttock is. What I don't know is why you want to see him."

"To ask him to stay his hand, of course. To show clemency, to temper the rule of law with mercy. Maybe I could give him a touch of the old Portia? 'The quality of mercy is not strained, it droppeth as the gentle rain from heaven upon the place beneath' and what-not."

"What are you babbling about?"

"It's a quotation. From 'The Merchant Of Venice'. By William Shakespeare. You see, there's this chap called Antonio…"

"I'm not asking about the damn' quotation. It's your plan to try and soft soap a high ranking member of the Clogwyn Mawr police force that I'm worried about. That's against the law, I should think. You could be seen as trying to exert improper influence, to subvert the course of justice, you'll probably get yourself thrown into a cell!"

There was a sudden clattering noise as a dark shape threw itself against the window and made a squawk like a banshee in a bad mood. When Ruby had first met Bessie, this remarkable incident would have caused her to blench, tremble, quiver and quake. No longer. When she was with Bessie, wild creatures were constantly making a nuisance of themselves at the most unexpected moments. Ruby was now used to this. The creature flinging itself at the window was Wenceslas, Bessie's not-entirely-tame carrion crow. Bessie went to the window, unlatched it and the crow immediately flew in and perched on the edge of the table. Bessie gave it an oat biscuit. One without any chocolate. She believed that chocolate was bad for crows so she had baked one specially.

"The thing is," Ruby continued, as though nothing out of the ordinary had occurred, "that Gwendolyn has only three days left."

"Left before what?"

"Before they charge her. With murder."

"I thought they already had."

"Yes, I did too, at first. But I phoned our local bobby, PC Ian Tucker, and he explained that it's a bit more complicated than that. It appears that Gwendolyn has been arrested on suspicion of murder. But she hasn't yet been formally charged."

"Does that matter?"

"Surprisingly, it does. The way it works is that they arrest you. Then, if they think they've got a good case against you – which is what, I am given to understand, is known in the business as 'bang to rights' – they charge you. If they don't charge you they have to release you within twenty-four hours."

"They arrested Gwendolyn yesterday, didn't they? So that means they have to charge her today."

"But she's innocent!"

"Innocent? Gwendolyn Gormly is as guilty as sin."

Wenceslas the crow, who had just finished his oat biscuit, looked Bessie in the eye and gave a raucous 'Caw!'"

"There, you see!" said Bessie.

"What?"

"Wenceslas," said Bessie. "He agrees with me. Gwendolyn Gormly is guilty."

Ruby was temporarily lost for words. "But it's a crow," she said at last.

Bessie considered that observation to be both irrelevant and offensive. She put out her arm to Wenceslas and the bird hopped on. It fixed Ruby with its beady eye, gave two caws, shook its head vigorously and then hopped off Bessie's hand and flew through the window which Bessie had opened for it.

"I take that back," said Bessie. "He thinks she's innocent."

"Well then," Ruby decided that her previous low estimation of the legal opinions of crows might have been too hastily formed, "that's all the more reason to go and see Detective Inspector Gruttock."

"I have some bread to bake first," Bessie said. "We can leave at one o'clock."

17. A Cold And Rat-Infested Cell

"Miss Lake, Mrs Morgan, please take a seat."

Ruby looked around the cramped office. It contained one desk and two chairs. One of those chairs was currently occupied by Detective Inspector Gruttock.

"I don't think we'll both fit," said Ruby, indicating the single vacant seat.

"I beg your pardon? Oh! Oh, yes, I see. Just a moment." Detective Inspector Gruttock picked up the telephone receiver on his desk, pressed a button and said, "Wisty, is that you? You're not busy, I suppose? What? No, making tea doesn't count. We need a chair. Yes, that's right. A chair. To sit on. Bring one in, would you? No, not after you've made the tea. Now. Come on, lad, snap to it!"

Detective Inspector Gruttock put down the phone, smiled at Ruby and steepled his fingers in a contemplative manner. "Good man, Sergeant Wisty. He'll get this sorted out with his customary efficiency."

Time passed.

"I could stand," Ruby suggested.

"No, no, I won't hear of it."

"*You* could stand," Bessie suggested.

Detective Inspector Gruttock smiled. "Don't worry, any minute now…"

The door to the office opened. A thick-set, burly sergeant lumbered in carrying a folded deckchair. This he placed against the wall, scowled at Detective Inspector Gruttock, then left without a word, slamming the door as he went.

"Resourceful," the Detective Inspector remarked. "My men are boundlessly resourceful. We are suffering a shortage of chairs, you see. Please, ladies, make yourselves comfortable."

Ruby unfolded the deckchair and sat in it. It sagged uncomfortably. Bessie sat in the other chair.

"Now, ladies, how may I be of assistance? I was told you have information pertaining to a case currently under investigation. I pride myself that we are always open to working hand in glove with the public which we so faithfully serve. That being so, speak on! Unburden yourself of such information as you may have."

"Gwendolyn Gormly…" Ruby began.

Detective Inspector Gruttuck sniffed significantly and said, "Ah!"

"…is innocent," Ruby concluded.

"I beg your pardon?"

"Gwendolyn Gormly," Ruby repeated, "is innocent."

"Ah." Detective Inspector Gruttock steepled his fingers again, gave another significant sniff and added, "That, of course, is for the court to decide."

"You haven't got a shred of evidence," Ruby protested.

The Detective Inspector permitted himself to indulge in a small smirk. "On the contrary, madam. We have an embarrassment of evidence. Indeed, I cannot recall a case in my entire career in which the evidence has been so overwhelming."

"You are relying on the testimony of an unreliable witness," Ruby protested. "Look, I happen to have met Mrs Williams-Jenkins. She's a sweet, dear old lady. But a bit loopy. She believes in ghosts, you know."

"So does the Archbishop of Canterbury. That does not make his testimony inadmissible."

"Not the Holy Ghost! I'm talking about little Victorian flower-sellers that communicate from beyond the veil through the mechanism of wine glasses pushed around on a table."

"Really, madam, I have no idea what you are talking about. In any case, I fail to see what Mrs Williams-Jenkins has to do with all this."

"She discovered the body, didn't she? It was she who claimed to have seen Gwendolyn at the scene of the crime. Pah!"

"I attended the scene myself, madam. Mrs Williams-Jenkins dialled 999. I was on the scene within twenty minutes. Well, possibly half an hour. Miss Gormly was still there. Nobody else was in the house. Just Miss Gormly."

"And Mrs Williams-Jenkins," Ruby said.

The Inspector conceded that Mrs Williams-Jenkins was there too for it had been she who had had contacted the police.

"And Miss Hicks!" Ruby exclaimed triumphantly. "You see, there were lots of people there. The crime scene was a mess. Not at all, um, contained, as it should have been."

"The crime scene was as undisturbed as any I have ever attended, madam. Mrs Williams-Jenkins, it seems, is an avid reader of what are known as 'police procedural' novels and, based on her reading of those, she was particularly careful to avoid touching or moving anything. The unfortunate victim, Miss Hicks, being deceased at the time, was certainly in no position to do anything. Which just leaves Gwendolyn Gormly and the cat. Miss Gormly was sitting quietly with Mrs Williams-Jenkins in the lounge of the bungalow when we arrived. And the cat was locked in the pantry so it too was innocent of any possible disturbance of the crime scene."

"Has Gwendolyn been charged?" asked Ruby.

The question caught Detective Inspector Gruttock off guard. "Charged? Charged, you say? Has she been charged?"

"Come, come, man! Either she has or she hasn't."

"Ah, no, the laws of the land are not so simple. They are, indeed, subtle and complex. I fear that to an untrained mind the ramifications would be quite impossible to explain."

"Balls!" said Bessie.

Detective Inspector Gruttock looked startled. Had the eminently respectable woman of mature years who was presently sitting in the chair at the other side of his desk really said what he thought she had said?

"I assure you, madam," he began – but he said no more because Bessie interrupted him: "We have every right to know if she has been charged and if you don't tell us immediately I shall contact my MP." Detective Inspector Gruttock opened and closed his mouth like a goldfish trying to gobble down some particularly recalcitrant ants' eggs. "And while I'm at it," Bessie continued, "I'll make a complaint to the Chief Constable too." She was not entirely sure whether or not the Chief Constable had authority over a Detective Inspector so, for good measure, she added, "And the newspapers!"

The mention of the newspapers did the trick. Detective Inspector Gruttock broke out into a cold sweat. His surly, authoritative manner had vanished as quickly and completely as the bubbles in cheap Prosecco. "No. No, Miss Gormly has not been charged," he blathered. "Not *yet*."

"Then you can't know that she will ever go to court," said Ruby.

"I never said she would."

"You said her innocence is for the court to decide."

"I may have said that but what I meant was…"

"Your suggestion," Ruby interrupted, "that Miss Gormly will of necessity find herself in court, well, that shows a clear and, um…"

"Improper," whispered Bessie.

"A clear and improper bias," Ruby went on, "prejudicial to, um, the fair and impartial, um…"

"What my friend is trying to say," interrupted Bessie, "is that your assumption of Miss Gormly's guilt demonstrates an institutional bias which calls into doubt the entire police investigation of the case. Police corruption is, as you know, something of which the public greatly disapproves. As does the Home Secretary. So when the Home Secretary reads in the newspaper…"

"Home Secretary!" Detective Inspector Gruttuck now looked considerably ruffled. His face had taken on an unhealthy deep pink colour, his fingers were fidgeting rather than steepling and his lips were twitching with the effort to form coherent words. Finally they succeeded. "Well, really, madam. I am quite sure that the Home Secretary has better things to do than take an interest in a minor investigation in a small village in the west of Wales."

"Minor?" said Bessie. "Minor, did you say? You call a murder, 'minor', do you? Not to mention two attempted murders." Bessie ground to a halt. No sooner were the words out of her mouth than she realised she might have said more than was entirely prudent.

An air of pomposity settled itself comfortably around Detective Inspector Gruttock. His surly, authoritative manner reasserted itself. "Attempted murders, did you say? Which attempted murders might those be?"

"Well, there was…." Bessie attempted to shrug it off. "It's nothing, really."

"Let me be the judge of that. You do realise, I suppose, that withholding evidence may be construed as a crime?"

"We thought you already knew," Ruby said. "I mean, I suppose you must have interviewed everyone at Coot Hall."

"Coot Hall? I fail to see the relevance."

"Oh!" Ruby put a theatrical tone of surprise into her voice. "Then your investigations haven't even progressed that far. Perhaps I can assist." And she told the detective inspector all about the attempted strangling of a Sergeant-Major and the ejection of a spiritual medium through an open window.

"I am aghast," Detective Inspector Gruttock said. "Had we been aware of these incidents we should have been able to charge Miss Gormly immediately. The case against her now looks very grim indeed."

"So will you let me speak to her?" persisted Ruby.

"No."

"Why not?"

"Why should I? Are you any relation?"

"No."

"A close friend?"

"No."

"Well then. If I let any Tom, Dick or Harry hold interviews with murderers… I mean, with people who have been arrested on suspicion of murder, well, I should soon be running a fairground sideshow instead of a police force."

"Where is she?" said Ruby. "Is she here? In this police station. Languishing in a cold and rat-infested cell?"

"I am not at liberty to tell you."

"So you admit that her cell is cold and rat-infested?"

"Certainly not."

"I have the right to speak to her. You can't stop me."

"You have no such right. And I can indeed stop you. Look, madam, you may think you are Perry Mason but in fact you are a member of the public with no familial or amical connection to Miss Gormly."

"I go to her wine bar!" insisted Ruby.

"That doesn't count!" Detective Inspector Gruttock had by now dispensed with any attempt at politeness. He was a busy man, he said, he did not have the time to engage in silly arguments with members of the public and if Bessie and Ruby would be kind enough to leave his office, leave the police station and, ideally, leave Clogwyn Mawr altogether, he would be extremely obliged.

"When are you releasing her?" Ruby asked as a parting shot.

"She may not be released at all," said Detective Inspector Gruttock. "Now, ladies, good day."

Detective Inspector Gruttock had stood up, walked across the room and opened the door – all of which was clearly more physical exertion that he was used to, for he was audibly panting. "Wisty!" he called, "See these ladies out, will you. And make sure they don't come back in again."

18. The Backstreets Of Clogwyn Mawr

"Well," said Ruby, "That went well, I think"

They were sitting at a window table of the Cockleshell Tea Shoppe drinking tea and eating buttered scones.

"We made things worse than they were before," Bessie said. "What possessed me to mention the attempted murders at Coot Hall I don't know. Now the police will start investigating those too. They'll be added to the list of Gwendolyn Gormly's crimes. We should never have come here. We should never have spoken to that man Gruttock."

"I disagree. I'm glad we spoke to Detective Inspector Gruttock. I've learn something very important."

"You have? What?"

"He knows that Gwendolyn is innocent," Ruby said.

"You think so?"

"Oh, yes. He hasn't got a scrap of evidence."

Bessie chewed her scone with exaggerated distaste; it was not a scone she would have been happy to unleash upon the world if she had baked it herself. "What about the fact that Gwendolyn was found at the scene of the crime with the murder weapon and the victim's blood on her hands?"

Ruby poured some more tea into their cups. "Circumstantial. It wouldn't stand up in a court of law. A good barrister would pull it to shreds. It would make a laughing stock of the police."

Ten minutes later, Ruby and Bessie were walking down a back street just past the "Celtic Coin-Op Launderama". There was, Ruby had told Bessie, something she wanted to look at. As far as Bessie could see, the street was unremarkable. There were lines of solid, stone-built terraced houses with doors that opened directly onto the pavement.

"You see," said Ruby, "if the police had watertight evidence they would have charged Gwendolyn by now. They can charge someone straight away, you know. In most cases, they have to charge someone within twenty-four hours of the arrest."

"And if they don't?"

"Then the arrested person walks free. Now, they arrested Gwendolyn yesterday evening. At six o'clock, so Police Constable Tucker told me. It's…" Ruby looked at her watch, "just gone half past two now."

"So in three and a half hours she'll be free?"

"No. The police applied for an extension."

"Is that legal?"

"We can only hope so. They can keep Gwendolyn in custody for ninety-six hours. That's four days. But a day has almost gone. So there are just three days left. Ah, there it is!"

Ruby had paused in front of an unremarkable terraced house with a dark green door and shutters over its windows. Next to the door there was a small brass name plate.

"And what is this exactly?" Bessie asked.

The words engraved on the brass nameplate were so small that Ruby was obliged to lean closer in order to read them. "It is," she said, "according to this sign, The Clogwyn Mawr Non-Political Working Men's Association, a private members' club. Entry by appointment only."

"A gentlemen's club in Clogwyn Mawr!" Bessie said. "Very fancy. Getting ideas above their station, I should say!"

"It's not an ordinary gentlemen's club," said Ruby. "This is what is more popularly known as the Hell Fire Club!"

"Doesn't look anything special," Bessie said. "Just a couple of terraced houses knocked into one by the looks of it."

"I must say I'm a bit disappointed," said Ruby. "It's not quite as, well, debauched as I'd been expecting."

"Debauched? What are you talking about? This is Clogwyn Mawr, not Tangiers."

Never having visited Tangiers, Ruby was unsure whether Bessie's colourful view of the Moroccan holiday resort was justified. She took her point, however. It was possible to imagine that Tangiers might contain secretive clubs catering to depraved tastes but it stretched credulity to imagine that such dens of vice could be found in the backstreets of Clogwyn Mawr.

"I thought it might at least have had a neon sign," Ruby said, wistfully, "with the club's name flashing on and off and possibly an animated Satan wielding a pitchfork. And a…"

"And a what?"

"Shh!"

"Why? What's the matter?"

From the corner of her eye, Ruby noticed a man on the other side of the street. He was wearing a long, dark overcoat and a flat cap pulled down over his forehead. He was walking very slowly and he was ostentatiously looking in any direction other than towards Ruby.

"I've seen that man before," Ruby whispered.

Bessie glanced sideways at him. "Wasn't he in the police station? One of Inspector Gruttock's men?"

"Sergeant Wisty. Why's he following us?"

"He might not be. Maybe he's just going for a walk and he happened to stroll down here."

"Follow me." Ruby turned around and began to walk briskly back the way they had come.

"There's something about the local police force that makes me wonder if they are really on our side," Ruby said. "We need to move fast. Three days from now, Gwendolyn Gormley will be charged with the murder of Miss Winifred Elizabeth Hicks. Unless we prove her innocent."

"And how are we going to do that?"

"I shall have to go to the Hell Fire Club."

Bessie swore in Welsh. Her command of Welsh curses was extensive and impressive. She gave vent to a selection of colourful and highly descriptive expressions which, however, were wasted upon Ruby whose knowledge of the Welsh language was not extensive.

19. The Smuggler's Itch

"The Hell Fire Club? My word! I hope you are not considering going there."

The man speaking was a slim, elegant gentleman with silver hair, penetrating grey eyes and an even more penetrating intellect. He spoke in a precise and dignified manner, enunciating each word clearly and pausing slightly between sentences as though to emphasise the implicit punctuation. This was Professor Lucian Henry Caradoc Prothero. Some of the locals simply called him The Professor. Nobody, apart from Bessie, called him Lucian. Bessie and Lucian were friends of long standing. In fact, Ruby strongly suspected that once, a long time ago, they had been a good deal more than just friends. But Lucian had moved away from the village to pursue an academic career while Bessie had stayed on; she had become a teacher in the village school and married a young man called Gethin who had died soon afterwards (Bessie had never said much to Ruby on that subject and Ruby did not care to probe) and Bessie had lived alone ever since.

"But, you see," said Ruby, "I think the Hell Fire Club is an important piece in the jigsaw. In fact, I think it's where the secret lies."

"I really must caution you most strongly against such a reckless endeavour," Professor Prothero said. "By all accounts, the Hell Fire Club is not a suitable place to be frequented by a respectable lady such as yourself."

Bessie was having none of it. "For Goodness' sake, Lucian. Ruby's a grown woman. You're talking to her like a child. I'm sure she will be able to look after herself. Now then, I think it's my turn to get in the drinks. What will it be, same again?"

The three of them were sitting at a corner table in the public bar of The Smuggler's Itch. There are two pubs in Clogwyn Bach – The Cat and Ferret, and The Smuggler's Itch. Respectable people, so they say, go to The Cat and Ferret. The Smuggler's Itch has a bad reputation.

To hear some of the locals talk about it, it would be easy to imagine that The Smuggler's Itch must combine the dissolute excesses of one of the Emperor Caligula's more lavish orgies with the seedy sleaziness of a Victorian opium den. In fact, it was in essence not much different from The Cat and Ferret – it had slate-tiled floors, whitewashed walls, solid oak tables and a big open fireplace. It was, however, in a back street at the less fashionable end of the village and the beer was a few pence cheaper than in the village's other pub. It also suffered from an extremely limited wine list: you could have house red or house white and that was it. Unlike The Cat and Ferret, it had a juke box whose selection of records appeared not to have been changed since the mid 1960s. At that moment it was playing "Crying in the Rain" by The Everly Brothers.

Ruby pushed her half-empty glass of red wine to one side. While it would be untrue to say it tasted of vinegar, it would be equally untrue to say it tasted of wine. "I'll have a half of bitter," she said.

Bessie had not yet finished her glass of orange juice so the professor went to the bar and ordered one pint and one half of a cloudy brown liquid that was humorously called "best bitter"; it was certainly bitter but its claim to being best was dubious since the pub sold no other bitter to which it might be compared. When the professor returned the three of them huddled closer around the table while Ruby consulted a small ring-bound pad of lined paper.

She had made notes prior to setting off for the pub. The notes all related to the three supposed crimes of Gwendolyn Gormly – two attempted murders and one actual murder. She had been puzzling over her notes all afternoon and had been hoping that Professor Prothero might be able to help her to cut through the clutter to find the clues which must (Ruby hoped) be hiding in plain sight. The professor was a man of fierce intelligence. While his speciality was not criminology but, rather, something called "antiquities", his brain operated in an analytical and methodical way which contrasted sharply with Ruby's more haphazardly intuitive approach.

"I think," said Ruby, "that the person, or persons, behind the attempted murders at Coot Hall, must also be the person or persons guilty of the actual murder of Miss Hicks."

"Indeed?" said the professor. "And what, may I ask, leads you to that assumption?"

"What?" Ruby looked at him blankly. "Well, don't you agree?"

"Whether I agree or not is immaterial. My agreement or disagreement would be based purely on conjecture. And on what would my conjecture be based? At present, on nothing. If you believe the events to be connected, you must convince me."

Bessie shook her head and tutted. "He's always been like this," she told Ruby. "He's the most infuriating man I've ever known."

The professor smiled at Bessie. "Which is why you find me so fascinating." Turning to Ruby, he said, "Now, Miss Lake, I suggest you go through your list and let us see if we can bring to light any relevant facts rather than rely upon supposition."

Ruby read the first item which she had written on her notepad: "Attempted Murder, Number One. The strangulation in the bathroom. Gwendolyn Gormly is found, by me, on the floor of the bathroom in the west wing of Coot Hall, apparently throttling Sergeant-Major Selwyn 'Stonker' Stippleton with a pair of tights. It was subsequently discovered that the Sergeant-Major had been rendered unconscious by a thump on the head with a glass bottle of bath salts. The tights were of a make called Nuits de Monmartre. This is an unusual brand. Quite expensive. It happens to be the brand of tights which Gwendolyn herself wears. When challenged, she stated that she had brought a spare pair of tights in her overnight case and she claimed that someone had stolen them."

Ruby looked up: "So what are we to make of that? On the face of it, all the evidence points to Gwendolyn's guilt. And yet she claims that someone else had tied the tights around the Sergeant-Major's throat and that she was not, as it appeared, trying to throttle him but, on the contrary, she was trying to stop him from being throttled."

"It was you who saw her 'in the act', so to speak," the professor said. "Is her explanation credible?"

Ruby took a sip of her beer. "It certainly looked as though she was strangling him. But I can't be certain."

"You said the bathroom was in the west wing. That suggests there may be another bathroom."

"There is," said Ruby, "in the east wing."

"Where was Sergeant-Major Stippleton's bedroom?"

"One floor above everyone else's in the attic. There's a little staircase in the corner of the east wing that leads up to the attic level. That's where the servants had their rooms once upon a time, I'm told, back in the days when the Coots of Coot Hall lived in the Downton Abbey style."

"And Miss Gormly's bedroom? Where was that?"

"In the east wing, right at the front of the house overlooking the Drawing Room which, as I'll explain shortly, is significant in the second murder attempt."

"Never mind that for the moment," said Professor Prothero. "One attempted murder at a time is quite enough to be going on with. The question that arises is why did Gwendolyn Gormly go to the bathroom in the west wing when there was a nearer bathroom in the east wing?"

"Guru Lennie was occupying the bathroom in the east wing at the time. Or so he says."

"You don't believe him?"

"I don't know. Do you?"

Professor Prothero smiled. "I don't know the man. And even if I did, I wouldn't believe him."

"Why not?"

"Because I don't make a habit of believing people. Believing what a person tells you in the absence of evidence is not a sound methodology for establishing the truth. Carry on. What is the second item in your list?"

"Well, the second murder attempt."

"Ha!" Professor Prothero sipped his beer and wiped away the froth from his top lip. "We have not yet established that the two incidents in Coot Hall were, in fact, murder attempts."

"What else could they have been?"

"Accidents. Pranks. Stratagems to divert attention from… well, who knows what? But no matter. For the time being, I suppose we may as well suppose that they were attempted murder, though we must be prepared to dismiss that supposition if the facts contradict it. Go, on, then. The second 'murder attempt'."

Ruby narrated the essential details: she had been sitting in the Drawing Room looking through the window when she had been startled to see Madame Evadne Miskyn whizzing past the window in a distinctly downward direction; then she summarized Madame Evadne's account of hearing the shutters in Gwendolyn's room blowing in the wind, how she had entered the room and gone to the window to shut it when she was suddenly pushed from the window by an unknown assailant; how Madame Evadne had assumed the assailant to be Gwendolyn Gormly who had been hiding behind the curtains of her four-poster bed; and how that assumption had been contradicted by Nye Clump who had stated that Gwendolyn had been with him in his room playing card games at the time of the assault.

"Do we know which card games they were playing?" asked the professor.

"Nye said they were playing Happy Families."

"Indeed? And are you quite sure that is not a euphemism for some other activity which does not involve cards?"

Bessie nudged the professor in the ribs. "Lucian!" she said. "Behave yourself!" And then to Ruby, "Don't be fooled by his grey hair and cultured voice. I knew him when he was a snotty-nosed little boy. He was wicked then and he's wicked now."

"I don't know what you're talking about," Professor Prothero replied with a magisterial air of hurt dignity. "There is one quite inexplicable detail in the curious list of events which you have just narrated," he said to Ruby.

"Yes," Ruby replied, "I know. We don't know why Gwendolyn Gormly was in Nye's bedroom."

"What? Oh no, there's nothing mysterious about that. Nothing at all. I can think of several, er, plausible explanations. No, the detail to which I was referring is this: why was the window open?"

"The window?"

"In Gwendolyn Gormly's bedroom. It was a bitterly cold night with a wind that was making the shutters bang. Nobody in their right mind would open the bedroom window on such a night. Certainly they would not open it to such an extent that a human being could be ejected from it. That a simple push caused Madame Evadne to plunge through the window suggests that it must have been fully open. That is surely most curious. Don't you think?"

"Well, when you put it that way, yes, yes, I suppose it is."

"Make a note of it," the professor commanded. Ruby did so.

At the other end of the bar a trio of very drunken men had started singing at the tops of their voices. The juke box was playing Harry Nilssons' moving rendition of the song "Can't Live, If Living Is Without You". The drunken men were singing a rumbustious version of "Oh, Sir Jasper, Do Not Touch Me". There is, in Wales, a lyrical and beautiful musical tradition called "penillion" in which one melody is improvised over a totally different melody. It is conceivable that a virtuoso penillion singer might be able to make "Oh, Sir Jasper, Do Not Touch Me" sound exquisite when sung over the tune of "Can't Live, If Living Is Without You". The three drunken men were not penillion virtuosi, however, and the end result was far from melodious.

"Next item on the list if you please!" Professor Prothero had to raise his voice to make himself heard over the discordant racket.

"If Gwendolyn Gormly isn't guilty…"

"Which," interposed the professor, "has yet to be proven."

"…then which of the other people who were at Coot Hall on the night in question might have had a motive?"

"A motive for what?" Bessie asked. "There were three crimes. Sergeant-Major Stippleton was knocked unconscious with a jar of bath salts and then strangled with a pair of tights. Madame Evadne was pushed out of a window. Miss Hicks was done to death with a wine bottle. Are we looking for one motive or three?"

"Oh!" Ruby smiled uncertainly. "I wasn't thinking of any of them."

"What!"

"Well, you see, I don't think they were the intended victims."

"What?" Bessie's eyes were growing wide with incredulity.

"I mean, there's no direct connection, is there? A retired Sergeant-Major, a spiritualistic medium of dubious repute and an elderly spinster who wasn't even at Coot Hall on the night of the first two attacks."

"You think they were unconnected?" Bessie said. "I find that hard to believe."

"No. I didn't say they are unconnected. I said there was no *direct* connection. There is one *indirect* connection, though."

"Which is?"

"Gwendolyn Gormly."

"Well yes," Bessie harrumphed, "we know that already."

"But I don't think she's connected in the way the murderer wants us to think she is."

Professor Prothero smiled. "That was something I too was beginning to have doubts about."

"Gwendolyn Gormly," Ruby went on, "is not the perpetrator of these crimes. She's the victim. Someone has set her up. Framed her. Someone made two attempts to stitch her up at Coot Hall. When neither of those worked out, that unknown person finally managed to frame Gwendolyn for the murder of Miss Hicks."

"That is certainly a possibility worthy of consideration," the professor cautioned. "However, it is too soon to jump to conclusions. Let's just say that we know that there is a common factor that links the murder of Miss Hicks and the two attempted murders at Coot Hall. That common factor is Gwendolyn Gormly. If we can think of anyone who might have a grievance against any of the three victims, we should make a note of it. Have you written down a list of the people who were at Coot Hall on the night of the two attempted murders?"

"I have. Not only that, I've also done some research. Online, you know. To help fill in any gaps in their histories."

"Marvellous. Then perhaps you could go through your list one by one. Please proceed."

"But first," said Ruby, "I think we should have some more drinks. Another orange juice, Bessie?"

Bessie held out her glass. "And shove a tot of vodka into it this time!"

20. The List Of Suspects

"Suspect Number One," Ruby said. "Nathaniel Snibb. Nice man. Tall, slim. Polite. Rich. The latter end of middle aged, I'd say. By which I mean in his mid-fifties."

"In the prime of his youth!" the professor said.

"Made his fortune from mass-produced pickled onions and gherkins before deciding that there was more to life than malt vinegar and vegetables. In short, he got the spiritual craze. Met Guru Lennie when they were on a TV chat show together. Between them they concocted the idea of a country retreat catering to spiritual seekers with plenty of spare cash to fritter away on luxury weekends with added aura-readings. When Coot Hall came on the market, he snapped it up."

"Has he a motive for murder, as far as you can tell?"

"No."

"Or a grievance against Gwendolyn Gormly?"

"Not as far as I know. Though I have heard a rumour that Gwendolyn had hoped the buy the Hall herself, so maybe there was some rivalry between them."

The professor looked surprised. "Is Gwendolyn really so wealthy?"

Ruby shrugged.

"I wouldn't be surprised if Nathaniel Snibb may have other interests in Gwendolyn," said Bessie.

"Such as?" said the professor.

"It's not for me to say. But what I will say is that he winked at her."

"Winked?"

"Like this." Bessie winked and made it look strangely lascivious. "You saw him winking, didn't you, Ruby? Not long after we arrived in Coot Hall on that snowy evening."

Ruby confirmed that she had indeed observed what appeared to be a wink in the general direction of Gwendolyn Gormly.

"So Nathaniel Snibb winked at Gwendolyn Gormly," the professor said. "An interesting detail but not, I think, a guarantee of a debauched clandestine relationship,"

The drunken men at the other end of the bar had moved on, as drunken men in Wales inevitably do, from smutty songs to hymns. They were at that moment inflicting melodic violence upon the stirring hymn, "Cwm Rhondda", known in English as "Guide Me, O Thou Great Redeemer". The juke box, meanwhile, had moved on to Elvis Presley's "Jail House Rock". The harmonising of the two songs was far from successful.

"And what of this so-called Guru Lennie?" the professor asked. "What do you know about him?"

"He's an odd little man," Ruby said. "He rather reminds me of an overgrown hamster. Plump, smiles a lot. Tends to wear inappropriately garish kaftans. His full name is Leonard Micklesworth. He's fifty-three. He was born in Doncaster in the West Riding of Yorkshire. Not all that far away from where I grew up, as a matter of fact."

Ruby's family came from the small village of Slackton Ings, on the outskirts of Bradford, about forty miles from Doncaster, though as an actress she had spent most of her adult life in London.

"He's worked in all sorts of jobs – everything from stacking shelves in a supermarket to repairing washing machines – but then, about ten years ago, he was visited by the spectre of an African shaman who informed Lennie that he had a special gift that allowed him more or less free access to the spirit world."

"And how do you know all this?" asked Professor Prothero.

"I found the information on his web site. Anyway, after the shaman had been in touch, Lennie set up a business to provide 'spiritual counselling' over the internet. His job at Coot Hall is probably likely to bring him a more secure income."

"And what is that job, exactly?"

"He's sort of manager as far as I can work out. Nathaniel Snibb is the owner but he doesn't actually live in Coot Hall; he has a big estate close to his pickle factory north of Newport. As far as the paying customers will be concerned, Coot Hall, or 'The Retreat' as they prefer to call it, is run by Guru Lennie and his second-in-command – a woman by the name of Evadne Miskyn, who prefers to be known as Madame Evadne."

"Is she French?"

"No, why?"

"Had she been French, the desire to be called 'Madame' would be unexceptional. Since she is not, we must assume it to be an affectation. Which leads me to wonder if she might not be quite who she pretends to be."

"Oh, that she isn't!" said Ruby. "Well, anyway, not according to Gwendolyn. She accused Madame Evadne of having been a seaside fortune teller who scammed her clients using shabby tricks to make them think she was reading their minds."

"And is the accusation justified?"

"I don't know. Gwendolyn certainly thinks it is, which may provide a motive for Madame Evadne to try to frame Gwendolyn for murder."

"Oh, I can't believe that," Bessie protested. "Madame Evadne was pushed out of a window. She's a victim, not the perpetrator."

"An interesting conundrum," Professor Prothero mused. "Is there, in fact, any evidence, other than Madame Evadne's testimony, that someone pushed her from the window?"

"I saw her fall," said Ruby.

"Indeed," said the professor. "You saw her fall but did you see her pushed?"

"No, but…"

"The snow beneath the window was deep, you said. So it is quite possible that she might have realised that she would come to no harm if…"

Bessie interrupted. "Lucian! For Goodness' sake! You are surely not suggesting that Madame Evadne threw herself out of the window just to pin the blame on Gwendolyn? No, indeed, I can't believe it."

"Bessie, my dear, I am saying no such thing. What I am saying is that we have a witness, namely Ruby, who saw the woman falling. We have no witness who saw her being pushed. On to the next item on your list, I think."

Ruby consulted her notes.

"Sergeant-Major Selwyn 'Stonker' Stippleton. While at the Hall, I couldn't form a clear idea of what sort of man he was. He seemed, I don't know..."

"Too much like a Sergeant-Major?" Bessie suggested.

"Yes, I suppose he did. He was like every British Army Sergeant-Major I've ever seen in a film or on a TV show. You know the sort, 'Chest out, shoulders back' and 'What do you think you're doing, you horrible little man?' – all that sort of thing."

"Did he mention anything about his Army experience?" the professor asked. "Where he had served, in which regiment and so forth?"

"He mentioned something about India," Bessie said.

"India?" the professor raised his eyebrows. "Did he indeed? Do you remember what he had to say?"

"Nothing much," said Ruby. "Some cock and bull story about a fakir who made a prediction when the Sergeant-Major was stationed in... oh, I can't recall where."

"Agra," said Bessie. "I remember it was Agra because that's where the Taj Mahal is."

"Yes indeed," Professor Prothero said. "Agra is in Uttar Pradesh. I know it well. I would be surprised if there were any British troops stationed in Agra these days, however. They tended to make themselves scarce after the partition of India in 1947. I suspect that either Sergeant-Major Stippleton is a great deal older than he appears or else his memory is playing tricks on him. Perhaps he was confusing India with some other country altogether."

"Or he was lying," said Bessie.

"I hesitate to accuse anyone of lying," said the professor, "but that is a possibility which we may have to consider."

"If he lied about that, maybe he lied about being bumped over the head and strangled with a pair of tights," Ruby suggested.

"That would be a reasonable conjecture," the professor agreed, "apart from the fact that he was indeed bumped over the head and strangled with a pair of tights. What's the next item on your list?"

"Ah, now this is where the Hell Fire Club enters the story. Clarissa Winthrop. Who, as far as I can gather, appears to be Nathaniel Snibb's romantic interest."

"Mr Snibb is not married?" the professor asked.

"I wondered that myself so I used my formidable internet-searching talents to find out. It would seem he has never found the right woman. Until now, at any rate."

"You think that Clarissa and he may be considering matrimony?"

"I think Clarissa Winthrop is after his pickled onion fortune. I formed the opinion that she was a bit of a gold-digger."

"And what has that to do with the Hell Fire Club?"

"Oh, it was just something Gwendolyn said. She intimated that Clarissa Winthrop frequented the notorious club. It was after the séance. Did I mention we had a séance?"

"You did not."

"Well, we did. We had to push a glass around on a table to see if it spelled out a message."

"I didn't take part," Bessie said portentously. "There are forces you should not meddle with, in my view."

"Well anyway, the planchette spelled out the words 'Gwendolyn Gormly is guilty'. This was before the first murder attempt so it didn't make any sense at the time. What was she supposed to be guilty of? Now, of course, it seems quite prescient. So much so that you have to wonder if the real murderer was the one who was pushing the glass."

"Unless, of course, the planchette really was being controlled by a visitation from the astral plane," said the professor. "Now, on to the next item on your list…"

Ruby glanced at her note pad. "That's it. All the salient facts."

"There were no servants, no cooks, no other guests at Coot Hall the night you were there?"

"Well, there was Bronwen, of course. You know Bronwen Price. A local girl. She certainly had nothing to do with it. I'd trust her with my life."

"How often people have said that about the worst villains in history! However, I also know Bronwen and for the time being I'll give her the benefit of the doubt."

"There was the cook," Bessie reminded Ruby. "Ebenezer Evans. Nice man. He didn't take part in the séance either. He and I went down to the kitchen. We had a cup of tea and a piece of seed cake and we talked about bats."

"Bats."

"Pipistrelles. They have a great many of them living in the loft at Coot Hall."

"Can we be sure he is really a cook or do we cast doubt on his professed biography as we did with the Sergeant-Major?"

"Oh, he's a cook all right. His seed cake was almost as good as mine."

"There was that other chap too," Ruby said. "The one who let us in. What was his name? Crickspittle?"

"Craigysbytol," Bessie corrected.

"Whatever. He looked a nasty piece of work, if you ask me. He kept appearing and disappearing at odd moments. I wouldn't trust him further than I could throw him."

"And there was Nye too," Bessie added.

"Nye would be Aneurin Clump, I presume?" the professor said. "A friend of yours, Ruby, I am given to understand."

"I suppose so." Ruby seemed uncomfortable talking about him. "It was Nye who told Guru Lennie about me. Guru Lennie was looking for someone to do voice projection and enunciation training. For the guests at The Retreat when it opens. Nye thought I'd be good at it."

"And it was also Nye who was with Gwendolyn in his bedroom..." the professor said.

"Playing 'Happy Families'," said Bessie, with a scowling expression that suggested she did not believe this for one moment.

"...when Madame Evadne fell from the window of Gwendolyn's bedroom?" the professor went on. "Hmmm..."

"Oh, I am quite certain that Nye isn't involved in all this," Ruby said. "He's was a teacher. Speaks French like a native."

"Sadly," the professor said, "the ability to speak French is not a guarantee of a blameless life. Consider the Marquis de Sade. Have you any more notes for us to consider?"

"Nope. That's it."

"Of all the people present at Coot Hall on the night of the attacks upon Sergeant-Major Stippleton and Madame Evadne, are there any who may be excluded from our enquiry? By which, I mean, anyone who has a solid alibi?"

"Well, when the Sergeant-Major was attacked, I think we were all in our rooms. All except for Guru Lennie who claims to have been in the bathroom in the east wing which was why Gwendolyn went to the bathroom in the west wing."

"So only Gwendolyn Gormly has an alibi?"

"I beg your pardon?"

"The Sergeant-Major is able to account for Gwendolyn's location at, or shortly after, the attack. Whereas nobody else can provide a witness. The rest of you could have been anywhere and up to anything."

"But Gwendolyn was on the floor strangling the Sergeant-Major!" Ruby protested.

"Piffle!" snapped the professor. "You yourself have said that you could not be certain that Gwendolyn was strangling the man. Since you are the only witness, we may discount that as unreliable evidence. Now, what about the second event – the launching of the female spiritualist from the window of Gwendolyn Gormly's bedroom? Who has an alibi for that?"

"I have," said Ruby. "I was sitting in the Drawing Room when I saw her fall past the window."

"Sadly nobody else was in the Drawing Room with you, so unless the falling spiritualist happened to glance in your direction as she plummeted past the window and thus confirm your story, you can produce no witness to verify your claim."

Ruby spluttered incoherently, "But, but…"

"What about everyone else?"

"All in bed. It was half past three in the morning."

"All except for Nye Clump and Gwendolyn Gormly who were playing card games in Mr Clump's room."

"So they say," muttered Bessie.

"So once again, Gwendolyn has an alibi. Assuming, that is, that we are to trust Mr Clump's testimony."

"All of which confirms my belief," said Ruby, "that Gwendolyn Gormly is innocent. The more I think about this, the more convinced I am that the two attempted murders and the one successful murder were all aimed at incriminating Gwendolyn Gormly. Whoever is behind those attacks was determined to prove the planchette's prediction correct – that Gwendolyn Gormly was guilty."

"Did anybody at Coot Hall know Miss Gormly prior to that night?"

"Guru Lennie and Nathaniel Snibb did, I think. Gwendolyn seemed to know Madame Evadne too."

"Did you get any sense that there was an existing animosity between any of them?"

"She had an argument with Guru Lennie. According to Nye Clump, Gwendolyn had thought that Nathaniel Snibb would appoint her as the manager of The Retreat but, in fact, he appointed Guru Lennie. When she didn't get that job, I think Guru Lennie may have given her some hope that he would appoint her as his chief spiritual advisor – but, in fact, it was Madame Evadne who got that job."

"So," said the professor, "first Gwendolyn wanted to buy Coot Hall but was outbid by Nathaniel Snibb. Then she expected Nathaniel Snibb to make her the manager of The Retreat, whereas he appointed Guru Lennie instead. And finally she had hopes that Guru Lennie would give her yet another permeant position which was, in fact, given to Madame Evadne? And what position did Gwendolyn eventually secure, might I ask?"

"Part-time aura-reading," said Ruby.

"I have no idea what that means," the professor commented. "I shall, assume, however, that the position is a good deal more menial than that of the owner, manager or chief spiritual advisor. Thus, there may have been a certain amount of friction between Gwendolyn and any or all of those three persons: Nathaniel Snibb, Guru Lennie and Madame Evadne."

"There was definitely friction between Gwendolyn and Madame Evadne," Ruby recalled. "As I said earlier, they had an argument during which Gwendolyn accused Madame Evadne of being a fraudulent seaside fortune teller."

"Gwendolyn had a few snipes at that Clarissa woman too," Bessie reminded Ruby.

"Oh yes. I have a strong feeling that there was some bad blood between Gwendolyn and Clarissa. Something to do with the Hell Fire Club in Clogwyn Mawr."

"Why was Mrs Williams-Jenkins there?" the professor asked. "It was my understanding that the event was intended to introduce the fulltime staff members at The Retreat to those people, like Ruby, Nye and Gwendolyn, who had been offered part-time employment."

"Yes, I thought that was a bit funny," Ruby conceded. "According to Guru Lennie, they were soft-soaping Mrs Williams-Jenkins in the hope that she'd recommend The Retreat as a suitable investment to her wealthy friends."

"She mentioned Miss Hicks," Bessie said. "Apparently she had been due to attend too but had been put off by the bad weather."

"Only to be murdered a week later in her own home!" Ruby added.

"Have either Miss Hicks or Mrs Williams-Jenkins actually committed any funds to The Retreat, do you know?"

"I really couldn't say," said Ruby. "As far as I could see, Mrs Williams-Jenkins was a bit of an outsider. She didn't seem to know anyone. I mean, if she'd already invested money in the place, I'd expect her to be on pretty intimate terms either with Guru Lennie or with Nathaniel Snibb. To be honest, I was surprised that they even wanted outside investors. By all accounts, Nathaniel Snibb is absolutely rolling in cash thanks to his picked onion fortune."

"Maybe he is not as financially secure as he would like us to believe?"

"That thought," said Ruby, "had already occurred to me. That's why I have to go to the Hell Fire Club."

"I confess, I fail to see the connection."

"Well, isn't it obvious? Gwendolyn accused Clarissa of some shady goings on in the club. Clarissa is sticking to Nathaniel Snibb like a limpet to a rock. The Hell Fire Club caters to gentlemen seeking what is known in popular parlance as a 'good time'. Does Clarissa known something that might be embarrassing to Nathaniel Snibb? Could she be blackmailing him? The only way to find out is to go to the club myself and have a good poke around."

"I admire your tenacity," said Professor Prothero, "but I really do think you are taking an unnecessary risk. What if you should get yourself into a, well, how can I put it? – into a compromising situation?"

"Oh, I shall take a chaperone."

Bessie gave Ruby a quizzical look. "You're not getting me to go there, if that's what you are thinking."

"Oh no," said Ruby, "it wouldn't be proper for two women to go together to a place like the Hell Fire Club. I shall be accompanied by a man."

"Oh!" Bessie's curiosity got the better of her. "And who might that be?"

"A young man from the village," Ruby said. "Quite a bit younger than me, as a matter of fact. I've always rather fancied a toy boy!"

But before investigating the Hell Fire Club, Ruby had decided to take a closer look at the scene of the murder.

21. The Scene Of The Crime

Bessie was driving slowly past the privet hedge in order that she and Ruby would have the chance to get a good, long look at the bungalow. It looked cold and lonely in the bleak morning light.

"What a beautiful location!" Bessie said.

"But the bungalow is quite small," Ruby said.

Bessie gave Ruby one of her "What on earth are you talking about?" looks. The bungalow was twice the size of Bessie's little cottage. It stood in an acre or so of its own land. The lawn at the front was well-tended and there were a few small evergreen trees lining the gravel path that led to the front door.

"You call that small?" Bessie said. "It's huge!"

By that time they had driven past the bungalow and were proceeding down a narrow country lane enclosed by hedges. "Pull over here!" Ruby commanded.

Bessie slammed on the brakes and her little yellow Mini skidded to a halt in in front of a wooden, five-bar gate. "What is it now?"

"I'm going to take a look."

"We've had a look."

"Not close enough."

Ruby had already opened the car door and was on her way out.

"I can't park here," Bessie shouted.

"Why not? You're not blocking the road."

The snow had thawed, leaving an open area of churned mud right in front of the gate where Bessie had stopped.

"But a tractor might come along," Bessie protested. "It might want to get into the field. My car's in the way."

"Then stay in the car," Ruby said, "and you can move it if a tractor arrives. Meanwhile, I'm going to investigate!"

"Wait a minute!" Bessie was out of the car in two seconds flat. "You're not going anywhere without me!"

"What about the tractor?"

"It can wait!"

And so the two of them trudged back up the narrow road towards 'The Brambles', the bungalow belonging to the late Miss Winifred Elizabeth Hicks. It was a neat but unremarkable little house – not much more than a big oblong structure, all on one level. Its walls were pebble-dashed with pink-coloured stones and its roof was made of crinkly terracotta roof tiles into the interstices of which small mounds of green moss had inserted themselves.

"It looks rather 1950s, don't you think?" said Ruby.

"I have no idea what you mean," Bessie replied. "To me it looks like a very pleasant little bungalow."

"Aha!" said Ruby, "so you agree!"

"Agree to what?"

"That it's little."

"I agree to no such thing. Miss Hicks was an elderly spinster and lived alone. It's bigger than she could possibly require."

"You've missed out an important detail," Ruby said. "Miss Hicks was a *rich* elderly spinster."

"How do you know?"

"I'm fairly sure that Nathaniel Snibb was doing his best to extract money from her. You will recall that Miss Hicks and Mrs Williams-Jenkins were the only two people invited to that fateful soirée at Coot Hall who were not, in some way, either involved with the running of The Retreat or who might become so involved."

"There was me too! I'm not rich."

"The point I'm making, Bessie, is that Miss Hicks and Mrs Williams-Jenkins were potential benefactors. Investors, perhaps? Which is why Mr Snibb was so mortified when Miss Hicks was unable to attend his little get-together on the night of the séance.

"But the thing that baffles me is this: if she was rich enough to throw away money in the direction of a pickled onion millionaire, why was she living in such a relatively modest little bungalow?"

Bessie shrugged. "Not everyone wants to live in a mansion."

Ruby was not listening. She was already striding up the gravel drive towards the front door of the bungalow.

"You can't go there!" Bessie protested.

"Why not?"

"It's private property."

"Who's going to object?"

"Well, it's a crime scene."

"Oh, the police aren't interested any more. They've been and gone ages ago. Look at this!" Ruby had her nose close to one of the windows and was staring into the room beyond.

"Look at what?" Bessie too stared in through the window. "It's a living room. Settee. Armchairs. TV. Shelves with some knickknacks on them. Nothing special as far as I can see."

"Exactly!" said Ruby. "Nothing special. I don't think she was as wealthy as Nathaniel Snibb thought."

Ruby had moved towards the back of the house and was now peering in through another window. "The scene of the crime!" she said. "The kitchen. Nothing special here either. A fairly ordinary washing machine, dish-washer, sink, gas hob, electric oven."

"It's a kitchen. What were you expecting?"

"The kitchen is a long way from the front door."

"It's at the back of the house," said Bessie. "Of course it's a long way from the front door."

"In fact," said Ruby, "I don't think the main hallway goes straight from the front door to the kitchen."

"Why should it?"

"Look. The back garden has a path that leads to that gate back there." Ruby walked down the path towards a small wooden gate with a latch. "But what's beyond this?" She opened the latch and walked through the gate. Beyond the gate the path continued between trees.

"Woodland!" Ruby said.

"So I see." Bessie was unimpressed.

A few yards further on, the path between the trees opened onto a small bridleway. From the hoof-prints in the mud, this appeared to be a popular spot for horse riding. To the right, the bridleway disappeared into dense woodland. To the left it opened onto a small road.

"Someone could have parked a car down there," Ruby said.

"Why would they bother? There is a garage adjoining the house."

Ruby ignored that comment. She went back through the gate and up towards the bungalow. She walked around the side of the building and up to the front door. She peered into the living room again. There was a door on its left and a door in the far wall.

"I think, if you came in by the front door, you would have to go through the living room in order to get to the kitchen," Ruby said.

"Quite possibly," Bessie agreed, "though I can't see why that's important."

"It's important because Miss Hicks was killed in the kitchen."

Bessie thought about that for a few moments then she shrugged. "I still can't see why that's important."

"Come on, Bessie," Ruby commanded, "we haven't got time to dawdle here. We have more important things to do."

22. LUNCH AT 'THE FAT OWL'

The village of Cwmhyfryd nestles at the bottom of a shallow, wooded valley. A small river runs through the village and on either side of the river there are two rows of terraced houses. A small bridge crosses the river and at one end of the bridge there is a pub called The Fat Owl.

Ruby imagined how idyllic it must have looked when it had lain, glittering and white, beneath a blanket of newly-fallen snow. But now, since the thaw had set in, it looked bleak and drear beneath a sky of sullen grey with only occasional traces of dirty snow lingering at the edges of pavements and gutters.

When Ruby and Bessie arrived in the village they made their way directly towards The Fat Owl. According to the chalk-written words on a blackboard attached to the outside wall of the pub, "delicious home-made food" including "our world-famous steak and ale pie" was being served within and, since it was lunch time and they had eaten nothing since breakfast, Ruby and Bessie decided to put the world-famous pie to the test.

They bought a half of mild and a glass of ginger beer at the bar then went to sit at a corner table, next to a window overlooking a small garden adjoining the river. They gave their order to a plump, rosy-cheeked woman who babbled relentlessly about the state of the weather (cold), the state of the world (depressing) and the state of the steak and ale pie (delicious). Ten minutes later she was back at their table holding two enormous, steaming plates piled high with massive portions of gravy-oozing pie. "Watch the plates," she warned, "or you'll burn your fingers." Ruby and Bessie did as they were told – they watched the plates and they did not burn their fingers. "Back in two ticks with your veg," the woman added. While her assessment of the number of ticks required to fetch the vegetables was optimistic, she nonetheless returned within a minute holding a little dish of green peas and carrots and another, somewhat bigger dish, of roast potatoes. "Anything else you want, my loves, don't be afraid to ask."

"Is there anywhere around here where I might walk my dog?" Ruby asked.

Bessie nearly choked on her ginger beer.

"There's the fields across the river," the woman said, "only you'll need Wellington boots this time of year. Maybe you'd be better going up into the woods behind the pub…."

"We've just come from that direction," Ruby said. "We passed a lovely little bungalow called The Brambles. There are some woodland walks up there, aren't there? Or do the woods belong to the owner of the bungalow? I wouldn't want to trespass."

"Oh, you don't know then?" The rosy glow in the woman's cheeks faded slightly. "The lady who lived in that bungalow. Well, it's all a bit tragic, I'm afraid."

"Oh, you don't mean…! Oh, I heard about that on the radio. That was the lady who was murdered. How awful. You knew her well, I suppose? A regular at the pub, was she?"

The plump woman laughed. "Not her! She didn't approve of drinking, you see."

Bessie muttered approvingly.

"Religious, I expect," Ruby commented.

The plump woman laughed again. "Far from it. She was as atheistic as they come. A bit of a Marxist is what I heard. Religion is the opium of the people and all that stuff. "

"Oh!" Ruby was too startled to think what to say next. She contented herself with, "This pie looks wonderful." And that was that.

Later, as they drove away in Bessie's car, Ruby said, "Miss Hicks doesn't sound like the sort of person who'd be likely to invest large sums of money in a fancy resort dedicated to the spiritual enlightenment of the idle rich, does she? For one thing, it seems she was not wealthy. For another thing, she was resolutely materialistic."

"What are you getting at?" Bessie asked. "Do you think we have a serial killer with a grudge against elderly atheists?"

“Stranger things have happened,” Ruby commented, gnomically.

23. The Tractor, The Bentley And The Chauffeur

"Take the right-hand turning just here," Ruby said, as Bessie drove her little car at a speed that would have been unexceptional on the M4 but which, on the narrow, twisty, pot-holed lanes of the Welsh countryside, demonstrated a lust for thrills and a scant regard for safety which seemed at odds with Bessie's sensible maturity.

The tyres screeched as the yellow Mini Minor made a sharp ninety-degree turn into an even narrower and more profoundly pot-holed lane than the one which it had just left.

Ruby braced herself against the dashboard, the blood draining from her face. "You could slow down a bit," she said.

"I'm already going at a snail's pace," replied Bessie. "What's in this direction anyway?"

Ruby had a road map unfolded in her lap. She ran her finger down the line representing the road they had taken from Cwmhyfryd. "It's a place called Co-ed DeRue," said Ruby.

"Never heard of it. Are you sure you've got the right map?"

"Of course I have. Look, There's Coom High-fried. And here's Co-ed DeRue."

"Give it to me." Bessie slowed the car to a touch under sixty miles per hour and took the map from Ruby.

"I think you may need to stop," said Ruby, her breathing now coming in panicky gasps.

"Stop? Not at all. Just show me where the…"

"STOP!!!!" screeched Ruby.

Bessie slammed on the brakes. The little car slewed across the lane and its rear end slammed into a big beech hedge. It was only then that Bessie noticed the tractor towering over the little car, just two or three yards away from it. The farmer sitting in the seat of the tractor was red faced and shouting. Ruby did not know what he was shouting as he was doing so in the Welsh language. Bessie gave as good as she got. She wound down her window, leant out and cursed poetically in the language of the bards. The cursing continued for a minute or two longer until some sort of mutual agreement was arrived at. Bessie then reversed her car, which fortunately had suffered no significant damage, until she arrived at a place wide enough for the tractor to pass. As it did so, the driver leaned out of the cab, smiled, waved and said something quite friendly-sounding in Welsh. Bessie smiled back, waved and she too said something that sounded as though it might be the Welsh equivalent of "Have a nice day."

"What was all that about?" Ruby asked.

Bessie affected not to understand the question.

"You were effing and blinding at one another one moment and the next you waving and smiling like long lost friends."

"He recognised me."

"I beg your pardon?"

"The farmer. Gwilym Prhys. He was one of my boys, years ago, when I was teaching school. Many's the time I gave him a good telling-off when he was a boy and just because he's a bit older now I'm not afraid to give him a good telling off if he deserves it. I did. And he was duly chastised."

Ruby considered pointing out that on this occasion it had not been Gwilym Prhys who had been in the wrong but Bessie Morgan who had been driving at a reckless speed without keeping her eyes on the road. However, since both Bessie and Gwilym appeared to be content with the relative apportioning of blame, Ruby thought it better to let sleeping dogs lie.

"Now, let's take a look at this map. You said we'd come from Coom High-fried. I take it you meant Cwmhyfryd…"

"That's what I said!" Ruby protested.

"But as for the place we are going to. There's nowhere called Co-ed DeRue on the map as far as I can see."

"There! There!" Ruby jabbed a finger at a location just two miles or so distant, according to the map.

"Coed Derw!" Bessie exclaimed. (She pronounced the name "Coyd" to rhyme with "Floyd" and "Derw" to rhyme with "Dare who?"). "It means the Oak Wood. And that's all that's there, as far as I can remember. Acres and acres of trees. Why on earth do you want to go there?"

"It's where Mrs Williams-Jenkins lives," Ruby said.

"So what? What has she got to do with anything? She must be well into her eighties. You're not suggesting that she's the killer, are you?"

"As your friend Professor Prothero would say, we can't rule out any possibility at this stage. Not until we have hard evidence."

"Oh, I wouldn't pay any attention to that old fool."

"But in any case, no, I very much doubt if Mrs Williams-Jenkins strangled Sergeant-Major Stippleton, pushed Madame Evadne out of a window and battered Miss Hicks to death with a wine bottle. On the other hand, she is the only person, other than Gwendolyn, who was present at the scenes of all three crimes either at the time they were being committed or very soon afterwards. It was, you may recall, she who arrived at Miss Hicks's house and found Gwendolyn lurking over the body."

The house in which Mrs Williams-Jenkins lived was named The Dingle. It was, thought Ruby, a quaint name that suggested a small, white-plastered thatched cottage. In fact, The Dingle was huge. Not, it is true, on the same monumental scale as Coot Hall but certainly much bigger than seemed quite appropriate for an elderly widow living alone.

The house looked rather splendid with its numerous mullioned windows, tall chimney stacks and substantial conservatory. The gardens, though not at their best at this time of year, were also on a magnificent scale. A gravelled driveway led past a pair of big wrought-iron gates from the road to the front door. Parked on the driveway was a large, silver-grey car which Ruby (who knew very little about cars) at first took to be a Rolls-Royce but then she recalled that Mrs Williams-Jenkins had mentioned her Bentley; Ruby assumed that the silver-grey car must be the Bentley to which she had been referring. It was not a modern car. It had the shape and styling of a classic model. From the 1950s perhaps. At any rate, it was not the sort of car that someone on a tight budget would be able to afford.

The impression of wealth was confirmed by the presence of a uniformed chauffeur who was buffing up the shine on the radiator grill with the help of a chamois leather. The chauffeur was smartly dressed in a dark suit with a peaked cap. He had a thin, rat-like face with beady little eyes which were, at that moment, focussed upon Ruby.

"Shall I stop?" Bessie asked. She was driving very slowly past the gates to give Ruby plenty of opportunity to take a good look at the house.

"Stop?" said Ruby. "Why ever would you want to stop?"

"I thought you might be planning to pay a call."

"Certainly not! Drive on! Drive on!"

As the yellow Mini drove past, the chauffeur's eyes followed it. There was something about the expression on the man's face that seemed to radiate a malignant contempt. It made Ruby's blood run cold.

24. Member Number 273

"You have got to be kidding!"

Ruby liked Matt. He was youngish, tallish, good-lookingish and charmingish. But he was also infuriatingly conventional. When she had mentioned the idea of a night out at the Hell Fire Club, Matt had not only looked shocked, he had actually squeaked. Well, it had sounded like a squeak, though it might have been a suppressed scream. They were sitting at a table in the Little Cloggy Café on the High Street at the time and, since Matt was far too timid to give vent to a full throated scream in public, a squeak was the noise he made.

"Good Lord," Ruby complained, "to hear you talk, you'd think I was suggesting taking you to a Roman Orgy. It's a private drinking club in Clogwyn Mawr, for goodness' sake. I hardly think it's likely to be a hotbed of depravity!"

"I've heard stories about it."

"What stories?"

"There are women there."

"There are women here too." Ruby leant forward to whisper into Matt's ear. "There are two women at this very moment having coffee and sandwiches over by the window. What's more, just in case you hadn't noticed, I happen to be a woman myself."

"You are different, though. I don't mean women like you or them two drinking coffee. I mean, you know… *women*."

Ruby was well aware that Matt's romantic inclinations tended more towards the male of the species. However, she felt that Matt's obsessive fear of seeing women in a private club bordered on the pathological.

"You must get over these prejudices," Ruby said. "I can't be expected to go alone. I need someone to escort me."

"I'll get a reputation!" whispered Matt.

"Of course you won't. Nobody'll see you. Only me."

"And anyone else who happens to be in the club."

"There won't be anyone who knows you. It's a very exclusive club."

"How are you going to get in, then? Don't you have to be a member or something?"

"Ladies aren't members. It's a gentlemen's club. Only men are members."

"Is that legal? I mean, isn't it sex discrimination or something?"

"The modern world of sexual equality has not yet encroached upon Clogwyn Mawr, I fear."

"Well, anyway, if you're not a member, they won't let us in, will they?"

"They'll let you in. Because you *are* a member."

"No I'm not!"

"Yes, you are, as a matter of fact. Here's your membership card."

Ruby rummaged in her handbag and brought out a small rectangle of cardboard upon which was printed the words "NPWMA Club, Clogwyn Mawr. Member Number: 273" and, beneath that, "Name:".

"You just have to print your name in the blank space provided and sign it on the line below that."

"Where did you get this?" Matt asked.

"I have my ways," Ruby said enigmatically.

The card had, in fact, been obtained for Ruby by PC Ian Tucker, the local police constable. He did not explain how he had obtained it and Ruby knew better than to enquire. Perhaps the club had been raided by the police? All she cared about was that it was a valid card and, once Matt wrote his signature upon it, the card would provide entrance for Matt and one guest. That guest would be Ruby.

Matt looked at the card closely. "What's NPWMA mean? I thought it was called the Hell Fire Club?"

"It masquerades as The Clogwyn Mawr Non-Political Working Men's Association," Ruby explained. "The Hell Fire Club is, it seems, a sort of a nickname."

"Oh God! Ruby! I don't want to go there."

"Matt…" Ruby looked crestfallen. She was very good at looking crestfallen. She had learnt the art many years ago while at drama school. "Think of all the things I've done for you."

Matt thought of them. Ruby had indeed done a few things for Matt in the past. Some of them, such as helping him prepare a cottage for a photo session he had done for a magazine (Matt wrote books and the magazine feature provided some much-needed publicity) had been very useful. Others, such as getting him involved in murder investigations, had been a pain in the neck. He was of the opinion that taking Ruby to the Hell Fire Club would definitely be at the pain-in-the-neck end of the spectrum.

"It's something to do with the woman Gwendolyn killed, isn't it?" Matt said.

"Matt!" Ruby looked at him sternly. "I'm surprised to hear you repeating malicious gossip. There's nothing to suggest that Gwendolyn killed that woman."

"She was found at the scene – with the murder weapon!"

"Well, yes," Ruby conceded, "there is that. But apart from that, the police haven't got a thing on her."

"Oh, Ruby, Ruby, what are you getting me involved in?"

"Nothing. Nothing at all," Ruby said cheerfully. "Don't worry, Matt, it'll just be a quiet night out. We'll have a few drinks and a chat. Nothing more than that."

25. The Hell Fire Club

The woman looked Matt up and then she looked him down. Then, just for good measure, she looked him up and down all over again. A woman of mature years, she was wearing a black, silky evening gown that gave the impression that it had been designed for a person of somewhat less maturity. The gown was low-cut and snug-fitting. There was quite a lot of the woman to fit into the gown and not all of her did.

"I don't reco'nise you, see, my darling, that's the thing."

"I…"

"He's new," Ruby interrupted. She put her arm around Matt's waist. "You're a new member, aren't you, sweetie?"

"Sweetie?" Matt mouthed back at Ruby; he grasped her fingers and made an unsuccessful effort to prise them from his waist.

"Introduced, was you?" the woman asked. "Who was it what introduced you, then, my darling?"

"Well, I, er…" Ruby giggled somewhat hysterically as though sharing a secret joke. "I should think you wouldn't ask a question like that. I was told this was a discreet club."

"So it might be, but, nonetheless… if I doesn't reco'nise someone, I has to establish who that someone is, my darling. You wouldn't believe the riff-raff we gets in here sometimes."

"It's all right, Violet," a voice said in the darkness behind the woman, "they're with me."

The woman in the snugly-fitting evening gown – Violet – glanced around. "You should have said, my darling. Only, see, I didn't reco'nise this gent' here and I can't be letting in just any-one…"

The man who had spoken stepped through a door that led from the inner reaches of the Hell Fire Club into the dimly-lit foyer.

"My God!" To Matt's enormous relief, Ruby ceased clutching his waist and put her hand over her mouth in shock. "What on earth are you doing here?"

It took Matt a few seconds longer than Ruby to recognise the man who had just entered the foyer. When he did, he was even more shocked than Ruby. It was Ian Tucker, the village constable of Clogwyn Bach.

"I'm a member," Ian said. "I thought you knew. That's how I got the membership card for Matt. New members have to be recommended by old members."

"But," Matt was not at all sure what was the appropriate thing to say to a policeman who had secured his membership to what was, by all accounts, an establishment whose business hovered on the wrong side of the law. He had been considering saying something along the lines of "I thought the police would be raiding a dive like this, not recruiting members." On further consideration, he decided that, in the circumstances, this might not be diplomatic, so what he actually said was, "I thought you'd be on duty tonight."

Ian smiled. "What you were really thinking is that the police should be raiding a dive like this, not recruiting members."

Matt blushed. He hoped it was too dark for Ian to notice. "Not at all, not at all," he blathered. "I just meant, well, you know…" He lowered his voice so that Violet, who was sitting at the entrance counter a few feet away, filling out her football pools, might not hear what he said. "You know. You hear the rumours…"

"Not all of which are true," Ian said. "Though some are. Come on, follow me."

Ian turned and pulled aside a dark velvet drape that was covering the entrance to a room beyond. As Matt and Ruby followed him, they heard Violet mutter, "The riff-riff we gets in here these days, you wouldn't believe…"

It took a few moments for Ruby's eyesight to adjust to the deeper darkness of the inner room. The only part of the room which was moderately well illuminated was the bar at the far end. This was a small bar, around eight feet in length, with rows of inverted spirit bottles attached to the wall behind the counter upon which slouched a large man who appeared to be watching something on his mobile phone.

As her eyes gradually acclimatised, Ruby saw that the rest of the room was taken up with a dozen or so tables, most of which were unoccupied, though shadowy figures could be seen sitting at two or three of them. The room itself was, Ruby estimated, only about forty feet or so in length and about twenty feet in width – which was precisely the size of two rooms in an old terraced house whose dividing wall had been removed. The Hell Fire Club was not the sort of nightclub with lavish dance floors and a stage. But nor, at first sight, was it quite the sink of depravity that its reputation suggested.

"I've got a table over here," Ian said. He led them to a table about midway along the far wall. "I'll get you something to drink. What would you like?"

"Wine" and "Beer", Ruby and Matt said simultaneously.

"The beer's awful," Ian said. "The red wine is just about drinkable though. I'll get a bottle, if that's all right with you, Matt."

Matt smiled sheepishly. "Perfect."

"Odd place," Ruby observed when Ian had left them in order to get the wine. "Not much going on, is there?"

She peered into the darkness which, she now realised, was slightly illuminated by faint dots of light spinning slowly around the walls. These dots were produced by a light shining onto a small mirrored ball that turned dejectedly at the centre of the ceiling.

"What are you looking for?" Matt asked. "I thought you were expecting to find clues. I can hardly see my hand in front of my face so if there's any clues, we'd never even notice them."

"Maybe we'll hear something?" Ruby said, hopefully.

They listened. There was desultory chatter coming from a couple of the other tables. There was also some 1960s jazz music being piped at low volume through a couple of crackly wall speakers. Ruby tried to identify the music. She thought it might be Acker Bilk. Or possibly Kenny Ball. Then again, since Acker Bilk and Kenny Ball were the only 1960s jazz musicians she had ever heard of, her guesses might have been wide of the mark.

"There." Ian placed three glasses on the table and proceeded to fill them from the bottle he was holding. "It's not a fine old vintage but at least it's got alcohol in it."

"Are you really a member?" Ruby said.

Ian sat, picked up his glass, swirled it, sniffed it like a connoisseur, gulped down a mouthful, winced and said, "Of course, I am. Ever since last night."

"Last night! You became a member last night! Why?"

"Detective Inspector Gruttock's idea."

"Gruttock! Is he a member too?"

"I don't know. I didn't ask. He got hold of a membership card for me. Told me to join. So I did."

"Why?"

"He seems to think you are on to something."

"Me? I can't imagine what he… Oh! Now I understand."

"What?"

"Yesterday. Bessie and I paid a visit to Detective Inspector Gruttock."

"And you told him you were planning to come to the Hell Fire Club?"

"No. But after we'd visited the Detective Inspector we came to take a look at the club. From the outside. We were seen. By one of your colleagues. A certain Sergeant Wisty."

"Wisty!" Ian broke into a broad grin. "You mean he followed you?"

"That's exactly what I mean."

"So Gruttock is so short of clues he's trying to pinch your leads."

"Excuse me," Matt said, "but I still don't know what clues you are looking for."

"Neither do I," Ian and Ruby said in unison.

Ruby continued: "Gwendolyn mentioned the Hell Fire Club when we were at Coot Hall. She dropped some fairly big hints that Clarissa Winthrop, Sir Nathaniel's lady friend, had been here – and might have had reasons to regret it. Of course, if Gwendolyn had seen Clarissa here, that presumably means that Gwendolyn had been here too. And if Gwendolyn had been here, maybe she saw something going on. Something that someone wouldn't want the world to know about. Something that would make it worth someone else's while to shut Gwendolyn up – for good!"

"You think Clarissa tried to bump Gwendolyn off?" Matt asked.

Ian scratched his head. "Wait a minute. Nobody tried to bump Gwendolyn off, did they? I thought it was Gwendolyn who was going around trying to bump off other people."

"It's complicated," Ruby said. "All I'm saying is that if Clarissa came to the Hell Fire Club and Gwendolyn also came to the Hell Fire Club, it might be worthwhile finding out who they came with. As I understand it, it's normal club policy for men to become members and bring women as guests. Did Nathaniel Snibb bring Clarissa here, I wonder? In which case, Nathaniel must be a member. Maybe he committed an indiscretion here?"

"And Clarissa is blackmailing him?" Ian suggested.

"Maybe it's Gwendolyn who's blackmailing him," Matt added.

"Or maybe Clarissa was with someone else. And that person is blackmailing Clarissa, to keep it quiet so that Nathaniel Snibb doesn't find out."

"Maybe, maybe, maybe…" Ian said. "My head's starting to ache with all the maybes. I'm not sure this is really getting us anywhere."

"If we could only find a way to get a look at the membership book," Ruby said, "maybe that would help."

"Another maybe," Ian moaned.

"Don't they keep the membership details on a computer?" Matt asked.

"No," Ian said. "They reckon that compromises membership privacy."

"How do you know that?"

"Detective Inspector Gruttock told me."

"And how does he know that?"

"I didn't think it would do my career prospects much good to ask," said Ian.

"OK. Well, how about this for an idea," said Matt. "I go out to the foyer and have a word with the woman there. What's her name?"

"Violet."

"I tell Violet that Ruby wants to see here."

"Why would I want to see her?" Ruby asked.

"I'll say it's a woman's matter."

"What sort of woman's matter?"

Matt frowned. "How would I know? You can think of something. So anyway, Violet comes with me to see Ruby. Meanwhile Ian pops out into the foyer and take a sly look at the book."

"Even if Violet fell for it, it wouldn't do any good," Ian said.

"Why not?"

"Because nobody signs in using their real names. I signed in as 'D. Duck'. I noticed that the names above me included 'A. Schwarzenegger' and 'H. Bogart'. It's safer to use false names just in case."

"In case of what?" said Ruby.

Ian shrugged but declined to speculate. The implication seemed to be that even if the police had not yet raided the Hell Fire Club, they might decide to do so in future.

"I signed in using my real name," Matt groaned.

Ian sucked his teeth meaningfully. "Risky, risky."

"So if the membership book won't tell us anything," said Ruby, "I suppose we'll have to ask around. Somehow I don't think Violet would be a mine of information. I got the impression she didn't much warm to us."

"There's always Mick the barman," Ian said. "Mind you, I'm not sure what I'd ask him. People here don't tell the barman their real names. It's a shame we haven't got some photos to show around."

"Oh, how infuriating!" Ruby hissed. "I'm sure there is something here, some clue, if only we knew where to look."

Feeling rather despondent, Ruby excused herself since she needed to "powder her nose". When she returned, a few minutes later, her mood has undergone a dramatic transformation. Indeed, she was so excited that her words came all out in an incoherent babble.

"Calm it, Ruby," Matt said. "You're not making any sense."

"You didn't sniff anything you shouldn't have when you were in the ladies, did you?" Ian asked. At any other time, Ruby would have been horrified at the suggestion and she would have treated Ian to the sharp end of her tongue. At that moment, however, she was in such a good mood that he could have accused her of people-smuggling and she would have laughed it off.

"Sit down," said Matt, "take a deep breath and start all over again."

Ruby followed Matt's instructions. She sat down. She took a deep breath. She took a good glug of red wine, ignoring its tart astringency. And then she started all over again. "You'll never guess who I saw in the ladies' toilets!"

Matt and Ian agreed that they never would guess and so Ruby told them – "Gwendolyn Gormly!"

26. Photographic Evidence

"You are mistaken," Ian said. "You can't have seen Gwendolyn in the ladies' toilets. I know for a fact that she's in custody."

"A photo," Ruby explained. "On the wall. There's a big corkboard over the hand-drying machine. And on the corkboard there are pictures of people sitting at tables, laughing, drinking, wearing silly hats…"

"Silly hats?" said Matt.

"The photos may have been taken at Christmas. At any rate, there are photos of numerous Hell Fire Club customers."

"Hmm, that's worth knowing," Ian said, possibly thinking of the likelihood of a future raid on the establishment.

"I thought they kept their customers all hush-hush," Matt said.

"Not in the Ladies' conveniences, they don't. There's a picture of Gwendolyn. And what's more, Clarissa is in the same photograph. They are sitting on either side of a dumpy little man. Gwendolyn's smiling at the camera. The man is smiling at Gwendolyn. Clarissa looks as though she's gritting her teeth and considering killing one or both of them."

"Is it a clue?" Matt asked.

"I don't know."

"The man in the photograph, is it Nathaniel Snibb?" asked Ian.

Ruby produced the photograph from her pocket and placed it upon the table. "No," she said, "I don't know who it is."

"You nicked the picture!" Ian commented.

"I thought it might come in useful."

"Did you recognise anyone in any of the other photographs?" Matt asked.

Ruby shook her head. "Nobody. But I wonder? Do you think there may be another corkboard in the gents' toilets? Maybe there are other people we might recognise. People who were in Coot Hall on the night of the attempted murders?"

"I'll go and take a look," Ian said.

"I'll come with you," Matt added.

They returned in less than a minute.

"Anything?"

"There was a corkboard," Ian said.

"There were lots of photos on it," Matt added.

"Did you recognise anyone?"

"Well, that's the thing," said Ian. "Since neither Matt nor I were at Coot Hall on the night in question…"

"We wouldn't recognise anyone who was there even if we saw them," added Matt.

"So you'll have to go and look," Ian concluded.

"Me?" Ruby was aghast. "Go to the gentlemen's toilets? I don't think so."

"Don't worry," said Ian, "there probably won't be anyone else in there."

"Probably?"

"And even if there were," Matt said, "in a club like this, I doubt if anyone would be scandalised."

"It probably happens all the time," Ian said.

"It's you best chance of finding more clues," Matt added.

He was right, of course. It was Ruby's best chance. She would just have to stroll in there as though she regularly made use of the men's facilities and scorned anyone conventional enough to think it improper. She stood, walked boldly towards the gents', which were situated to the left of the bar, pushed open the door and strode in. A minute later, she strode out again.

She sat down at her table, refilled her glass from the bottle and downed it in one. "Gah! This wine is foul," she said. "It makes the stuff Gwendolyn serves at her wine bar taste like Château Lafite Rothschild. Not," she added, "that I've ever tasted Château Lafite Rothschild. But if I manage to prove Gwendolyn's innocence, I reckon she owes me a bottle."

"Well," said Matt, "did you recognise anyone in the photos?"

"I did," said Ruby. She took a crumpled photograph from the pocket of her jacket. "This," she said, "is Sergeant-Major Selwyn 'Stonker' Stippleton."

The photograph showed the Sergeant-Major smiling broadly. He had his arm around the shoulder of another man, whom Ruby did not recognise. The other man too was smiling, possibly due to excessive consumption of alcohol since both he and the Sergeant-Major were holding huge cocktail glasses brim-full of an iridescent greenish sort of fluid.

"Sergeant-Major Stippleton is, supposedly, the fitness instructor at The Retreat," Ruby explained. "Though, as far as I can see, he does not appear to be any fitter than I am. He is also supposedly a self-defence instructor, which, bearing in mind that he got himself knocked unconscious with a jar of bath salts and strangled with a pair of ladies' tights, does not inspire great confidence in his abilities. In fact, I am not even totally convinced that he is a real Sergeant-Major. There are one or two details in his autobiography which leave room for doubt."

"He's a bit dodgy, then?" suggested Ian.

"Decidedly dodgy," Ruby agreed.

Matt asked if Ruby had seen photographs of anyone else she had recognised.

"Well," she made a shrugging gesture, "there were one or two others who looked vaguely familiar but I couldn't identify anyone with any certainty."

In fact, she had quite clearly recognised Emrys Greenalge – Muriel's husband – in one photograph. Emrys was sitting very close to an extremely voluptuous woman who definitely was not Muriel. Ruby wondered if Matt and Ian had recognised Emrys too but had been too discreet to mention it. Oh well, that was none of Ruby's business.

For a moment or two she had also thought she had recognised someone else: a ruggedly handsome man with fair hair and a most attractive smile. Nye Clump! But on looking more closely at the photograph, she had to admit that it was impossible to be sure. The man was in the background, in the shadows and slightly out of focus. "Your suspicious nature may be getting the better of you," she told herself.

The important thing was that she now knew that no less than three people who had been at Coot Hall that fateful night had also, at some time or another, been to the Hell Fire Club: Sergeant-Major Selwyn 'Stonker' Stippleton, Clarissa Winthrop and Gwendolyn Gormly. It was all quite confusing. Even so, Ruby felt quite sure that if she could only understand the significance of the Hell Fire Club, she would be closer to understanding why Gwendolyn Gormly was taking the rap for a murder which she did not commit.

The night wore on but the Hell Fire had no intention of living up to its sordid reputation. Of unbridled debauchery there was no sign. A middle-aged couple sitting at a table on the other side of the threadbare dance floor had a short but lively argument. A small, mouse-like man wearing a cheap single-breasted suit and half-moon glasses approached Ruby and asked if she would care to accompany him in a cha-cha-cha. Ruby informed him politely but firmly that she could think of nothing that would give her less pleasure so the mouse-like man retreated to a corner table where a matronly woman was knitting a pullover. "She's a hostess," Ian informed Ruby. "You know – a good-time girl." Ruby found this hard to believe but, knowing nothing of the erotic nightlife of Clogwyn Mawr, could not dismiss the possibility out of hand.

"I've got an idea," Ian said all of a sudden. "Give me that picture."

For a moment, Ruby could not think which picture Ian meant. Then, remembering the photograph which she had purloined earlier in the evening from the gentleman's convenience, she took it from a pocket and handed it to Ian. He immediately walked across to the bar. Ian exchanged a few words with the barman, then showed him the photograph. They talked for a minute or two longer then Ian returned to the table. He threw the photograph across to Ruby. "You were right," he said. "The Sergeant-Major is not who he claims to be."

"The barman knows him?" Ruby asked.

"Mick knows everyone who comes in here," Ian said. "The man you know as Sergeant-Major Selwyn 'Stonker' Stippleton is in fact a junk dealer from Swansea by the name of Ernie Smallman."

"A junk dealer! Are you sure?"

"He calls himself an antique dealer but according to Mick he sells a lot of old tat. You know the kind of thing – he gets some wonky old wardrobe, sands it down, gives it a coat of varnish and suddenly it's a rare Chippendale armoire."

"How does Mick the barman know all this?"

"Mick's done a bit of business with Mr Smallman, or Sergeant-Major Stippleton or whoever he claims to be."

"Buying or selling?"

"You think Mick would be in the market for fake antiques? No. Mick sells. Some of the old folk around here have good furniture. When they die, their families don't want it. Too old-fashioned for them. There's a lucrative trade in snapping up house contents at bargain basement prices."

"I suppose," Ruby suggested, "that he might have been a Sergeant-Major before he became an antique dealer?"

"Possible," said Ian, "but that doesn't explain why he'd change his name."

It was a few minutes after midnight when they left the club. Either its orgiastic reputation had been grossly exaggerated or else the Hell Fire Club on a wet Wednesday evening in early February was not operating on all thrusters. At any rate, nothing of any significance was going on there and both Ruby and Matt felt that their time would be more productively spent getting back to their respective homes and doing some serious sleeping.

On the way out, Ruby noticed another corkboard to which pictures had been attached. She had not noticed it on the way in as it was directly behind the counter at which Violet had been standing and had therefore been obscured by Violet's less than sylph-like form. Violet was nowhere to be seen now, however, so Ruby and Matt were able to take an unimpeded look at the photographs. Matt was staring open-mouthed at one photograph in particular. "My God!" he said. "Is that who I think it is?"

Ruby squinted her eyes to get a closer look. "My God!" she said. "I do believe it is! It's hard to recognise him at that angle."

The person in the photograph was a popular singer and TV personality, known for his good deeds and clean-living lifestyle. He was certainly doing some good deeds in the photograph but they weren't entirely compatible with his clean-living image.

"Good grief!" said Ruby then. By way of emphasis, she said it again. "Good grief!" Then, realising that she had not explained why she had said "Good grief!" twice, she turned to Matt and said, "I recognise him." She pointed to a tall, slim, balding man wearing a dark suit, round-lensed glasses and a silly smile. He was sitting next to the clean-living singer who had originally attracted their attention. "It's Nathaniel Snibb!"

"The pickled onion magnate!" Matt gasped.

"The very same. Good grief!"

"Is that the same 'good grief' or a different one?"

"A different one," said Ruby.

There in the shadows, just to the left of Nathaniel Snibb, was another familiar face. Matt's jaw fell open when he saw it. "Good grief!" he echoed. "Gwendolyn Gormly!"

"Yet again!" said Ruby. "Gwendolyn does seem to keep popping up, doesn't she!"

As they opened the door to leave the club, a tall man in a dark coat roughly pushed past Ruby. There was something very familiar about the man. Ian, Matt and Ruby were back on the street before it occurred to Ruby where she had seen him before. It was the man named Wilkins. Mrs Williams-Jenkins's chauffeur.

27. Bessie's Cat

"I'm no nearer solving this than when I started!"

Ruby was sitting in her kitchen with a steaming mug of tea in one hand and her mobile phone in the other. It was half-past nine in the morning, rain was lashing against the window, obscuring the otherwise dramatic view of the bay far down below and she was in no mood to be talking business with her agent, Max.

"Never mind that," Max said. "I've got a client for you. A radio commercial for haemorrhoid cream. They specifically asked for you."

"Forgive me if I'm not flattered. Are you telling me that when your client heard my voice, he immediately thought of haemorrhoid cream?"

"My client is a woman, as a matter of fact. She was listening to one of your audio books. The one about the lascivious pirate."

"Oh God! 'Passionate Pirates Of Port Royal'. I knew I should have used an assumed name. I'm not sure that narrating these audio books is really very good for my acting career."

"What acting career!" There was a bitterness in Max's voice that Ruby could not fail to notice. "You haven't done any acting since you went to that godforsaken dump in the back of beyond, have you."

"It's called Clogwyn Bach," said Ruby tersely, "and it's actually rather beautiful." A gust of wind rattled the windows and a rumble of thunder boomed out across the sea. "In summer it is, anyway. Look, Max, I realise you're doing your best to find work for me and I appreciate that, I really do."

"It doesn't sound like it."

"But just at the moment I have a critical deadline to meet. Even more critical than narrating one of Miss Cicely P. Tuberose's semi-pornographic historical novels. Even more critical, in fact, than waxing enthusiastic about the soothing effects of a haemorrhoid cream."

Max did not seem greatly impressed. Ruby appeared to be spending all her time assisting the local police force in solving murders, these days. Had she been astute enough to promote her crime-solving talents for the purposes of publicity, Max would have been the first to congratulate her. But when he had suggested that she make herself available for interviews on daytime television, she had been curt in her dismissal of the idea.

Max had even approached a book publisher with the proposal that Ruby should write her autobiography, provisionally entitled, "Murder Is My Business (How I Solve Crimes That Baffle The Police)" but Ruby had wanted nothing to do with it. Max could not understand her. Having retired from acting, her only source of income was derived from narrating audio-books and recording radio commercials. She made no secret of the fact that she hated doing them. Her involvement in some sensational murder investigations was a potential goldmine waiting to be exploited. And yet, she was absolutely dead set against doing so.

"I think you're wasting your time on this one," Max said. "I read a bit about the murder in The Times. Old woman clobbered to death with wine bottle. Murderer arrested at the scene of the crime. It's an open and shut case."

"So everyone keeps telling me. But I don't believe it. I've now got less than twenty-four hours to prove that Gwendolyn Gormly is innocent."

"And if you don't?"

Yes, what if I don't? That thought had already occurred to Ruby. The odds were stacked against her finding any evidence that might cast doubt upon Gwendolyn's guilt. And yet, she had to try.

"Call me again on Monday," Ruby said. "By then, I'll either have succeeded or I'll have failed."

"If you've succeeded, will you be in the mood to do the haemorrhoid cream commercial?"

"No. Not at all. But if I fail, I'll record as many haemorrhoid cream commercials as you like. I shall regard it as my punishment."

*

"Well, you've done all you can. There's really nothing more you can do, is there?"

Ruby had dropped in on Bessie. As always, her kitchen was warm, comforting and smelled of baking. On any other day, just sitting there talking to Bessie and stroking her cat would have made her feel calm and contented. But today, she just could not relax. She had been too hopeful of finding something at the Hell Fire Club that would exonerate Gwendolyn. The only things she had discovered were photographs of Gwendolyn, Clarissa, Nathaniel Snibb and Sergeant-Major Selwyn 'Stonker' Stippleton. She had also learnt that the Sergeant-Major was not a Sergeant-Major at all (which was not really news since she had already suspected he was not all he claimed to be) and that he conducted a dubious antique business in the name of Ernie Smallman somewhere in Swansea. That might be of interest to the officials at the Inland Revenue. It might even be of interest to rival antique dealers. But it was surely not a motive for murder. Ruby sat at Bessie's table, morosely stroking the cat and watching the rain lash against the window.

Wait a minute! Ruby thought, *Bessie hasn't got a cat!* "My God, Bessie! You've got a cat!" she said.

"Moggie. That's his name."

He was a fine, fat, tabby cat and he was purring loudly as Ruby stroked him.

"But you've never had a cat before."

"Oh, years ago, I did. But not recently. Moggie turned up a few days ago. I was pottering about in the garden, the door was open and he wandered in. He seems to have decided that he likes it here so he's staying."

"Staying! But he's someone's cat. You can't just keep someone else's cat. It's cat-napping."

"No, Moggie doesn't belong to anyone. He's a stray. He's been wandering around for months. I give him a pilchard or a sardine every once in a while. But until a few days ago he'd never come inside the house. Then one day last week he strode in through the front door, bold as brass. Now he's discovered the chairs and the cushions and how warm it is in the kitchen, I don't think he's likely to leave again."

The cat looked up at Bessie, yawned, showing a fine set of needle sharp teeth, and then slid off Ruby's lap and onto the floor. It padded across to Bessie, stuck its tail straight up in the air and ingratiated itself against Bessie's legs, mewing at her pitifully.

The cat had Bessie well-trained. Without a moment's hesitation, Bessie stood up, walked across to the door to her pantry, which was set into the wall on the right of her Aga, came out with a tin of pilchards, scooped one of the sauce-covered fish into a saucer and placed it on the floor where the cat scoffed it up greedily.

Ruby's jaw hung slack. "The pantry," she muttered.

Bessie gave Ruby an odd look. From Ruby's expression, you would imagine that she had seen something shocking or exciting or exhilarating, whereas she was, in fact, just staring at Bessie's pantry. The pantry was a tiny, walk-in room, not much more than a store cupboard. There was nothing shocking or exciting or exhilarating about it.

"The cat was in the pantry!" Ruby said. "Why, Bessie? Why was the cat in the pantry?"

Bessie shook her head. "He wasn't in the pantry. The cat has been sitting on your lap all this while."

"Not your cat. The victim's cat. Miss Hicks's cat. Don't you remember? When we went to Clogwyn Mawr police station to talk to Detective Inspector Gruttock. He told us that when he had arrived at Miss Hicks's bungalow, the victim was lying on the floor of the kitchen, Gwendolyn was sitting in the living room with Mrs Williams-Jenkins… and the cat was locked in the pantry. That's why he was sure that it couldn't have contaminated the murder scene. But why would anyone lock a cat in a pantry?"

"By mistake, I suppose?" suggested Bessie.

"By mistake, by mistake? No, I don't believe it. It's such a strange thing to do that it can't be accidental. A cat locked in a pantry at a murder scene. It's just too bizarre."

Bessie did not look convinced. "If you say so."

"But what does it mean?"

Moggie, having finished his pilchard, padded over to Ruby and rubbed against her legs. "What does it mean, Moggie?"

"Miaow!" The cat knew but it wasn't saying.

28. The Mystery Of The Locked Pantry

"The cat?" There was a slightly hysterical edge to Constable Ian Tucker's voice. "What's the cat got to do with anything?"

It was half past eleven and Ruby was sitting in her kitchen once more, staring at the rain pounding against the window. She could barely keep her eyes away from the clock on her kitchen wall. The second hand was ticking relentlessly as though counting away the seconds of Gwendolyn Gormly's fate. Ruby had phoned Ian Tucker in the hope that he might be able to shed light on the mystery of the cat which had been locked inside Miss Hicks's pantry.

"Detective Inspector Gruttock happened to mention the cat," Ruby said. "I thought you might know something about it."

"What is there to know? It was a cat. A scrawny looking cat, it was. Probably had fleas."

"The fleas are inconsequential. It's the cat I'm interested in. Did you actually see it?"

"See it? It was me who found it."

"You did? Wonderful! Tell me everything you know."

"Sorry, I have no idea what you want me to say. I'm not a cat expert. One cat is much like another cat as far as I'm concerned."

"Tell me how you found it. Where was it? What was it doing? All that sort of thing."

Ian sighed. The sigh gave the strong impression that he had better things to do than talk about cats. But he knew that once Ruby was determined to find something out she would give him no peace.

"Truth is," he said, "there's not much to tell. I got to the bungalow about half-past two, I suppose. The scene-of-crime people were already there. They were busy in the kitchen, documenting and photographing and putting things in plastic bags. I think they may have been taking fingerprints. Maybe collecting fibre samples."

"Yes, yes, yes." Ruby was getting impatient. "I'm sure they did a very thorough job. But that's not what I'm interested in. It's the cat I want to know about. Where was the cat wile all this was going on?"

"In the pantry."

"Why was it in the pantry? That's what's puzzling me."

"It was after the fish."

"The fish! Nobody's mentioned fish before."

"It was a murder investigation. The fish didn't seem important."

"Well, perhaps it was. Look, I think you've missed out some details. You said there were some forensics people in the bungalow. Did one of them lock the cat in the pantry?"

"Why would they do that? No. They didn't know it was there. I found it."

"How did you do that?"

"I heard a miaow. There was a door in the wall. I thought it was a toilet or a washroom. But it turned out to be a pantry. The miaow was coming from behind the door. I had to get permission to open the door, of course, but everything had already been photographed and examined; and, in any case, nobody was interested in the pantry on account of the fact that the murder had been done in the kitchen and the body was still lying on the floor. Anyhow, when I opened the pantry door, the cat flew out like a bat out of Hell. It ran straight through the house towards the front door. Someone opened the door and out it scooted."

"You let the cat get away?" Ruby was unable to keep the tone of astonishment out of her voice.

"Yes," Ian was chuckling to himself. "We didn't think it was the murderer, you see."

"Oh, very droll. Nor did you think that it was odd that there was a cat locked in the pantry, I suppose?"

"Not at all. Like I was saying before, it was there for the fish. There was a big fillet of fresh cod, or maybe haddock, on a plate in there. There wasn't much left of the fish by the time I saw it though, because the cat had been eating it."

"The fish might explain the cat's motive," Ruby conceded, "but not its method. How did it get into the pantry? Miss Hicks surely wouldn't have locked her cat in there with a fillet of fresh haddock."

"Ah, well, that's where you are making a mistake."

"I am?"

"You are assuming it was Miss Hicks's cat."

"Wasn't it?"

"No. Miss Hicks didn't have a cat. In fact, she was allergic to cats. We talked to her neighbours. They told us she'd cross a road rather than go anywhere near a cat."

"Then whose cat was it?"

"Not sure. None of the neighbours were missing a cat. It was probably a stray. There are quite a few stray cats around, you know."

Ruby thought of Bessie's recent feline acquisition. "Yes, so I gather. But that makes it even more peculiar that the cat was in the pantry. Why would Miss Hicks lock a stray cat in her pantry?"

"It probably got in there somehow without her knowing about it. Through a window, I expect."

"Is there a window in the pantry?"

"Yes. A small one. But it doesn't open."

"Were there any other windows open in the house that day?" Ruby recalled that the weather had been cold and windy on the day in question.

"Well…" Ian hesitated, "I can't be sure but… I don't think so."

"Someone must have checked, surely."

"Now I think back, I'm pretty sure there weren't any open windows. Maybe the cat came in through the front door."

"Why would anyone keep their door open on a cold, wet day in February? And even if Miss Hicks had been so eccentric as to have done so, why would she then lock the cat in her pantry with a fillet of fresh haddock?"

"I can see what you are saying," Ian conceded, "but…"

"But *what?*"

"Well, when all's said and done, it's just a cat. I don't think it's got anything to do with the murder."

But Ruby did not agree. She thought the cat may well have had something quite significant to do with the murder. But she did not know what.

29. The Eventful Life Of Miss Winifred Elizabeth Hicks

Winifred Elizabeth Hicks had been an explorer and poet. Ruby discovered this fact within moments of searching online. When still a young woman Miss Hicks had left her home in a small Derbyshire village and set sail for West Africa. She arrived at Freetown in Sierra Leone, she worked her way through central Africa, along the way encountering enraged elephants, an amorous prince and several species of venomous snake. She later wrote a best-selling book recounting her adventures. The income from that book funded her travels to Indonesia, India and Outer Mongolia. At the age of fifty, she suddenly decided that exploring was not her true calling but poetry was. She returned to Britain, bought a small but expensive flat in Belgravia and set about writing several books of poems about life, love, loss and grief. The books did not sell well. Her income was soon so depleted that she was obliged to sell her Belgravia residence and seek more modest accommodation. She found a neglected bungalow called 'The Brambles' in a secluded spot close to the village of Cwmhyfryd in South-west Wales.

While Winifred Hicks had never married she was certainly not celibate. Her amorous encounters with princes, potentates, warriors and street-peddlers were fulsomely documented in her travel books. When she came to live in Wales she met a fisherman named Alwyn Evans who, by all accounts, became the one great love of her life. She was far too Bohemian even to consider the possibility of marriage so Alwyn moved in with Winifred and stayed with her until the day he died, from a heart condition, just two years earlier.

One day, a few months after Alwyn's death, Miss Hicks happened to find herself sharing a table with a woman of about her own age in the café at the Farmer's Market in Cwmhyfryd. That woman was Mrs Lowri Williams-Jenkins. Rather quickly, the two women found they had more in common than just their age for they had both recently lost the man they loved. What was more, Mrs Williams-Jenkins not only knew who Miss Hicks was but she had also read all of her books – even the ones devoted to poetry. They soon found themselves talking about old times, the ambitions which Mrs Williams-Jenkins had once had (she had wanted to be a ballet dancer) but had not achieved; and the wealth which Miss Hicks had accumulated and had let slip through her fingers.

But most of all, they also talked about their late partners: Alwyn Evans, a fisherman and Harold Williams-Jenkins, a banker. For both women, the loss of the man they loved was a grievous one. Few people understood how dreadful a loss it was. Younger people seemed to think that the older a person became, the less the death of a loved one mattered to them. What is more, Miss Hicks had the impression that some of her neighbours did not truly think that the loss of her beloved Alwyn (her "live-in lover" as she had heard him being called) could possibly be as devastating as the loss of a husband. The sanctity of marriage was held in high esteem in Cwmhyfryd. Those whose relationships were not thus sanctified were living in sin – an idea which, at her advanced age, Miss Hicks considered rather curious.

*

Ruby had been surprised to discover that Miss Hicks was sufficiently famous to merit her own web site. The web site had not, in fact, been created or maintained by Miss Hicks herself but by a group of dedicated fans of her writing. There were photographs too. The young pigtailed schoolgirl, then the bronzed and athletic explorer, the literary figure of her more mature years seen in the company of some quite well-known intellectuals and writers. And finally the frail old woman sitting in the garden of her bungalow.

Until she had seen the photographs, Ruby had thought of Miss Hicks as no more than a minor character in a drama. Now Ruby saw Winifred Elizabeth Hicks as a real person who had lived a full and interesting life and whose final years had been cruelly taken from her in an act of pitiless, cold barbarity.

The web site devoted to the life and works of Winifred Elizabeth Hicks made no mention of her friendship with Mrs Williams-Jenkins. Ruby had learnt of that from Mrs Lowri Williams-Jenkins herself. That morning, Ruby had phoned Mrs Williams-Jenkins to ask if she knew anything about the mysterious cat which had been locked in Miss Hicks's pantry. Mrs Williams-Jenkins said that she did not, other than the fact that it was a filthy, mangy creature which had scurried from the house the moment it had been released. She had not seen the cat on any previous occasion and she was quite sure that it did not belong to Miss Hicks. For Miss Hicks had not been a cat lover; indeed, she had gone to some lengths to avoid the creatures due to an allergic reaction.

At that point, Mrs Williams-Jenkins's voice had broken slightly and Ruby realised that talking about her old friend was upsetting her. Ruby offered her condolences but, even so, she was determined not to allow emotion come between her and her investigation. Once Mrs Williams-Jenkins had regained her composure, Ruby took the opportunity to ask how it was that she had been the first person to arrive at the bungalow on the day of the murder.

"Oh, Winifred, that is Miss Hicks, telephoned me. She was clearly distressed. She said something about Gwendolyn. So naturally, I went straight to her bungalow to see what the matter was. And the rest you know. My poor, dear friend was lying on the floor of her kitchen. There was blood all over the place." Mrs Williams-Jenkins's voice cracked again and she paused before continuing. "That evil woman was there. Gwendolyn! And to think that I may have been responsible."

"You?" Ruby said, "What do you mean?"

"It was I who mentioned Gwendolyn to Miss Hicks. I had met Gwendolyn at the soirée at Coot Hall, as you may remember. She had struck me as a most intelligent and sensitive person at the time and, of course, a natural psychic."

"Of course," Ruby said, noncommittally.

"Why Winifred decided to ring Gwendolyn Gormly that morning, I cannot say. Prior to that, Winifred had shown no interest in consulting her. She was rather sceptical of spiritual matters, you know. But what is an equal mystery to me is why Gwendolyn should have wished to harm dear, sweet Winifred. They had never met previously, to my certain knowledge. What on earth can have possessed that wicked woman? Perhaps she was possessed by something that is not of this earth?"

"Yes." Ruby thought it unwise to pursue that topic of discussion any further. She did not want to enter into a debate on the mysteries of life after death. "If you don't mind my asking, what precisely did Miss Hicks say about Gwendolyn? When she phoned you, I mean."

"Oh, I'm afraid I don't know. I didn't actually speak to her, you see."

"You didn't?"

"No. I was in my conservatory, pruning my winter jasmine. I often spend my mornings in the conservatory. I find it most relaxing."

"So who took the phone call?"

"Wilkins. My chauffeur. If you want to know precisely what Winifred had to say about that monstrous woman, Gwendolyn Gormly, you would need to speak to him."

"Do you remember what time it was when Miss Hicks phoned?"

Mrs Williams-Jenkins made a little huffing noise. Ruby had the impression that she was laughing to herself. "You are a very impertinent young woman, Miss Lake."

"Young?" Ruby thought. It was not often that she was called that these days!

"However, I know of your reputation. You have a history of solving crimes which baffle the police. No, no, don't contradict me. Modesty does not become you. It is my belief that the local police force has reached an *impasse*. Rumour has reached my ear that while they currently have the hideous Gwendolyn under lock and key, it is not at all unlikely that they shall soon set her free again. Can you believe such a thing?"

"Mmmm." This was another topic of discussion that Ruby did not want to pursue. She tried to make her "Mmmm" sound ambiguous.

"Well, frankly, if you can pin the goods on the vile Gormly, I would be all too pleased to assist."

"Mmmm."

"Suffice to say, Wilkins rushed into the conservatory to tell me about the phone call which he had received from Winifred Hicks. I naturally phoned her back immediately. But answer came there none. So Wilkins suggested that we get into the car and go to The Brambles, Miss Hicks's cottage, at once. Which is what we did. The rest, of course, you know."

Ruby had hoped that her phone-call to Mrs Williams-Jenkins might provide her with some information which would help to cast doubt upon Gwendolyn's guilt. In fact, it only strengthened the case against Gwendolyn. It appeared that, in her panicked phone-call to Mrs Williams-Jenkins, Miss Hicks had even mentioned Gwendolyn by name. And then, minutes later (the two women lived only a few miles from one another) Mrs Williams-Jenkins arrived at Miss Hicks's bungalow to find a grisly scene featuring Gwendolyn, a wine bottle and a corpse.

"Blast it all!" Ruby said to herself. "It's all too damn' convenient. There's far too much evidence against Gwendolyn. It doesn't make any blasted sense!"

30. THE POPULARITY OF PICKLES

That afternoon, the skies were grey and lowering. The weather mirrored Ruby's mood. She had tried her best to find some breach in the wall of evidence which was growing around Gwendolyn Gormly but to no avail. The more Ruby delved into the mystery surrounding the murder at The Brambles, the more solid became the case against Gwendolyn. Instead of undermining that case, Ruby's efforts only seemed to strengthen it. She decided she needed to get out of the house. Perhaps a brisk walk and a breath of fresh air would stimulate the old brain cells!

She trudged down the hill into the village and made straight for "Food'n'News", the little shop run by her friend Muriel Greenalge and her husband Emrys. A fine drizzle was falling by the time she arrived which may have helped to explain why she was the only customer there. She had no real reason to be there and she struggled to think of some things to buy.

"We've got a two-for-one offer on Exotic Magnolia Roll-on Deodorant," Muriel suggested.

"Two for one," Emrys confirmed. "Exotic Magnolia."

"I'll take one," said Ruby.

"Two," Emrys said. "Since it's a two-for-one offer."

"The bourbon creams are nice this week," said Muriel.

"Very nice they are," Emrys said, "the bourbon creams."

Ruby had bought more bourbon creams from Muriel and Emrys's shop than she had any expectation of being able to eat in her lifetime. She glanced around the shelves looking for something with which she was not already supplied in abundance.

"Pickled onions would make a nice change," she said at last.

"Which flavour?" asked Muriel. "We've got Hot Spiced Mexican Tortilla and we've got Hawaiian Chilli and Pineapple."

"Hawaiian Chilli and Pineapple," Emrys confirmed. When they were together Muriel and Emrys showed a great reluctance for one of them speak a whole sentence without the other making some small contribution to it. This created the disconcerting auditory illusion of a single voice echoing around the cavernous recesses of the tiny shop.

Ruby was suddenly inspired. "Have you any Snibb pickled onions?"

Emrys looked at Muriel. Muriel looked at Emrys.

"Snibb?" said Muriel.

"Pickled onions?" said Emrys.

Muriel's face projected sadness as she looked back at Ruby. "Not Snibb's pickled onions," she said. "We haven't sold Snibb's pickled onions since… ooh, how long, Emrys?"

"Two years, I'd say, wouldn't you, Muriel?"

"I would, Emrys. I'd say it must be at least two years since we had a jar of Snibb's pickled onions on the premises. They don't sell, do they, Emrys?"

"They don't, Muriel. The one thing I'd say about Snibb's pickled onions is that they don't sell."

"Really?" Ruby was not a connoisseur of pickled onions and the merits and demerits of competing brands was an unknown world to her. "I thought they were amongst the most sought-after pickled onions in the land."

"Not any more they aren't," said Muriel.

"They aren't," affirmed Emrys. "Not any more."

"They are a bit old fashioned, that's the problem," said Muriel.

"Old fashioned," agreed Emrys. "You only have to look at their ingredients: onions, vinegar, spices. That's not what people want. Not these days."

"They don't?" said Ruby.

"They don't," said Emrys.

"Then what do they want?" said Ruby.

Muriel's face broke out into a smile. "Hot Spiced Mexican Tortilla flavoured pickled onions, that's what they want."

"And Hawaiian Chilli and Pineapple flavoured pickled onions," added Emrys.

"We've got plenty of both of them," Muriel said brightly.

Ruby considered the possibility of buying a jar. She did not consider it for long, however. "I'll take some chocolate bourbon biscuits," she said.

"Good choice," said Muriel.

"You can't have too many chocolate bourbon biscuits," said Emrys.

Ruby did not think this was literally true.

*

When she got back home, Ruby went up to her office, turned on her laptop computer and searched for "Snibb's Pickled Onions". Apart from the ubiquitous advertising ("Snibb's Pickled Onions – traditional pickles with an extra zing") there were several news items about "market share" and "stock values", both of which were declining; also some details about a failed takeover bid and an acrimonious resignation from the board. Earlier in the week a rather technical article had been published in the Financial Times which made reference to something called a "profit warning".

Ruby had never understood big business. Her only investments had been in a rather poor pension plan, and her knowledge of stocks and shares was non-existent. She did, however, know enough to realise that Snibb's Pickles was not a thriving company. The days when the pickle-eaters of Britain thronged to traditional pickles with an extra zing were long gone. Now they demanded more esoteric pickles enhanced by spices from the exotic orient and fruits from far Hawaii. Her assumption that Nathaniel Snibb was rolling in dough to such a degree that he could create a New Age retreat in a remote corner of South-west Wales on a mere whim might not be entirely justified. In fact, his finances seemed to be decidedly shaky. All of which caused Ruby to wonder where he was getting the money to pour into the extensive refurbishments of Coot Hall.

31. The Sergeant-Major's Secret

"It was always a long shot," Bessie said philosophically, as they sat together in Bessie's kitchen. "Trying to prove that Gwendolyn is innocent, I mean. The trouble with you is that you only see the good in people. But there's no getting away from the fact that some people are just naturally bad. I don't like to talk ill of anyone but I would have to say that I would struggle to find a single good thing to say about Gwendolyn Gormly. She's a nasty piece of work and she always has been."

Ruby had to agree. She too had never liked Gwendolyn; she was cold, callous, mean, argumentative, avaricious and hard-hearted. Ruby had disliked Gwendolyn the first time she had met her and she had not grown to like her on further acquaintance. There were many people in the village who hated Gwendolyn with a passion and some of them had personal reasons for their hatred. If Gwendolyn was sentenced to life imprisonment with no possibility of parole, there would be no grieving and lamentation in Clogwyn Bach. Indeed, Ruby suspected that many of the locals would greet the news with approval, excitement and celebration.

But in Ruby's view, it really did not matter how unpleasant or how widely disliked Gwendolyn might be, if she was not guilty of murder then she should go free without a stain on her character. But Ruby's belief in Gwendolyn's innocence was not widely shared. Most people had assumed her guilt from the outset.

Having left Bessie's cottage and returned to her own cottage, Ruby felt at a loose end. She looked at her wrist-watch: 2:35. In under nineteen and a half hours, Gwendolyn Gormly would be charged with the murder of Miss Winifred Elizabeth Hicks. And there was nothing Ruby could do about it.

"Oh well," she said to herself, "you did your best." And the thought came unbidden to her mind, "But your best was not enough."

She trudged upstairs to her little office, turned on her laptop computer, took out the manuscript of Miss Cicely P. Tuberose's latest blockbuster novel, "Lady Harriet and the Hot-Blooded Hussar", and, after pressing the recording button on her audio software, she began to read with, she hoped, a credible simulation of enthusiasm.

She was three pages into Chapter One (Lady Harriet had been captured by a gang of brigands when the hot-blooded hussar who had, mysteriously, been bathing naked in a mountain stream, having heard her cries for help, came running through the thicket waving his cutlass) when she was disturbed by a low, thrumming, rumbling sound from the road outside. It sounded like a motorbike. She pressed the Stop button of her audio-software. Background noises of galloping horses she might have got away with but a motorbike intruding upon the cutlass-wielding hussar would, she felt, be unlikely to be received kindly by listeners to the audio-book.

She waited a few seconds to give the motorbike time to move out of recording distance. She realised, however, that she could no longer hear it at all. Then there came the loud ringing of her doorbell.

Ruby uttered a few well-chosen imprecations, slammed down her dog-eared copy of "Lady Harriet and the Hot-Blooded Hussar" upon the desk next to her computer and stumped angrily downstairs with the intention of giving a piece of her mind to whoever it was who had driven their blasted motorbike up to her cottage. Probably a delivery driver who's got lost, she thought. She opened the door and was about to say, in a strident tone, "What the bloody hell do you want?" when the words caught in her throat. The man standing there, wearing a black leather jacket and holding a crash helmet in his gauntleted hands, was Sergeant-Major Selwyn 'Stinker' Stippleton.

His brash, assertive manner had withered on the vine. He stood there, with his eyes downcast, shuffling his feet, looking like an overgrown child who had been summoned to the headmaster's study. "Good afternoon, Miss Lake," he said, timidly. "There's a few things I think we needs to talk about. I wonder if I might…" He looked up, smiled ingratiatingly, and with one leather-gloved hand, he gave a tentative twirl of his moustache.

Ruby had no idea what had occasioned his visit but she thought it might well have something to do with Gwendolyn Gormly. "Oh, come in! Come in!" she said, smiling encouragement. "Awful weather we're having. Perhaps you'd like some tea?"

"Very kind of you. A mug of tea is just what I could do with."

So off they went into Ruby's kitchen.

*

"A nasty little man is what he is, though I probably shouldn't be saying so."

"I'm sure he's only doing his job to the best of his ability," Ruby said, "though I must admit that he does seem a little – how shall I put it? – officious at times."

The Sergeant-Major slurped his tea, wiped a few drops from his moustache with the back of his hand, cleared his throat, sniffed and added, "There was plenty like him that I knew in the Army. I knows the type well and I doesn't like 'em."

The object of the Sergeant-Major's scorn was Detective Inspector Arthur Gruttock who had arrived at Coot Hall at the ungodly hour of eight-thirty that morning and had not left again until shortly after two. In the intervening period, he had spoken to everyone at the Hall, often in a highly condescending manner. He had been particularly condescending to Sergeant-Major Stippleton, something to which the Sergeant-Major took particular exception.

"Do you know, he accused me of falsifying my rank?"

Ruby tutted into her tea as though such a terrible idea had never occurred to her. In fact, had it not been for her intervention, she doubted whether Detective Inspector Gruttock would even have bothered interviewing Sergeant-Major Stippleton, let alone questioning his rank. It had been Ruby who had told the inspector of the strange events following the séance at Coot Hall, events of which the inspector had previously been unaware. And it had been Ruby who had recognised the Sergeant-Major in a photograph at the Hell Fire Club. No doubt, Constable Ian Tucker had conveyed that information to Detective Inspector Gruttock.

"I recall you saying that you were in India?" Ruby said.

"A terrible, strange, hot country it is too. Stationed in Agra we was. Then in Jaipur. Did I tell you about an old fakir I met who…"

"Yes, yes, I think you did mention him. Which regiment were you in, out of curiosity?"

The Sergeant-Major was unaccountably busy removing biscuit crumbs from his moustache. He appeared not to have heard the question. "Lovely cuppa tea, if I may say so. I likes a good strong cup meself. None of this maiden's water what some serve."

Ruby would have loved to have pressed her visitor further on the matter of his military experience. From the first time she had met the Sergeant-Major, she had felt there was something unconvincing about him. According to the barman at the Hell Fire Club, the putative Sergeant-Major was in reality Mr Ernie Smallman, a Swansea antique dealer of dubious repute. Ruby supposed that if that were indeed the case, Detective Inspector Gruttock would have been able to unearth the truth and Ruby might be able to get the story out of Ian Tucker later on. However, for the time being, it was not the crimes of Sergeant-Major Stippleton (aka Ernie Smallman) which were of interest to her but those of Gwendolyn Gormly.

"I'm sorry to hear you've had a trying morning," Ruby said, "but I still don't understand why you've come to see me of all people."

"Ah, yes, well, I was coming to that…"

"Yes?"

"You was at the Clogwyn Mawr Non-Political Club, I believe."

At first, Ruby could not think what the Sergeant-Major was talking about. Then she recalled the brass plate set into the wall outside the Hell Fire Club. It purported to be a working men's club of no particular political affiliation.

"Oh, yes, I was taken there by a friend."

The Sergeant-Major put a thumb down the inside of his collar as though to loosen it. From the ruddy colour of his face, he seemed to be feeling the heat, which was odd since Ruby's kitchen was unheated and the day was far from balmy.

"I, um. I went there once."

"Oh yes?"

"With a friend."

"Did you like it?"

"A very close friend."

"Oh?"

"A gentleman friend."

"Ah?"

"A very close gentleman friend."

Ruby was gaining the distinct impression that the Sergeant-Major was beating about the bush, avoiding the subject and leading her on a wild goose chase. He was also becoming decidedly red in the face.

"Is everything all right? If you are too warm, by all means take off your jacket."

The Sergeant-Major cleared his throat. "A chartered accountant from a small village near Newport. My friend, I mean. The friend I went to the club in Clogwyn Mawr with."

"Ah?" Ruby paused, awaiting more information but none was forthcoming. "Oh!" Suddenly illumination broke upon her. "You mean you have a boyfriend!"

The Sergeant-Major glanced away, smoothed his moustache, coughed, then glanced back again. "This is not something that is widely known."

"Oh, but really, nobody cares. I myself have several gay friends here in Clogwyn Bach. There's really no problem. Not in this day and age."

"My gentleman friend is married. With two teenaged children, a boy and a girl. He belongs to the golf club. He has a BMW car and a West Highland terrier dog."

"A West Highland terrier dog, 'ey?" said Ruby. "Ah, well, I can see how that might put another complexion on matters."

"The point is, that you 'as seen me in the company of this gentleman. In a certain photograph."

Ruby at once recalled the photograph she had found in the Hell Fire Club in which the Sergeant-Major was pictured holding a large cocktail in one hand while his other arm was draped around the shoulders of a man whom Ruby had not seen before.

"And I would be grateful if you could forget you saw me," the Sergeant-Major went on. "Detective Inspector Gruttock was most interested in obtaining a copy of the photograph what you saw. Apparently the detective inspector went to the Non-Political Club in Clogwyn Mawr but the aforementioned photograph was no longer there."

"That's because I have it," said Ruby.

"You has?"

"I has. I mean, I have. You can have it if you like."

The Sergeant-Major's face went rapidly from red to white. "I don't want it! No, you must destroy it. Burn it. Cast the ashes out to sea. The sooner that photograph is removed from this Earth the happier I will be."

"Oh well, if you like…" Ruby stopped in her tracks. While she did not understand why the Sergeant-Major was so exercised about an entirely innocent photograph of him and a chartered accountant from Newport, it occurred to her that the photograph might be used to her advantage. If she were to agree to destroy it, she might reasonably expect some recompense for her actions. The thing she most wanted was information. And the Sergeant-Major (for want of any compelling evidence to the contrary, she would continue to think of him as Sergeant-Major Selwyn 'Stonker' Stippleton), while lacking in first-hand knowledge of the murder of Miss Winifred Elizabeth Hicks, was overburdened with first-hand knowledge of the attempt upon his own life. Ruby was convinced that the perpetrator of those two offences, and also of the attempt upon Madame Evadne's life, was one and the same person.

Ruby explained the urgency of her investigation to the Sergeant-Major and he assured her that he would be only too pleased to furnish her with any information that she required. Ruby wanted to know all his memories of the events leading up to the attack upon him in the bathroom.

"I'd gone back to my room, 'and't I? After all that malarkey with the wine glass and the spirit messages which, I may say, I consider to be a load of baloney. Ghosts talking through wine glasses! Whoever heard of such tomfoolery? A proper Ouija board, now, that's a different kettle of fish altogether. But a wine glass? Pah!

"Anyways, I'd had a hard day working out, you see, in the gym, which is on the ground floor, at the back. I'm to be the fitness instructor, as you may know, so I 'as to keep myself in tip top shape which, as you can no doubt see, is exactly what I do."

Ruby smiled noncommittally. To her inexpert eye, the Sergeant-Major's physique bordered on the flabby but she did not think it prudent to say so.

"At about twenty-two 'undred hours which in layman's terms is ten o'clock, I decided I would just have the time to have a quick wash and brush-up before going downstairs for a few drinks."

Ruby interrupted him. "Was this at ten o'clock precisely?"

"Not precisely. It would have been a few minutes before. I remember thinking that Nathaniel Snibb had suggested we meet up at quarter past ten which gave me about twenty minutes. So that must have meant that the time was about five to, um, twenty-two hundred hours. Or, as you might say, twenty-one hundred hours and fifty-five minutes."

"Five to ten," said Ruby.

"In layman's terms, yes. I proceeded down the stairs…"

"Which stairs would these be?"

"The stairs from my room. You see, I 'as a room on the top floor of the house. At the front-right corner."

"Two storeys above the Drawing Room?"

"Exactly. The top floor was where they had the servants' quarters in years gone by. The ceilings of the rooms are a bit low but apart from that, I 'as nothing to complain about. Of course, when you 'as lived in tents in the blazing heat of the Sahara or the perishin' cold of the arctic, even a broom cupboard can seem like luxury. In Jaipur once I lived for two weeks inside a termite mound that I had to excavate with my own hands. The enemy was hiding in the trees all around me, so I had to find a hide-out where they'd never think of looking. Then one day an ant-eater chanced along and…"

"Most interesting," Ruby commented. "If time wasn't so pressing, I'd love to hear more about your adventures. However…"

"Oh yes, sorry about that. I was getting carried away…"

Carried away to the extent of inventing ant-eaters which did not reside in India, Ruby thought.

"So I went downstairs to the bathroom in the east wing of the second floor of Coot Hall. But it was already in use. I could hear the tuneless tones of Guru Lennie proceeding from within. 'I'm Gonna Wash That Man Right Out Of My Hair' was the song he was warbling. You might know it? It is taken from the musical 'South Pacific' which tells the story of a nurse, a plantation owner and various assorted sailors on a tropical island. In the film, the nurse is played by Mitzi Gaynor."

"Is that relevant?"

"You wouldn't understand the song unless you knew about the plot of the musical. I can sing a bit if you like."

"On some other occasion, perhaps. What happened next?"

"After Mitzi Gaynor sings the song, you mean?"

"After you heard Guru Lennie singing in the bathroom."

"Oh. Well, I walks along the passage to the west wing. There's another bathroom there, you see."

"And what did you do then?"

"I opens the door."

"The sign on the door said 'Vacant'?"

"I would not have opened the door if it had said 'Engaged'. Then I goes inside. I was about to pull the string that dangles beside the door to turn the light on. And that's all I can remember. Everything went black and I woke up with a thumping headache and a pain like fire around my throat. And there I was, stretched out on the floor with Gwendolyn Gormly straddling me, throttling me with her tights!"

Ruby had heard all this before. Was there nothing that the Sergeant-Major could tell her which might provide a clue?

"Wait a minute! The light. You said you were about to pull the string to turn on the light. Do you mean that the bathroom was in darkness?"

"It was. If the light had been on I'd have seen my assailant and taken effective measures to deal with her."

"Or him," Ruby said. "I'm convinced it wasn't Gwendolyn who attacked you. But wasn't there enough light from the passageway to let you see if anyone was inside the bathroom?"

"The door shut behind me. I was in complete darkness."

"It shut behind you! Why didn't you switch the light on before letting it shut?"

"I gave the light cord a quick tug but it wouldn't come on. My arms were full, what with my towel and a clean shirt and my shaving soap and my razor and my aftershave and my hair pomade and other such necessaries of which a lady like yourself is no doubt unawares."

"The light wouldn't come on, you say? Why ever not?"

"It's a bit temperamental that bathroom light. You 'as to pull it in just the right way to get it to come on. I told myself that once I put down all the stuff I was carrying I'd be in a better position to mess around with the light. But by that time someone had struck me on the noddle and I was out for the count."

"Unless," said Ruby, "someone had deliberately tampered with the light to make sure it wouldn't come on. Then they could launch their attack under cover of darkness."

"I had already considered that possibility. I mentioned it to that detective inspector chap."

"And what did he say?"

"He said 'Oh, no, no, my dear fellow. That is not the way the criminal mind works.'"

"The man's an idiot," said Ruby.

"I 'as to admit that thought 'ad occurred to me too."

"I don't think you were the assailant's target at all," Ruby said.

The Sergeant-Major laughed sardonically. "If you'd 'ad the bump on the top of your head that I had on mine, you wouldn't say that."

"I think someone was hiding in the bathroom, in the darkness, waiting behind the door, or behind the shower curtains perhaps, for Gwendolyn Gormly to arrive. That person struck out with the jar of bath salts before realising that it was you, not she, who had entered the bathroom. Then, turning on the lights and realising their mistake, that same person…"

"Decided to strangle me with Gwendolyn's tights?"

"I admit that does sound implausible."

"Not to say bonkers."

“Suffice to say, it stretches credulity. But since that must be what actually happened, all that remains for me to do is find a logical explanation.”

32. Privates On Parade

"Good Lord. Really?"

Ruby was sitting in her little upstairs office staring blankly at the drizzly twilight world beyond the window. She had been taking a short break from narrating the latest exciting chapter of "Lady Harriet and the Hot-Blooded Hussar" when her mobile phone rang. It was Constable Ian Tucker. The news he gave her was startling.

"Are you sure that's correct?" Ruby asked. "Well, I only wish I'd known that a few hours ago. Yes, he called around. To my house. What? Oh no, it was nothing important. A social call, I suppose. What? You're asking why he'd want to socialise with me? Cheeky devil! Some people do, you know. After all, if I accept Guru Lennie's job offer to go and teach voice coaching and public speaking workshops, well, the Sergeant-Major – or Ernie Smallman, if that's really his name – will be my professional colleague."

By the time she put her phone back on her desk, Ruby's mind was reeling. She could no longer concentrate on the perfumed prose of Miss Cicely P. Tuberose so she decided to call it a day.

According to Ian Tucker, the full investigative might of the local police force had been deployed upon the mystery of Sergeant-Major Selwyn 'Stonker' Stippleton's dubious past. There was indeed more to the man than met the eye. His real name was Ernest Theodore Smallman and, as Ruby had already been informed, he had for a while owned a small antique shop on the outskirts of Newport. Whether or not that shop had operated on the wrong side of the British law, as Mick the barman at the Hell Fire Club had intimated, was a matter of unproven conjecture. At any rate, he did not have a criminal record.

Ernie Smallman was not, however, an antique trader of longstanding. Nor was he (or had he ever been) a Sergeant-Major in the British Army. What he had been was an actor. He had acted on stage, he had acted in films, he had been on television and he had been on the radio. For a horrible moment, Ruby wondered whether their paths might have crossed when she too had been active in that very profession. She tried to imagine what he might have looked like ten or twenty years ago: slimmer perhaps, possibly lacking the moustache and with a fuller head of hair. Eventually, with a feeling of relief, she concluded that she really did not remember him so their paths, in all probability, had not previously crossed.

Then she loaded up a web browser on her laptop computer and began searching. The name "Ernest Smallman" produced a surprisingly large number of matches. One was an estate agent, another was a lance-sergeant who died in 1916. She tried "Ernest Theodore Smallman". That resulted in far fewer matches but none of them were relevant. Then she tried "Ernie Smallman" and finally "Ernie Smallman actor". That was altogether more productive. There were several matches which linked to theatre reviews in provincial newspapers. Assuming they all referred to the same Ernie Smallman, he clearly tended to be cast in a particular type of role. He had played Colonel Carbery in Agatha Christie's "Appointment With Death" in Walsall, Sergeant Kite in a touring production of Farquhar's late Restoration comedy, "The Recruiting Officer" and – *Oh!* thought Ruby, *now it all makes sense!* – he played the part of Sergeant-Major Reg Drummond in a semi-professional production of Peter Nichols's musical comedy "Privates On Parade" which tells the story of an Army concert party during the Malayan Emergency of the 1940s.

No wonder he comes across as everyone's idea of a British Sergeant-Major (thought Ruby). He has created a character for himself based on the theatrical stereotype. Ruby had to concede that he was surprisingly effective in the role and he would have been entirely convincing if only he had bothered to get the history right.

Ruby could not help but laughing at the man's sheer bravado. It was probably the best performance he had ever given. But she also wondered why he had bothered. Why would a small-time actor and failed antique dealer impersonate a British Army Sergeant-Major? She also wondered how far he was prepared to take his performance. Might he have staged the entire business with the bottle of bath salts and the tights? Had he thumped himself over the head and tied the tights around his own neck? Ruby rather hoped not. In spite of his copious lies, she rather liked the man.

Ruby glanced at her watch. It had been almost an hour since Ernest Smallman (aka Sergeant-Major Selwyn 'Stonker' Stippleton) had left her bungalow. He would surely be back at Coot Hall by now. She rang the Hall. Guru Lennie answered. They passed the time of day, talked about the weather for a few moments and then Ruby asked if she could have a few words with the Sergeant-Major.

"Oh, he's only just come in!" cooed Guru Lennie. "Been out on that great, smelly motorbike of his. Hang on, love, I'll go and get him."

Twenty seconds later and the Sergeant-Major (Ruby could not get out of the habit of thinking of him in terms of his fictitious military rank) was on the line.

"I want a quick answer," she said. "Why did you quit the antique business?"

"Oh, well, I, er…"

"No shilly-shallying, man. I have the photograph, remember. If you give me the run-around, that photo will be in the hands of Detective Inspector Gruttock within the hour."

"Well, I'm not sure I can, really…"

"Your reticence is explained by the fact that Guru Lennie is hovering nearby and he will overhear what you tell me, is that what you are saying?"

"Yes."

"Very well. I'll ask the questions. You say, 'Yes' or 'No'? OK?"

"Yes."

"Was the antique business in trouble?"

"Yes."

"You'd been overcharging?"

"Well..."

"Yes or No?"

"Yes."

"Selling shoddy junk under the pretence of being fine old antiques?"

"Yes."

"In debt at the bank?"

"Yes."

"Irate customers threatening to do acts of violence upon you?"

"Yes."

"You don't have to say 'Yes' to all my questions, you know! The occasional 'No' would be acceptable."

"But it's all true."

"Good Lord! You amaze me. So am I to assume that you sought a way out of the mess you had created and, when you saw an advertisement for a fitness instructor at The Retreat at Coot Hall, you thought *that* might be the answer to all your problems? The perfect opportunity, in fact, to do a runner from your dodgy antique business. So you adopted the fictitious identity of Sergeant Selwyn 'Stonker' Stippleton, came to the interview, claimed to be a trained martial arts expert, fitness fanatic and all sorts of other baloney and you got the job."

"More or less. You got a few minor details wrong, but..."

"Oh! Really! You are annoying! I thought you were the killer."

"Me?"

"I'll explain later. First I have to track down the real villain." With those parting words, Ruby slammed the phone down. It was several minutes later when she realised that slamming down a mobile phone does not terminate the call. She hoped that nobody had been listening in on the other end as she had given vent to a string of imprecations worthy of, well, a Sergeant-Major.

33. Time Is Running Out!

Ruby could not concentrate on working. She could not concentrate on reading. She could not be bothered to watch the television or listen to the radio. She had less than twenty-four hours in which to prove Gwendolyn Gormly's innocence and so she sat at her kitchen table with a pencil and a pad of paper and she jotted down notes. She noted the names of all the people who had been at Coot Hall on the night of the séance. Alongside each name, she jotted down reasons why they might have wanted to do away with Gwendolyn and reasons (or 'alibis') why they could not have done so. On another page she made notes of all she knew about the two attempted murders at Coot Hall and the one successful murder at Miss Hicks's bungalow.

The manner in which the second attempted murder was effected remained a mystery while the final and successful murder was more mysterious still. But Ruby felt she now knew quite a lot about the assault upon the so-called 'Sergeant-Major'. Prior to the attempt upon his life, the bathroom in the eastern wing was occupied by Guru Lennie. For that reason, Gwendolyn was obliged to use the bath in the west wing. The would-be murderer was already hidden within, awaiting the arrival of Gwendolyn. It was purely by an unhappy coincidence that, just at that moment, the Sergeant-Major had decided to go for a wash and brush-up. He entered the bathroom, the door closed behind him, the killer, unable to see anything in the darkness, bopped him over the head. Only when the bathroom light was turned on did it become clear that the victim was the wrong person. Why the killer then proceeded to strangle the Sergeant-Major with Gwendolyn's tights Ruby could not imagine. That was a detail that would no doubt become clear when the killer was identified.

Having found so much information about the first murder attempt, Ruby tried to make some deductions about the second attempt in which Madame Evadne was ejected through the window of Gwendolyn's bedroom. What features did that have in common with the bathroom strangling? Ruby made notes:

"1) The victim went into a room

2) The room was in darkness

3) The killer mistook the victim for Gwendolyn"

Ruby stared at her notes. Then she added another note:

"3a) How could the killer mistake Madame Evadne for Gwendolyn?"

The bathroom, according to Sergeant-Major Stippleton, had been in total darkness. Gwendolyn's bedroom, however, was not. Ruby remembered sitting in the Drawing Room that night and watching the snow through the window. She had particularly noted the clarity with which she had been able to observe the snow due to the exterior lights at either side of the drive leading to the front door of Coot Hall. Gwendolyn's bedroom was directly above the Drawing Room. With the window fully open and Madame Evadne silhouetted against the light, it would have been quite impossible to mistake her for Gwendolyn. Ruby vividly recalled how small and dainty Madame Evadne was, whereas Gwendolyn could only be described as statuesque. So, did that mean that the killer had made no mistake but had indeed intended to throw Madame Evadne from the window?

Ruby's head was spinning. She had all the information she needed. She felt sure of it. All she had to do was put the facts together in the right order and then Gwendolyn Gormly's innocence would be revealed for all to see.

"Easier said than done," she mused.

It was then that she happened to glance at the calendar on her kitchen wall. She had written something on the blank square of tomorrow's date, Friday, 11th February. "Oh, blast!" She suddenly remembered that she had made an appointment with the hairdresser for half-past three.

"Well," she said aloud, "that'll have to be cancelled. I have far too much to do!"

But the following morning when, as she sat eating her breakfast and staring out at the rain beating against the window, she realised that she had nothing at all to do. She had exhausted every line of enquiry into the "Gwendolyn Gormly Affair". She had done her very best to solve it but she had failed. Innocent or not, Gwendolyn Gormly would no doubt be found guilty.

She ate a miserable lunch and then whiled away the time until three o'clock trying and failing to concentrate on reading a novel. Finally, with a heavy heart, Ruby put on her Wellington boots, a long overcoat and a rain-hat and went trudging down Fern Hill towards the Karenz Kutz hairdresser's in the High Street.

34. The Startling Revelations Of A Hairdresser

"What you need is a bit of body. It's limp, that's what it is. Your hair dangles whereas it should fizz."

"Fizz?" said Ruby sceptically. "I'm not sure I really want my hair to fizz."

"What you've got now," Rod the hairdresser said, stretching out a particularly droopy strand of Ruby's hair so that she could appreciate its repellence in the mirror, "is what is called a pageboy cut. I don't mean to be harsh but, well, for a lady of mature years, a pageboy cut is not exactly flattering."

"But you suggested it!" Ruby protested.

"Me!" Rod gasped to indicate that he had never heard such a dreadful calumny.

"Yes, you! You said it would make me look like Barbara Stanwyck."

"The actress? *I* said that?"

"You did."

"When was this?"

"I can't remember. A few months ago."

"Ah well, that explains it. Pageboy cuts were all the rage back then." He imbued the words "back then" with a suggestion of untold aeons. "But these days, you see, that wouldn't do at all."

"No? Then what *would* do?"

"Back-combing."

"Back-combing? I thought that went out in the 1980s."

"It's back again."

It was a quiet morning in Karenz Kutz. Other than Ruby, there were only two customers – a large woman who was snoring loudly beneath the comforting warm blast of a hairdryer, and a somewhat musclebound young man who was having his nostril hairs removed and his cuticles cut back by the proprietor, Cyndi (Karen, after whom the business was named, had departed for more profitable salons elsewhere). Ruby had been hoping for more of a crowd. She had, on past occasions, found that the hairdresser's was a peerless source of local gossip; and, having no further leads to follow in her enquiries, she had vainly hoped that local gossip might provide her with inspiration.

"…but if that's the case then we've lost our best customer. Do you fancy a cup of tea?" Rod had been nattering away all the time and Ruby had heard barely a word of what he had said since her mind had been wandering elsewhere.

"If *what's* the case?" she asked.

"If they come back into fashion."

"Sorry, Rod. I didn't catch what you were saying. You'll have to repeat it."

Rod gave a disapproving *tut!* To indicate that it really was the bane of his life when his clients did not bother to hang on every word of his glittering conversation. "Beehives! I said I was reading in the newspaper that they reckon beehive hairdos are coming back. You know, like in the 1960s. Dusty Springfield. Dolly Parton. Hair like helmets. Well, our local queen of the beehive would have been ahead of the trend, wouldn't she. Only I don't suppose I'll be doing her hair again. Did you say you'd have a cuppa, petal?"

"You mean Gwendolyn? You do her hair? I hadn't realised."

"You think she does that all on her own? It's a two-hour job to get it just the way she likes it."

"Ha! I can't imagine Gwendolyn sitting still for two hours. Is she a difficult customer?"

"Oh, not at all. She drops it in. Two hours later she comes and collects it. I wish all my clients were that easy!"

"What?" Ruby frowned. She was trying to make sense of what Rod was telling her. "You don't mean to say?" She pictured Gwendolyn's mighty hairdo, towering over her head like one of those bearskin hats that Royal guardsmen wear – except their hats are black whereas Gwendolyn's beehive was platinum blonde. "You mean to say… it's a *wig*?"

Rod stopped teasing Ruby's hair and looked at her in the mirror with wide, astonished eyes. "Well, you didn't think that was all her own hair, did you?"

"A wig…" Ruby muttered. Then she said it again, louder this time: "A wig, a wig, a wig!"

The man having his cuticles done looked around and said, "If you are talking about me, love, you're wrong. Come and have a tug if you don't believe me."

Ruby apologised, assured him that his hair had not been the subject of her exclamation. Then she stood up, hugged Rod, kissed him full on the lips and said, "Rod, you are a bloody genius!"

Ruby left the salon, in high good humour. Cyndi turned to Rod and said, "What was that all about?"

Rod shrugged. "Beats me. I think she may have taken a fancy to me."

The woman under the hairdryer opened an eye. In spite of her snores, she did not want to miss a juicy bit of gossip.

35. The Cat Crept In

"I know how it was done, Bessie!"

"Are you going to stand in that rain shouting at me or are you coming inside?"

Ruby was so excited, that she had not even bothered to go home after having her hair done (she had decided to stick with the pageboy cut for the sake of simplicity, no matter how unfashionable it might be).

Once in Bessie's kitchen, Ruby quickly took off her overcoat and rain hat and hung them over the back of a vacant chair where they steamed gently in the heat of the Aga.

"Gwendolyn wears a wig!"

"You're making no sense, Ruby. Sit down while I make some tea and… No! Not there!"

There was an almighty *yowl!* As Bessie's cat, Moggie, leapt from the chair just before Ruby's posterior had settled down upon it.

"The cat!" Ruby exclaimed.

"What?"

"That's the other missing part of the puzzle. The cat in the pantry. If only I could solve the mystery of the cat in Miss Hick's pantry, everything else would fall into place. The window in her pantry doesn't open, Miss Hicks hated cats so she would never have let it in deliberately. So how did the cat get in?"

"Through the door like anyone else, I expect," said Bessie. "That's how Moggie gets in here."

"Through the door? Through a cat-flap in the door, you mean?"

"No. I told you before but I don't think you were paying any attention. I was pottering around in the garden one day and I happened to leave the door open. Moggie saw his chance, came in when I wasn't looking, and decided to stay."

"You left the door open?"

"I don't know why you sound so surprised. I don't lock the door every time I go into the garden."

"The door was open," Ruby repeated. She was clearly deep in thought. "The door was open. So the cat walked in!"

"Yes."

"That's it! Bessie, you are brilliant. The cat came in through the door. That's the answer. That's the solution to everything. What time is it?"

"Just turned quarter to five. Why?"

"You must drive me. Now! To the police station in Clogwyn Mawr!"

"You know who the murderer is?"

"No."

"Oh."

"But I do know that Gwendolyn Gormly is innocent. And this time I can prove it."

36. A Prisoner In Her Own Wine Bar

"Yes, ladies, what can I get you?"

Ruby, Maggie Pountice and Muriel Greenalge were sitting at a table by one of the big picture windows of Gwendolyn's Wine Bar. The bay beyond the window was plunged into darkness and the sea glinted in the pale light of the moon.

"I never thought I wouldn't be saying this, not to you of all people," Maggie said, "but I'm glad to see you back again, Gwendolyn. It was a terrible injustice is what it was, what them police done to you, my love."

Gwendolyn assayed a smile. It was the sort of smile that Cruella De Vil might have given upon spotting a clutch of Dalmatian puppies. "You'll be having a Guinness, I suppose, Maggie?"

"That I will."

"And you other ladies. White wine, is it?"

"That would be lovely," said Muriel.

As Gwendolyn tottered across the floor-tiles on her vertiginous stilettoes, Ruby leant across to her two friends and said in a whisper, "It's a wig."

"What is?" said Maggie.

"Gwendolyn's beehive."

All three women turned to look at Gwendolyn. Her precipitous blonde hairdo towered over her, with various gracefully arranged curls framing her highly-rouged cheeks.

"Get away!" said Maggie.

"How do you know?" asked Muriel.

"I have my informants," said Ruby.

"And that's how you solved the murder?" said Muriel.

Ruby leaned back in her chair. She glanced out through the window into the impenetrable darkness. The little matter of solving the murder was a delicate subject. She had been so excited by unravelling the details of how the two murder attempts had been undertaken at Coot Hall and also her solution to the mystery of the cat in the pantry that she had quite forgotten that she still had no idea who the murderer was.

When she had arrived at Clogwyn Mawr police station earlier that evening, Detective Inspector Gruttock had been on his way out, preparing to go home for the night. Ruby had been obliged to insist that he stay and hear what she had to say – "It's a matter of life and death!" she had exclaimed, somewhat over-dramatically. With great reluctance, the Inspector had agreed to give her ten minutes of his valuable time. In those ten minutes, Ruby outlined her theories relating to the assaults upon Sergeant-Major Stippleton and Madame Evadne. She was just about to embark upon her explanation of the significance of the cat in the pantry when the Detective Inspector had brusquely informed her that her time was up and he was heading for home. Ruby had glanced at her watch. It was five to six. In desperation she had cried, "But in five minutes Gwendolyn Gormly's fate will be sealed!"

The Inspector had looked at her blankly. Then he had laughed. "Gwendolyn Gormly?" he had said. "So that's what all this is about, is it? Oh, then you are too late, Miss Lake. Gwendolyn Gormly was taken away half an hour ago."

"Taken away!" Ruby had cried, imagining that her destination might be some high-security prison for dangerous felons.

"I believe her intention was to go to her wine bar in Clogwyn Bach," the Inspector had replied. "To which end, she summoned a taxi cab."

Now here Ruby was, sitting in Gwendolyn's Wine Bar, staring out through the picture window overlooking the bay. Muriel had asked if she had solved the murder. It was no good trying to bluff it out. She had to admit defeat.

"The truth is," Ruby said, "the murderer is still out there. I know how each of the three crimes was done but I don't know why and I don't know by whom."

"But the police released Gwendolyn," Muriel said. "So they must know she's innocent."

"That's not how it works, ladies." Gwendolyn was standing next to their table, with a bottle of wine in her hand. "Released on bail is what I am. At any moment of the day or night they can come for me again. I'm a prisoner in my own wine bar!"

"I'm so near to solving this," said Ruby. "If only I could work out who had the motive and the opportunity."

"A motive? To get their own back on me?" Gwendolyn laughed the harsh, throaty laugh that resulted from a lifetime's heavy smoking and drinking. "Look around this bar. The people sitting at the tables. Look around the village when you are out walking. Go to Coot Hall. Wander through the streets of Clogwyn Mawr. Almost everyone you see will have something against me. Don't think I don't know how much people hate me. No, don't bother denying it!" Gwendolyn paused to give the three women the opportunity to deny it. When none of them did, she carried on. "Every one of the people at Coot Hall that night had a motive to stab me in the back."

Gwendolyn picked up an empty wine glass from an adjoining table. Then she sat down at the same table as Ruby, Muriel and Maggie and poured herself a glass of their wine. "All right, then," she said to Ruby. "If you're so damn' clever, tell me what I have to do to nab the bastard who's set me up for murder?"

"I don't know," said Ruby.

"Hah!" Gwendolyn drank her wine in a single swig. "I thought as much."

"No," Ruby explained. "I don't know. But I think *you* do. All I need is for you to tell me."

Ruby asked Gwendolyn a few questions. Gwendolyn provided the answers. She explained how Miss Hicks had phoned her on the fateful day that was to be the last of Miss Hicks's life. She had asked Gwendolyn to visit her house to provide a "spiritual consultation". She had said that, upon arrival at her cottage, Gwendolyn should simply come through to the kitchen as the front door would be unlocked.

"The door was open when you arrived?" said Ruby.

"It was ajar," Gwendolyn confirmed. "I glanced inside. Nobody was there. I called out. There was no answer. So I went through to the kitchen. And that was when I saw the body. I tried to resuscitate her but it was obvious it was no good. There was blood everywhere."

Ruby then showed Gwendolyn the two photographs she had taken from the Hell Fire Club. Gwendolyn had nothing to say about the photograph showing Sergeant-Major Stippleton but when Ruby showed her the other photograph, Gwendolyn exploded in fury. So did Maggie Pountice. The photograph showed Gwendolyn and Clarissa sitting, one on each side of a portly, insignificant-looking man.

"Ken Collop!" Maggie and Gwendolyn exclaimed simultaneously.

"He stole my shop!" Maggie Pountice said and then, fixing Gwendolyn with a gimlet stare, she added, "And so did *she*!"

"That's a lie, you evil, miserable, nasty little..." Gwendolyn paused in order to think of an insult worthy of Maggie; Ruby took advantage of the pause to tell Gwendolyn to shut up. Gwendolyn was not used to being told to shut up. In fact, nobody ever dared to tell Gwendolyn to shut up. Gwendolyn was so outraged at being told to shut up that, for once in her life, she shut up.

"Ken Collop is the missing link in this whole messy business," Ruby said. "Now that I've found that link, I know who did the crimes, how they were done and why."

Muriel, Maggie and Gwendolyn stared at Ruby with wide eyes.

"Well?" said Maggie, when, after, half a minute of staring, Ruby had failed to say another word.

"Well *what*?"

"Who did it, how was it done and why?"

"Oh, I can't tell you that. Not now. Not here. It wouldn't be right. I shall phone Detective Inspector Gruttock in the morning. I'm sure he'll want to be there when I explain it all."

That night Ruby went to sleep contented. Tomorrow, she knew, was going to be rather an interesting day.

37. The Suspects Assemble

Ruby raised the brass lion's head knocker on the left of the two huge oak doors that were set into the main portico of Coot Hall and with it she stuck three resounding thumps that echoed into the hallway within. Almost immediately the creaking doors were opened just far enough to permit a malign, skeletal face to peer through the gap.

"What?" it said.

"My name is Ruby Lake."

"So?" said the wizened figure.

"I have an appointment."

"Who's the other one?" The shrivelled creature nodded in a surly manner towards Bessie who was standing on the steps immediately behind Ruby.

"This is Bessie Morgan. She has an appointment too."

"You've seen us before," Bessie snapped at the man. "Your memory seems to be as defective as your politeness. Now open the damn' door and show us in."

The man, whom Ruby called "Crickspittle" due to her inability to pronounce his Welsh name, rolled his eyes and made a tutting sound. Then he turned around and shuffled away down the hallway, leaving Ruby and Bessie to make their own way into Coot Hall while he slouched off towards the rear of the building in the general direction of the Sitting Room.

"Oh, ladies, ladies! How lovely to see you again!" Guru Lennie was standing in the middle of the great hallway. Clad in a purple and orange kaftan elaborately embroidered with gold thread, his hamster face rubicund and beaming, he extended his chubby arms towards them in the attitude in which Saint Francis of Assisi is often portrayed when there happen to be a few doves, lambs or rabbits in the immediate vicinity.

"My return, alas," said Ruby, "is not in quite the happy circumstances I might have wished."

Guru Lennie drew closer, gave Ruby a conspiratorial wink and whispered, "Dark deeds are about to be unveiled, I'm told."

"Perhaps," Ruby said. "Has the Detective Inspector arrived yet?"

"In the Sitting Room. Along with everyone else."

"Everyone?"

"Oh yes. The gang's all here, as you might say."

"Yes, I might say that, I suppose," Ruby agreed, "though the possibility is remote."

The Sitting Room looked much as it had on the night of the séance. The principal difference was that on that night the curtains had been drawn together whereas now, on this bleak February morning, they were fully open and the room was thus illuminated by a few struggling beams of thin, cold daylight which did nothing whatsoever to dispel the oppressive gloominess of the crimson velvet furnishings.

At once, Ruby saw that Guru Lennie had been entirely accurate: the gang was, indeed, all there. Leaning against the mantelpiece over the great fireplace stood Nathaniel Snibb, dressed as ever, in a dark suit as though he were preparing to go to the office. Next to him, Clarissa Winthrop lounged in a chic, loose-fitting navy-blue dress with a beige cardigan thrown artistically over her shoulders. She was coughing elegantly and wafting the air before her face with a well-manicured hand. In various armchairs sat Madame Evadne, Sergeant-Major Selwyn 'Stonker' Stippleton and Nye Clump. Nye smiled uncertainly at Ruby. Ruby raised her eyebrows, pursed her lips and nodded curtly in his general direction.

Sitting around the great oak table upon which, two weeks earlier, they had attempted to contact the spirit world with the aid of an inverted wine glass, were Ebenezer Estyn Evans the chef, and Bronwen Price the local girl who did Ruby's cleaning once a week and who also did occasional work at the Hall. In a dark corner of the room, partly obscured by a large potted palm, lurked the loathsome Crickspittle.

As on Ruby's first meeting with her, Mrs Lowri Williams-Jenkins occupied one end of the chaise-longue, perching on its very edge, looking frail and nervous like a temperamental budgerigar. At the other end of the chaise-longue, wearing a split-sided skirt which, with her legs crossed, showed rather more thigh than seemed entirely decorous, sat Gwendolyn Gormly, puffing on a cigarette the smoke from which wafted behind her in the direction of Nathaniel Snibb and Clarissa Winthrop. It was this smoke which occasioned the elegant little coughs and hand-wafting movements in which Clarissa was indulging.

There were two more people in the room who had not been present on the night of the séance. Standing just behind the chaise-longue, close to Mrs Williams-Jenkins, was her chauffeur Wilkins. Meanwhile, positioned at the centre of the room and commanding the attention of all its occupants, was Detective Inspector Gruttock. It was he who addressed Ruby and Bessie as they entered: "Ah, Miss Lake! Mrs Morgan! Thus, the company is assembled and we may proceed."

Ruby had telephoned Detective Inspector Gruttock earlier that morning and had informed him that she had all the information necessary for an arrest to be made so that the true perpetrator of the crimes which had erroneously been attributed to Gwendolyn Gormly might at last be apprehended. With his usual officious manner, Detective Inspector Gruttock had riposted that he was perfectly capable of finding his own information and making his own deductions and he certainly did not require the assistance (the actual term he had used was "meddling") of a member of the public in the making of an arrest. To which Ruby had replied, "It's Saturday."

"I fail to see the significance of that," the Inspector had harrumphed.

"I was surprised to find you at work. On a Saturday, that is."

He had harrumphed a bit more and then pompously informed Ruby that crime does not confine itself to weekdays between nine and five and nor does the work of a Detective Inspector of the South Wales Police Force. Here he had assayed a small laugh, to emphasise the uproarious humour of his remark.

"Then I take it you are stumped," Ruby had said. "So well and truly stumped that you are working on your day off in the hope of trying to find the killer who is still at large in the small, peaceful village of Clogwyn Bach. Since you have released your only suspect, I fear that the headlines in the Sunday newspapers may not reflect glowingly on you."

"Oh, yes, the, er… the newspapers. Oh," (here he had tried to inject a tone of devil-may-care indifference into his voice), "I don't concern myself with the tittle-tattle in the Sunday newspapers."

"A sound principle," Ruby had agreed. "And yet, think how very different those headlines would be if you were able to make an arrest this afternoon. Which, I might add, you certainly could do if only you would let me explain…"

"Ah, yes. Well now, there may be merits in what you say."

And thus it was arranged. A few phone calls were made to ensure that all the relevant participants in the events surrounding the three crimes of which Gwendolyn Gormly had been accused should gather once more at Coot Hall "to assist the police" (Detective Inspector Gruttock did not specifically mentioned Ruby Lake at this point) "in their ongoing and extensive enquiries."

Ruby took the opportunity to say hello to the people she knew. She was surprised to see Nathaniel Snibb there, she said, as she had understood he was not resident at the Hall but lived many miles distant; he explained that, since the formal opening of The Retreat was now just weeks away, he made it his habit to supervise developments at Coot Hall on weekends.

Mrs Williams-Jenkins greeted Ruby enthusiastically. "This is all so exciting!" she exclaimed, which, bearing in mind that the meeting had been occasioned by the death of her close friend Miss Hicks, Ruby thought an odd thing to say.

"Yes, yes, well never mind all this chitter-chatter," interrupted the Detective Inspector. "We are conducting a murder enquiry, not a vicarage tea party. Suffice to say that my own investigations have borne great fruits."

"Such as?" muttered Ruby but the Detective Inspector either did not hear the question or else he chose to ignore it.

"But before I give you all the latest, er, news on my investigations, I am given to understand that Miss Lake has a few words to say which may, or, indeed, may not, have some relevance to…"

Ruby got the distinct impression that the Detective Inspector planned to ramble on for some considerable time so she interrupted him. "Thank you so much, Inspector. Now if you'll please take a seat…"

"But I haven't finished!"

Ruby carried on without pausing: "I would like to explain to everybody here how a great crime was committed – namely, the murder of Miss Winifred Elizabeth Hicks – and how a great injustice was very nearly done to Miss Gwendolyn Gormly."

"Out with it, then!" said Gwendolyn, blowing out a long stream of smoke. "Tell me who the bastard is so I can deal with him." Then, glancing meaningfully from Mrs Williams-Jenkins to Clarissa Winthrop and finally to Madame Evadne, she added, "Or *her*."

"Oh, Good Lord!" mumbled Mrs Williams-Jenkins. "Surely you don't think that *I*… I'm a member of the Women's Institute, you know."

"I don't think that is a cast-iron alibi," Ruby commented. "However, you may put your mind at rest, Mrs Williams-Jenkins. You are certainly not implicated in these crimes."

"Oh!" Mrs Williams-Jenkins looked curiously upset at this. "Are you saying that I am so tediously conventional that I can't even be a suspect in a murder case?"

"Not at all," said Ruby. "You were a suspect."

Mrs Williams-Jenkins smiled broadly.

"But you have now been eliminated from my enquiry."

"Oh, how wonderful!"

"Though not," hissed Detective Inspector Gruttock, "from *my* enquiry, which is all that really matters."

"The elimination of suspects proved difficult," Ruby went on. "It was not helped by the fact that so many of the people here have practised to deceive."

"I certainly haven't!" protested Nathaniel Snibb.

"Not directly, perhaps," Ruby said. "Though I feel you may not have been quite as forthcoming as you might have been about your present financial difficulties."

"Financial difficulties?" Guru Lennie said. "Is that true, Nathaniel?"

"Well…"

"I'll come onto that later," Ruby said. "Let me begin with Madame Evadne, who purports to be a celebrity astrologer when, in fact, her most notable previous engagement was one season as 'Gypsy Evadne Vitalengro' at one of the less salubrious English seaside resorts."

"I did readings for celebrities!" Madame Evadne protested. "That fat bloke who used to be in East Enders came into my booth once. I told him he was on the cusp of a great change."

"What happened to him?" Mrs Williams-Jenkins asked.

"He got fired the next month. He'd been tampering with one of the makeup girls. Well, if he isn't a celebrity, who is, that's what I'd like to know?"

Ruby resisted the temptation to answer Madame Evadne's rhetorical question. "Then there was Sergeant-Major Selwyn 'Stonker' Stippleton. I don't wish to embarrass him by revealing information which he vouchsafed to me in private and which he may not wish to be made public. I must say, however, that the tales of his military exploits in India were embroidered to such an extent that, for a while, they led me to believe that he might be deliberately falsifying his history in order to hide a guilty past. There were, I later discovered, quite different reasons for that charade but they need not concern us now."

"We all 'as skelingtons in our closets, 'asn't we?" said the putative Sergeant-Major. "But my skelingtons is not criminal ones."

"Quite. The two attempted murders on the night of the séance were vital in setting me on the correct path. From the outset, it seemed to me self-evident that the person who had attacked Sergeant-Major Stippleton and Madame Evadne must be the same person who subsequently killed Miss Hicks. If I could figure out who was behind any one of those crimes, I would know who was behind all of them."

"A sound principle," said Nye Clump.

Ruby ignored him and she did so ostentatiously.

"I began with the first crime. The attack upon the Sergeant-Major. I didn't think it likely that he attacked himself, so his name was removed from my list of suspects. But that cast suspicion upon everyone else who was in Coot Hall that night. We had all retired to our bedrooms following the séance. Any one of you might have gone to the bathroom in the west wing to lie in wait. Apart from Guru Lennie, that is. He was in the bathroom on the east wing at the time. Both Sergeant-Major Stippleton and Gwendolyn heard him singing from within the bathroom. Indeed, it was his tenancy of that bathroom that caused both of them to go to the bathroom on the west wing.

"It is my contention that the would-be murderer was already hiding in the bathroom, waiting for Gwendolyn. The murderer had removed the bulb from the bathroom light so that Gwendolyn would be unable to see her assailant."

Inspector Gruttock harrumphed. "May one ask how you made the astonishing deduction that the light bulb was removed?"

"Oh, not astonishing at all. Sergeant-Major Stippleton told me that the bathroom was in darkness when he entered and the light was not illuminated when he pulled the cord designed to switch it on. I am sure he gave the same information to the police. Perhaps you assumed a mere electrical fault. Perhaps you are right, but I doubt it. I presume you took fingerprints from the lightbulb…"

Ruby waited some moments but Detective Inspector Gruttock was disinclined to confirm her presumption so she continued. "Had you done so, you would certainly have found the killer's fingerprints all over it.

"At any rate, Sergeant-Major Stippleton entered the bathroom in darkness. The murderer, unable to see who it was, assumed it to be Gwendolyn Gormly and that is why he was struck soundly over the head with a bottle of bath salts. Only when the killer replaced the lightbulb and the bathroom was once again flooded with light did the awful mistake become apparent."

"And the tights?" said the Detective Inspector.

"I shall come to the tights later. For the time being, let me consider the second crime. Once again, the killer hid, awaiting the arrival of Gwendolyn Gormly. This time the scene of the crime was Gwendolyn Gormly's bedroom. The killer opened the window wide in the expectation that, since it was such a cold and windy night, the first thing that Gwendolyn would do on returning to her bedroom would be to go to the window in order to close it. That would give the killer the perfect opportunity to push Gwendolyn through the window."

"Pah!" The sound which Madame Evadne uttered cannot be precisely rendered in words but suffice to say it was a sound that expressed no great admiration for Ruby's exposition of the crime in which Madame Evadne had been the victim. "If you are asking me to believe that someone could mistake a hulking great lummock like Gwendolyn Gormly..." – she turned to Gwendolyn and smiled sweetly – "No disrespect intended, my dear. If you are asking me to believe that I might be mistaken for *her*, you must be off your flaming rocker."

"That had me stumped for a while, too," Ruby admitted. "Madame Evadne is what we might call of a petite build whereas Gwendolyn is positively statuesque."

"Well-proportioned is the term I prefer," said Gwendolyn.

"The lights along the drive leading from the main road to Coot Hall were all illuminated that night and Gwendolyn's bedroom overlooked the drive. Anyone standing behind Madame Evadne would have seen her in silhouette. How on earth could such a small and dainty woman be mistaken for the towering form of Gwendolyn Gormly?"

"Are you suggesting that the prospective assassin might be short-sighted?" Nathiel Snibb asked and his eyes goggled at her through the thick bottle-glass lenses of his spectacles.

"Not necessarily," said Ruby. "Another reason was suggested to me by my hairdresser."

Clarissa Winthrop giggled. "Your hairdresser! So now he's an amateur detective too, is he?"

"There are some crimes," said Ruby, "which are more readily solved by a professional hairdresser than by an amateur detective. This is one such. By great good fortune, it turns out that my hairdresser is also Gwendolyn Gormly's hairdresser."

"Wait just one minute!" Gwendolyn protested. "The confidences between a hairdresser and his client are sacred. Like between a doctor and a patient or a priest and... well, whoever goes to a priest."

"That, I'm afraid, is not entirely true. Not only aren't hairdressers required to take the Hippocratic oath but anyone who has their hair done by Rod knows that if you want to keep a secret, you don't let Rod know about it. However, if Gwendolyn objects to my repeating what Rod told me, I shall remain silent on the matter. Sadly, that may mean that I will be unable to prove her innocence and I shall then hand her over to Detective Inspector Gruttock who…"

"Don't get so high-handed with me, Ruby-bloody-Lake! If you think I care what people say about me, you don't know me very well." Every eye in the room was on Gwendolyn. She glanced from one person to another and, as she did so, her smile broadened. "What Miss Ruby-la-de-dah-Lake is hinting at, and frankly I don't care who knows it, is that this…" She pointed to the magnificent blonde beehive hairdo towering above her head, "is not quite as nature intended. It's a wig. OK. In fact, I've got quite a few wigs. I swap them over when I fancy a new style."

"Is she bald?" Mrs Williams-Jenkins whispered loudly to Wilkins her chauffeur, who was standing directly behind her.

"As it happens," Gwendolyn said, "I have a very fine and lustrous head of hair. I just can't be bothered spending time tarting it up every day. Though what that's got to do with the murder I do not know."

"The point I am trying to make," said Ruby, "is that without your beehive hairdo, you would be twelve inches shorter. Late at night, when you would have slipped off your stiletto heels, you would be another six inches shorter. About the height, in fact, of Madame Evadne."

Guru Lennie put a hand over his heart and gasped. "So the killer could have mistaken Madame Evadne for Gwendolyn after all!"

"Only if he…" As Ruby said this, she noticed that Gwendolyn gave a dark and meaningful glance at Clarissa Winthrop. Ruby continued: "or *she* happened to know that Gwendolyn's beehive came off at night!"

"Anyone could have figured that out," Clarissa said. "That beehive is so big and stiff it wouldn't fit in most beds."

"I wouldn't know," said Gwendolyn. "I haven't tried out quite as many beds as you have, Clarissa dear."

"Ladies, ladies, please…" tutted Guru Lennie.

"Having established that the two attempted murders here in Coot Hall were perpetrated not *by* Gwendolyn Gormly but *against* her…"

Detective Inspector Gruttock chuckled. "Not quite 'established', I think. The burden of proof in British Law is set at a higher bar, I fear. Let us say that you have introduced an element of doubt."

"Quite so," agreed Ruby. "Let us say, at any rate, that the evidence against Gwendolyn's guilt relating to the two murder attempts at Coot Hall is of such a poor sort that it may be disregarded."

"Well, now…" Detective Inspector Gruttock was about to give his legal opinion on the matter but Ruby cut him off before he could get underway: "I now turn my attention to the more serious matter of the murder of Miss Hicks. The cat, of course, holds the secret to that."

"The cat?" said Detective Inspector Gruttock. "I fear, madam, that you are straying into the realms of fantasy. There was no cat involved in the murder of Miss Hicks."

"That is where you are wrong," said Ruby. "The cat explains everything."

38. Dramatic Events At Coot Hall

"I am referring, of course," Ruby said, "to the cat that was locked in the pantry."

"Really, I hardly think that…" Detective Inspector Gruttock once again attempted to interrupt Ruby and once again Ruby ignored him and continued: "The cat struck me as highly significant. Especially after I found out that Miss Hicks didn't have a cat. Not only did Miss Hicks not have a cat but she didn't even like cats. She was, in fact, allergic to cats. So why did she lock a cat in her pantry?

"The answer is, of course, that she didn't. She wouldn't have a cat in the house, let alone in her pantry. So how did it get there? Did Gwendolyn see the animal lurking outside, decide to let it into the house and then, on a whim, lock it in the pantry before bludgeoning the bungalow's owner to death with a wine bottle? That seems, wouldn't you say, Detective Inspector, improbable."

"Well, I, er…."

"Not just improbable but inconceivable. So we must assume that nobody deliberately let the cat into the house. Which means that it must have got in when nobody was looking. How? Through a window? The day was cold and there were no windows open. There is a single window in the pantry but that cannot be opened. Then the cat must have entered through the front door. According to Gwendolyn, the front door of Miss Hicks's cottage was ajar when she arrived. Miss Hicks had told Gwendolyn over the phone that she would leave the door open for her to enter. That was an odd thing to do, wasn't it? Why wouldn't she just answer the door when Gwendolyn rang?

"The reason was simple. It wasn't Miss Hicks who had phoned Gwendolyn!"

A gasp of astonishment ran around the room.

"No, not Miss Hicks but another woman altogether. Gwendolyn, you see, had never previously spoken to Miss Hicks so when someone phoned her, claiming to be Miss Hicks, Gwendolyn would not have known that the voice was that of an imposter.

"It was the imposter who had phoned Gwendolyn that morning under the pretext of asking for a private consultation. She arranged for Gwendolyn to arrive moments before she had also arranged for Mrs Williams-Jenkins to arrive. She had to leave the door open because by the time Gwendolyn arrived, Miss Hicks was already dead so could not, therefore, have gone to the door to open it. It was while the door was open that the cat saw its opportunity, went into the house and made straight for the pantry where it found a nice piece of haddock which Miss Hicks had been keeping for her dinner. I am assuming that the murderer, ignorant of the cat's presence, had shut the pantry door, thus confining the animal.

"I now direct your attention to the timing of the murder. And also of the timing of its discovery. In order to be incriminated, Gwendolyn would have to be found at the scene of the crime. Wait too long, and Gwendolyn might have taken the opportunity to scarper. She might even have summoned the police which would hardly be the sort of thing a murderer would do. But how could it be arranged that Gwendolyn would be found at precisely the right time? That's where Wilkins enters the story."

"Wilkins?" asked Guru Lennie.

"Mrs Williams-Jenkins's chauffeur."

"You trying to say I had something to do with it?" snapped the sharp-faced man standing just behind the chaise-longue on which sat his employer. "You must be kidding. I'm just a driver."

"Yes indeed. It was you, Mr Wilkins, who drove your employer, Mrs Williams-Jenkins, to Miss Hicks's bungalow. And you timed it to perfection."

"Oh yes," twittered Mrs Williams-Jenkins approvingly, "Wilkins is always most punctual."

Nathaniel Snibb raised an eyebrow. "Are you are suggesting that this man, Wilkins, is somehow involved in all this?"

"I am indeed," said Ruby.

"Then suspicion falls upon me again!" cried Mrs Williams-Jenkins, excitedly.

Wilkins glared at Ruby. "Off your rocker is what you are," he said with a smirk.

Undeterred, Ruby continued: "This is how it happened. That morning Clarissa Winthrop, disguising her voice, phoned Gwendolyn, pretending to be Miss Hicks."

"You lying bitch!" Clarissa snapped.

"I might have guessed," Gwendolyn hissed.

"Ladies, ladies, please…" said Guru Lennie.

"Pretending all the time to be Miss Hicks, Clarissa claimed that she was interested in having a psychic consultation and that Gwendolyn had been warmly recommended by her friend, Mrs Williams-Jenkins."

"Oh yes!" Mrs Williams-Jenkins agreed. "That's true. I could tell at our first meeting that Gwendolyn has the true 'gift'."

"Clarissa told Gwendolyn to come to Miss Hicks's cottage at one o'clock on the dot."

Clarissa laughed. "I never even knew this Hicks woman!"

"Some while before one o'clock," Ruby said, "Clarissa arrived at the bungalow on some pretext. It doesn't matter what. Maybe she said she was from the council or maybe she said she was collecting for charity. One way or another she managed to persuade Miss Hicks to let her into the house. Once inside, Clarissa killed Miss Hicks."

Clarissa laughed again. In a slightly hysterical tone of voice, she said, "Defamation of character is what this is. I hope you've got a good lawyer, Miss Lake, because I'll drag you through every court in the bleedin' land. You won't get away with this, I promise you!"

"Having committed the deadly deed," Ruby said, trying to keep the nervousness out of her voice, "Clarissa telephoned Mrs Williams-Jenkins's house. Wilkins, as had been prearranged, answered the phone. He told his employer that the phone-call had been from Miss Hicks. He claimed that Miss Hicks had cried out for help and that she had said something that sounded like 'Gwendolyn'. Mrs Williams-Jenkins had, naturally, tried to phone Miss Hicks at once to find out what the matter was. But there was no answer. So Wilkins offered to drive her to the bungalow. They arrived there at a minute or two past one.

"By that time, Clarissa had made her escape. As I discovered when I visited the bungalow, there is a path leading from the back garden, through a wooded area towards a small road. Clarissa no doubt parked her car there so that she could arrive and depart from the bungalow without anyone having seen her.

"At one o'clock – after Clarissa had left and just before Wilkins arrived with Miss Hicks – Gwendolyn turns up at the bungalow to keep her appointment. Finding the front door ajar, she does as she has been instructed. She walks through the house and into the kitchen. And that is where, moments later, Mrs Williams-Jenkins finds Gwendolyn, standing over the lifeless body of Miss Hicks. Gwendolyn, who had tried vainly to resuscitate the recumbent body, has blood on her hands. Nearby is a wine bottle of a sort that is readily identifiable as a type served at Gwendolyn's Wine Bar. In fact, anyone could have obtained that bottle from the bin reserved for empty bottles outside the wine bar."

"It's her wine bottle," Clarissa protested. "She brought it with her!"

"Oh no," Ruby said. "Anyone who knows Gwendolyn knows that she is far too cunning…"

"'Ere, watch what you are saying!" Gwendolyn hissed.

"I mean, 'astute', 'shrewd', 'perceptive'…"

"Yeah, that's more like it."

"…to do such a stupid thing as incriminate herself needlessly. Only someone less cunn… astute, would make such a mistake. It was another example of the same slinking stupidity which caused the killer to strangle the Sergeant-Major with a pair of tights."

"You're not saying I did that too, are you?" Clarissa said.

"Wait a minute!" Gwendolyn said. "It's all making sense now. I'd never have gone to that bathroom if Clarissa hadn't told me to. She said the bathroom in the east wing was in use so I should go to the one in the west wing! The bitch set me up!"

"Don't you call me a bitch!" Clarissa snapped. "If anyone here's a bitch it's…"

"Ladies, ladies, calm yourselves, please," muttered Guru Lennie, "this is all most unseemly."

"The tights were a nice touch," Ruby said. "They were doubtless purloined from Gwendolyn's room. Probably to throw us off the scent. Had Gwendolyn herself been found strangled with her own tights, as Clarissa had initially intended, perhaps the police might have concluded that she had committed suicide…"

"An auto-erotic procedure gone horribly wrong," suggested Detective Inspector Gruttock. "It happens all the time."

"An auto-*what?*" asked Mrs Williams-Jenkins.

"Or possibly, we were intended to assume that the tights had been stolen by one of Gwendolyn's gentleman friends…" Ruby glanced from Nathaniel Snibb to Nye Clump to Guru Lennie. The Guru went pale and muttered that, in spite of all the gossip, there was nothing between him and Gwendolyn.

"At any rate," Ruby continued, "when the Sergeant-Major became the accidental victim, Clarissa determined to use the tights to strangle him instead. So, having failed to kill Gwendolyn she would at least be able to make it seem as if Gwendolyn was a murderer, which would have been a satisfactory alternative to her original scheme."

"You're nuts!" Clarissa spat out. "Why would I do any of that?"

"Revenge," said Ruby, simply.

Detective Inspector Gruttock chuckled. "A most entertaining story, Miss Lake, but hardly one that is likely to stand up in a court of law. Miss Clarissa Winthrop has not the slightest motive for pursuing a series of attacks against Miss Gormly."

"Oh, but she has. And I can show you why!"

Here Ruby reached into an inside pocket of her jacket and took from it a small, crumpled photograph. "I discovered this," she said, "upon the wall of The Clogwyn Mawr Non-Political Working Men's Association."

"The *what?*" said Nathaniel Snibb. "You know this area, Sergeant-Major. Have you heard of the place?"

Sergeant-Major Stippleton coughed discreetly into his hand and, avoiding eye-contact, mumbled something about it being a place that was known to be of dubious repute.

Ruby aimed a meaningful glance at Nathaniel Snibb. "Perhaps you may know it by its alternative name," she said. "The Hell Fire Club."

Suddenly the room was in uproar. "You cheap little bitch!" Clarissa screamed and she made a lunge towards Ruby. The

Sergeant-Major sprang to his feet and, seizing her from behind by the elbows, pulled Clarissa away. Then Detective Inspector Gruttock jumped up and shouted, "Stay calm, everyone. As the official representative of the Law I shall take, oof!" The "oof!" was in response to one of Clarissa's elbows which, having momentarily escaped from the Sergeant-Major's grasp, made firm and energetic contact with the Detective Inspector's solar plexus. Gwendolyn Gormly, having elevated herself to the commanding height of her six inch heels, pointed a crimson-nailed finger at Clarissa Winthrop with all the menace of the Ghost Of Christmas Yet To Come. And, in a guttural voice she uttered two words that brought a chill into the room: "Ken Collop".

Clarissa screamed with the ferocity of a vampire confronted by a garlic-draped crucifix. The profanities that issued from her mouth need not be recorded in this narrative, colourful and expressive though they were. Their general import may be summarised thus: Gwendolyn Gormly was (in the view of Clarissa Winthrop) a jolly bad sort who had killed Ken Collop and thereby deprived Clarissa Winthrop of a very convenient source of wealth and comfort. When she said this, Nathaniel Snibb could be observed to recoil as though struck. He had clearly never supposed his lady friend capable of employing such vulgar language with such fluency. He had, in addition, known nothing of her association with a man by the name of Ken Collop. Of the pandemonium that ensued, nothing more needs to be said.

When, having recovered slightly from the elbow to the solar plexus, Detective Inspector Gruttock was able to make himself heard above the uproar, he announced that he was arresting Clarissa Winthrop on suspicion of murder, he was furthermore arresting the chauffeur Wilkins on suspicion of being an accessory to murder. That was when he noticed that Wilkins was nowhere to be seen.

Having seen which way the wind was blowing, Wilkins had taken advantage of the chaos to hotfoot it out of Coot Hall before anyone noticed his absence. In so doing he had underestimated Detective Inspector Gruttock. Knowing full well that people accused of murder or accessory to murder have a distinct tendency to skedaddle when you happen to be looking the other way, he had arranged for Sergeant Wisty and Constable Ian Tucker to be waiting on the steps of the Hall where they very easily apprehended the departing chauffeur before he could make his getaway.

39. Just Like Old Times

"It's just like old times," Muriel Greenalge sighed.

Muriel, Maggie, Bessie and Ruby were sitting in Gwendolyn's Wine Bar, at a table next to the window that overlooked the terrace and the beach beyond. It was a cold night in February and thin flakes of snow pattered against the window.

"Everything all right for you, ladies?" Gwendolyn Gormly towered over the table. "Another bottle of wine, maybe?"

Bessie, who did not habitually drink wine but had been prepared to make an exception in order to celebrate Ruby's successful resolution of the crimes that had been wrongly attributed to Gwendolyn, struggled to focus her eyes on the label of the wine bottle. She had already drunk two glasses of wine and her vision was fuzzy. "I'm paying," she said. "Another bottle of Gwendolyn's Gliborne.... Whatever this one's called."

"Gwendolyn's Gisborne Glug," Gwendolyn said. "A scintillating New Zealand sauvignon blanc that's bottled exclusively for this wine bar."

"And another pint of whatever that is that Maggie's drinking," added Bessie.

"Guinness," Maggie said. "And I'll have a packet of pork scratchings to go with it."

As Gwendolyn tottered away in the general direction of the bar, Maggie leaned across to Ruby and whispered. "Is that the same bottle?"

"That was used to bludgeon poor Miss Hicks to death?" Ruby said. "Not the actual bottle, of course. But similar."

Maggie quivered visibly with revulsion.

"What I can't work out," said Muriel, "is why Clarissa killed Miss Hicks. They'd never met before, had they?"

"It's quite simple," Ruby said. "When her two attempts to kill Gwendolyn had failed, Clarissa realised that, quite by accident, she had made it seem as though Gwendolyn was an unhinged would-be murderer who had tried to kill both Sergeant-Major Stippleton and Madame Evadne. But in order to confirm Gwendolyn's guilt Clarissa needed to pin an actual murder on her. She'd heard Mrs Williams-Jenkins talking about her friend, Miss Hicks, who lived alone. And so Clarissa simply picked Miss Hicks as an easy victim."

"The swine!" said Maggie.

"And all because she blamed Gwendolyn for killing Ken Collop," said Muriel.

In fact, since the arrest of Clarissa Winthrop, more details on the history of her relationship with the late Ken Collop had emerged and PC Ian Tucker had told Ruby all about it. Ken Collop had owned a number of properties throughout both Clogwyn Bach and Clogwyn Mawr and had been quite well off by local standards. One of the most lucrative of Ken's properties was the bingo hall in Clogwyn Mawr. Thus it was that he had attracted the attentions of a number of local women, notable among whom had been Gwendolyn. Soon Ken and Gwendolyn were romantically attached. Ken had proposed to Gwnedolyn; Gwendolyn had accepted. While a wedding date had not been set, Gwendolyn had convinced Ken of the merits of seeing a solicitor in order to arrange for his will to specify Gwendolyn as his principal beneficiary ("Best get the sordid legal details out of the way," Gwendolyn had told him, nonchalantly).

However, unknown to Gwendolyn, not long after making adjustments to his will in Gwendolyn's favour, Ken Collop had met another woman, one Clarissa Winthrop. Soon he and Clarissa had been having secret liaisons. Ken had become so besotted with Clarissa that one night, under the influence of Clarissa's amorous attentions and a large bottle of whisky, Ken had not only proposed to her but had also promised to let her run his bingo hall. Clarissa, being of a practical turn of mind, had suggested that the arrangement should be given appropriate legal status and Ken had drunkenly muttered something about needing to get his will changed.

The next day Ken Collop was dead. It was Gwendolyn who had found his lifeless body in the double bed that she and Ken shared in Gwendolyn's flat. The coroner said that Ken had died of a heart attack. Gwendolyn inherited everything: including Maggie Pountice's little shop and the bingo hall in Clogwyn Mawr. Meanwhile, Clarissa was left destitute.

"I suspect," said Ruby, "that, at first, Clarissa would have been content with simply making us all believe that Gwendolyn might have been complicit in the death of Ken Collop. Hence the accusatory message at the séance." Ruby explained the message which had been spelled out: "Gwendolyn Gormly is guilty".

"But when the séance ended in disarray, the exact nature of Gwendolyn's guilt couldn't be established by continuing to push a wine glass around. So Clarissa decided to take a more deadly form of retribution."

"Ken Collop's death unhinged her, that's what it did," commented Maggie.

"Mind you," said Muriel, "Clarissa bounced back again, didn't she? I mean, hooking up with the millionaire pickle magnate, Nathaniel Snibb."

"Whose pickle empire, it seems, is on the wane," Ruby said. "You told me yourself, nobody is interested in Snibb's old fashioned pickles any more. They want more exciting pickles."

"That is true," conceded Muriel. "We haven't sold Snibb's pickled onions in our shop for ages. There's no demand."

"The Retreat was Nathaniel Snibb's final, desperate attempt to stay rich. But when Gwendolyn turned up…"

"Clarissa finally snapped?" Muriel said.

"She was burning with rage and jealousy," Ruby added. "Especially when she saw Nathaniel Snibb flirting with Gwendolyn."

"He winked at her," Bessie interjected.

"Clarissa suddenly saw that her dreaded rival was still a danger to her. Maybe Gwendolyn would snatch Nathaniel Snibb out of her grasp, just as she had snatched Ken Collop?"

"But how did Mrs Williams-Jenkins's chauffeur get involved?" Muriel wanted to know.

"I think," said Ruby, "the chauffeur, Wilkins, had been in on it from the outset. In fact, I suspect it was he who had hatched the plot against Miss Hicks. He was in the perfect position to deceive his employer, Mrs Williams-Jenkins, into believing that it was Miss Hicks who had telephoned, when in fact, it had been Clarissa.

Wilkins was then able to drive Miss Hicks to the cottage just in time for her to find Gwendolyn on the scene of the crime."

"They're like Bonnie and Clyde," growled Maggie. "Working together, like, on the wrong side of the law."

Ruby was not entirely sure that the comparison was apposite. "Possibly," she said.

"But how did Clarissa even get to know Wilkins in the first place?"

"At the Hell Fire Club," said Ruby. "I happened to see Wilkins entering that depraved establishment. It was that which first made me wonder if he might in some way be involved."

"The Hell Fire Club!" Maggie exclaimed portentously.

"So where Clarissa met Ken Collop?" asked Muriel. "Ken was living with Gwendolyn at the time, after all."

"Once again, the Hell Fire Club in Clogwyn Mawr," said Ruby. "Everything goes back to the Hell Fire Club. That place holds innumerable secrets. It is where Clarissa met Ken Collop and where, at a later date, Nathaniel Coot met Clarissa."

"But Nathaniel Coot hadn't even heard of the Hell Fire Club," Bessie protested. "I particularly recall him saying so."

"I think you'll find, Bessie, that very few men will admit to having heard of it. In fact, a great many local men go to the club, often with the intention of meeting women."

Muriel looked shocked. "No! Whoever would have thought that things like that go on around here!"

Ruby recalled the photograph she had seen in which Muriel's husband, Emrys, had featured. She blushed at the thought of it. Muriel noticed: "You're blushing," Muriel said. "Is it because you know of some other local men who've been to that terrible place? Oh, do tell! I'd love to know!"

Just then a cold gust of air swept into the wine bar as the outer door was briefly opened and shut again. The four women turned to see who had entered. It was a slim, middle-aged, middle-height man with neat, fair hair and vivid blue eyes. He was wearing a long, dark overcoat which was liberally sprinkled with snowflakes. "Am I glad to be in the warmth at last! Oh, hello, Ruby."

"Hello, Nye," Ruby said coldly. She had not forgotten that it was Nye who had provided Gwendolyn with an alibi on the occasion of the second attempted murder when Madame Evadne had been thrust from the window of Gwendolyn's room at Coot Hall. He had claimed that he and Gwendolyn had been playing cards – Happy Families! – in Nye's room. It was a claim which, at the time, Ruby had not challenged since it had supported her argument in favour of Gwendolyn's innocence. On reflection, however, Ruby had decided that the claimed card game seemed improbable.

"Mind if I sit here?" Nye said.

"There's no room," Ruby said tersely.

"Well," said Muriel, "I was just thinking of going, as a matter of fact."

"Stay where you are!" Ruby hissed under her breath.

Nye smiled uncertainly. "Yes, well, nice to see you again, Ruby. You were marvellous, the way you solved that case, you know."

The tapping of stilettos across the floor tiles announced the arrival of Gwendolyn Gormly. She smiled at Nye with all the voluptuousness of a wolf welcoming a lamb into its den. "I've kept a table for you over here, Nye, my love," she said, and, putting an arm around his shoulders, she led him to a small table beneath a big potted palm, adjacent to the bar.

"That Gwendolyn Gormly is an evil bitch," said Muriel.

"She's got very low morals," Bessie added, which were strong words indeed by Bessie's standards.

"The world would be a better place without her," said Maggie.

Ruby struggled to think of something to say in support of Gwendolyn Gormly but she struggled in vain. She glanced out through the window. "The snow's getting quite heavy now," she said.

"Don't worry," said Maggie, "It won't stick."

Bessie's Teisen Lap Recipe

Teisen lap is a traditional Welsh fruit cake that is quickly made and tasty. By tradition it is made in a shallow baking dish though you may make it in a small cake tin if you prefer. The mixture of lard and butter gives it its typical crumbly texture but you may use all butter if you wish.

Ingredients

225g (8 ounces) flour
1tsp baking powder
55g (2 ounces) butter
55g (2 ounces) lard
55g (2 ounces) sugar
150g (5 ounces) currants
2 large eggs
½ freshly grated nutmeg
¼ pint milk

Method

Butter a shallow baking tin (the sort you might use for an apple pie). Sift flour and baking powder into a large bowl. Grate the nutmeg into the flour mixture. Rub in the butter and lard (or use 4oz butter and omit lard); or use a food processor. Mix in the sugar and currants. Beat eggs in a small bowl and fold them into the dry mixture. Add the milk and beat the mixture to make a soft dough. Heap the mixture into the baking tin and bake at 170 degree C (350 degrees F) for about 40 to 50 minutes until the top of the cake is golden brown and the centre is firm. Allow to cool and serve slices cut direct from the baking tin.

A Short Message

I hope you enjoyed this latest story set in the Welsh seaside village of Clogwyn Bach. If you have enjoyed this book, I would be enormously grateful if you could take a few moments to leave a short review on Amazon. You can do that by clicking one of the two links on the next page or (on other Amazon sites) by clicking the 'Write a Customer Review' button on the book page.

Thank you again for reading my book!

K T Mill

LEAVE A REVIEW

Amazon (USA)

https://tinyurl.com/5xb9y4k2
or
https://www.amazon.com/review/create-review?asin=1913132196

Amazon (UK)

https://tinyurl.com/m7wmf3p8
or
https://www.amazon.co.uk/review/create-review?asin=1913132196